The Avenged

A Novel

Charles Prandy

D1468270

To Lisa, Zoie, Kaia and Caiden. I write for you first.

Prologue

COLD PELLETS OF RAIN fall from the night sky and a brisk winter wind blows through the air, causing Detective Jacob Hayden's body to shiver. In his right hand is a black Ruger 380 handgun, which he holds by his side as he fiercely stares into the eyes of the man he's about to murder. He's never killed anyone before. The falling rain stings open wounds along his arms and torso. His torn white T-shirt is soaked and clinging to his body with blotches of red blood stains from where he was sliced with a knife.

Jacob takes a step closer to the man and raises the cold mass of steel that's wrapped in his hand. The rain falls harder, smacking him in the face and camouflaging the hot tears that fall from his eyes. This ends tonight. Everything ends now. All he needs to do is squeeze the trigger and the gun will blast, ending his struggle and torment. Yet, something inside of him fights back. Deep in the corner of his mind, he hears the echoing words that tell him justice can still be served. No, it can't. Despite the fact that revenge is the whispering rationale that plagues his inner soul, his conscience keeps him from doing what needs to be done.

He extends his arms and steadies his aim, resting his finger on the trigger. Maybe this isn't the only way? After everything that's happened to him and after all that he's been through, he suddenly doubts himself. He tensely lowers the gun, confused by his own emotions. As he does, the man he's been chasing for the past five months, bruised and beaten up, suddenly smirks.

"I knew you didn't have the balls to do it, you pansy."

Jacob's brows curl and white rage suddenly demolishes any doubt. His skin reddens as he sharply extends the Ruger once again. He clenches his jaw, but the deep wounds that have torn at his heart scream to be released.

"You don't deserve to live!" Jacob yells, more to convince himself than to reassure his enemy.

The man's smirk widens to a full smile and then he spits at Jacob. "So now you're going to be the big bad cop and shoot me? Is that it? You ain't nothin' but a piece of scum the garbage man left behind."

Jacob becomes engulfed with blind rage and swings his right leg, kicking the man between the legs. The man grunts and topples to the ground in pain.

"I should kill you right now, you son of a bitch. You took everything from me!"

Jacob raises and aims the gun. The man climbs back to his knees and eventually stands in a hunched-over position, holding his crotch. He coughs and then slowly stands to his full height. With rain pellets beating him in the face, his cold eyes speak before his mouth opens.

"And I'd do it all over again if I could."

The lasts words are too much for Jacob to handle. He yells as a rush of adrenaline bursts through his veins, causing his finger to squeeze the trigger. He continues squeezing, each bang becoming more deafening than the first, until there are no more bullets left to shoot. As the riveting sound from the jolting gun slowly dies and the adrenaline eases away, his eyes gloss over with fear as he stares at the end of the barrel, confused by what he just did.

Part One: The Detective

One

Five Months Earlier.

June, 2011 · Washington, D.C.

I'VE HEARD THE CRIES too many times, working as a homicide detective in Washington, D.C. A teenager gets murdered in the streets, shot by a coward with a gun and left for dead, leaving a grieving mother standing past the police tape, screaming and sobbing with family members over their lost child. They're the type of screams that haunt the mind in the middle of the night when sleep refuses to come. I've heard the cries too many times, and that morning was no different.

It was 2:33 a.m., a time when most people should be asleep, but the residents on Euclid Street were fully awake. The street was taped off, with yellow police tape keeping bystanders back far enough from the crime scene. Flashing red and blue lights rhythmically bounced off century-old row houses and cars parked along the curb in the dark night.

I'm Homicide Detective Jacob Hayden from the Third District. I had just arrived at the scene, where a young black male, thin and looking to be about six feet tall, was lying on his back. His lifeless eyes were wide open to the sky and his arms were spread apart. His white tank top and blue jeans were soaked with his own blood. In the background, I heard a woman crying louder than everyone else. The mother, I thought. The kid must live nearby for the mother to have gotten here so fast.

I knelt next to the victim, who couldn't have been older than seventeen or eighteen. Patches of thin hair covered his face where he was trying to grow a beard. What was he doing out at this time of morning? I didn't have to think too hard for the answer.

A few feet from the kid's body, officers placed yellow tabs around seven spent shell casings. From the looks of the shells, they were from a handgun, possibly a nine millimeter. The shells were bunched together, which led me to believe that the killer wasn't moving when he took the shots.

From behind me, I heard my partner, Charlie Evans, talking to another officer. Charlie was a younger cop who had just made detective last year. He was the University of Maryland's star quarterback about nine years ago until a defensive end swiftly bypassed a three-hundred-pound lineman and took Charlie down by the knees, ending his dreams of playing in the NFL. Charlie was six-four, slightly taller than me, with broad shoulders and boyish good looks, according to the women from the precinct. Charlie's thirty-one, a few years younger than me, but his smooth, bare skin made him look like he was still college-bound.

I stood up when I heard Charlie nearing. He rubbed his hands through his flowing sandy-blond hair as he looked down at the body.

"Kid's name is Melvin Johnson," Charlie said. "But on the street, he's known as Gimmick."

"Gimmick?" I responded. "Did he have a lot of tricks up his sleeve?"

"Not so much tonight."

I turned around and looked at the screaming woman. "Is that the mother?"

"Yeah, poor woman. Lives down the street. The gunshots woke her up and when she didn't see her son in his room, she came outside like everyone else, checking to see what happened."

"From the location of the spent shells, it looks like the killer walked right up on him," I said. "Do we know if anyone was with him at the time of the shooting?"

"No, you know how it is. No one saw nothing."

I nodded in agreement. I knew all too well how it was. "Somebody wanted this kid dead in a bad way. Look how many casings are on the ground. A nine-millimeter magazine can hold up to a dozen bullets. I count seven shells. Whoever did this wanted to make sure he was dead."

"You think it's drug related?"

"That's always a possibility, but I don't think so this time."

I motioned for Charlie to kneel and pointed to the kid's chest.

"Look at the entrance wounds. They're targeted at the kid's heart. The killer knew exactly where he was shooting."

"So what are you saying, this was a professional hit?"

"Looks like it to me. You've seen how some of these street kids shoot. The bullets are all over the place. Whoever did this knew how to use a gun."

"So where do we start?"

"Let's talk to the mother. She may know something without realizing it."

Two

I WAS HESITANT about interviewing the mother so shortly after her son had been killed, but I had little choice. None of the people in the neighborhood saw anything, or at least that's what they were saying, so the mother may be the only key to helping solve this murder. Sometimes when these kinds of murders happen, a witness emerges a few weeks later, but if my suspicions were correct and this was a professional hit, a few weeks may be too late to help this grieving mother.

Sitting in a small living room in the front of the house, Camille Johnson, the victim's mother, appeared to be trying her best to control her emotions. While sitting on a comfortable beige sofa, Camille offered Charlie and me lemonade, but we politely declined. As I looked around the room, I saw two framed pictures of Melvin Johnson in a football uniform that sat on the wooden end table next to the sofa. The grieving mother was in her late forties and thirty pounds overweight for her five-five frame. Her skin was the color of dark chocolate and she wore a ponytail that was streaked with grey. One of Camille's neighbors, a slender woman with a close haircut named Bonnie Randall, sat by her side. Bonnie looked to be in her late thirties, and her fitted pajamas showed off her toned figure.

Before questioning her, I offered my sincere condolences to Camille and told her that I'd do everything I could to find out who killed her son. She started to cry again, and hearing the pain in her sobs almost made me postpone the interview. I couldn't imagine what this woman was going through. My mind went back to a previous case where one mother told me that when her son was murdered, she literally felt a part of herself die. She said that she'd never be whole again. I assumed that Camille must be feeling that way; the same cold, empty, painful void that only a mother could feel.

"Ms. Johnson," I softly spoke, "did Melvin ever mention anything about anyone wanting to hurt him? Has anyone made any threats against him?"

Camille shook her head, "Melvin was a good kid. Everybody in the neighborhood liked him. He grew up in this neighborhood, everybody knew him."

"I'm sorry for having to ask you this, but was Melvin into drugs? Was he selling or doing drugs that you know of?"

"No, not that I know of," she answered as tears gently fell down her face. Her friend Bonnie held Camille's hand to comfort her.

"Have you seen anyone strange in the neighborhood over the past couple of days, someone that you've never seen before?"

"No, I work two jobs. I'm not home much, but I haven't seen anyone out of the ordinary." At this she broke down, loudly sobbing, "Oh, God! Why? Why my son?"

I took down notes in my notepad. Camille's answers were the same that I'd gotten from the dozen or so people outside. No one saw anything. No one knew anything. Melvin was a good kid who wasn't into anything illegal. The one question that was in the back of my mind wouldn't go away: if he wasn't into anything, then why was an eighteen-year-old kid out in the neighborhood at two o'clock in the morning?

At that thought, Bonnie, Camille's neighbor said something. "Now that you mention it, I did see Melvin walking away from a green Mercedes the other day. I'm sorry, I just remembered this." Then turning to Camille she said, "I'm sorry."

Without trying to appear too anxious, I sat up in my seat a little. This was the first real bit of information that anyone had given me.

"Was Melvin driving the car? Does he own a Mercedes?"

"No, he wasn't driving the car. I happened to glance out of my window and Melvin had just turned around and headed this way. The green Mercedes sped off like it was in a hurry."

"Did you get a look at the driver?"

"Sorry, no. The windows were tinted pretty dark. But Melvin appeared to be in a hurry, too."

Camille started crying again. I reached for her hand and squeezed it. "I'm going to find out who did this, Ms. Johnson. I promise."

There was something about this mother that made me make the promise that I normally wouldn't make. I glanced at Charlie and he gave me a look like "what are you doing?" I know the last thing I should do is promise anyone that I'll solve a case. It provides false hope because many times, cases go unsolved. The sorrow of loss in Camille's deep sobs was overwhelming, and I knew that this woman needed to know why her son had been killed.

"Ms. Johnson, do you mind if we look around Melvin's room?"

Camille nodded without looking up. Her tears appeared to be endless.

Melvin's room was the typical eighteen-year-old's room. Posters of the rappers Lil Wayne and Drake hung on the wall over a twin-sized bed that wasn't made. The room was small, and on the opposite side of the bed was a small desk with a laptop, an iPod sitting in a docking station, and a four-foot-high dresser next to the desk. Charlie applied his latex gloves and looked through the dresser and under the bed while I searched the closet. As far as evidence, there wasn't anything in the room that was of any use. The laptop would be taken to the station for forensics to go through to see if Melvin was hiding anything inside it. Other than that, the room was clean of anything incriminating.

Charlie and I walked back to the living room and found Camille and Bonnie sitting in the same positions that they were in before we went into Melvin's room. I reached into my pocket and pulled out my card.

"Ms. Johnson, if you can think of anything, please give me a call."

She nodded and held the card in her hand.

"Again, we're sorry for your loss."

So far the only lead we had was a green Mercedes that seemingly sped off after the driver had a conversation with Melvin. Who was driving the Mercedes? And did they have anything to do with Melvin's murder? It wasn't much to go on, but at least it's a start.

Three

TWO HOURS LATER, AT the Third District station on V Street, Charlie and I sat at our desks reviewing a multi-page printout of Department of Motor Vehicle records. There were more than three thousand registered green Mercedes in the District. Bonnie said that she didn't know much about cars and wasn't sure if the Mercedes was a late-model or older-model car. She only knew that it was a Mercedes because she recognized the emblem on the hood. I followed a hunch and narrowed the search to later-model cars because I assumed that whoever Melvin was talking to was probably someone younger with money and wouldn't waste time driving an older-model car.

Unfortunately, the young kids who sell drugs, once they get a little money, like to drive flashy cars. The fortunate part is that I could narrow my search for later-model cars that were newer than the year 2007. I found that there were fewer than seven hundred green Mercedes registered in the District that were newer than the year 2007. That's still a lot, but much less than the original number.

The early morning sun rays started to seep into the station. I told Charlie that we should head home and rejuvenate ourselves. The day was going to be long, trying to find the green Mercedes and also canvassing the streets in search of Melvin's killer. Thirty minutes later, I pulled in front of my house, exhausted. I'd been at my shift for over twelve hours and needed to relax before hitting the streets again. I'm glad I only live ten minutes from the station.

When I opened the front door, the smell of sizzling bacon and fresh waffles immediately hit my nostrils. My stomach came alive with hunger. In the kitchen, my in-laws, Mama J and Pops, were cooking over the stove in the place where my wife, Theresa, normally stood.

"From the smell of things, I'd say you guys need to open your own bed and breakfast. Those waffles smell heavenly."

Mama J turned around and smiled, holding a plate with two golden, crisp Belgian waffles.

"We knew you'd be home from your shift any time now, so I thought I'd whip up some breakfast."

Adding an in-law suite in the basement had been the best investment that I'd ever made. From time to time, Theresa's parents would come and stay at the house to cook and clean. They liked being in the city, even though their house was only about forty-five minutes away in Germantown, Maryland. My wife, Theresa, was a fifth year ER resident at Georgetown University Hospital and worked long shifts like me, so many times we'd come home without having cooked or cleaned the house. Mama J and Pops started coming over so often that I decided to finish the basement so they could have a comfortable place to sleep when they stayed over.

I loved having them here. They reminded me of my parents, who had passed away shortly after I was sworn in to the force ten years ago. My parents had been older when they had me. My mother was forty and my father was forty-four. They had already been married for twenty years and felt like having a child was the next step to completing their lives. In my sophomore year of college, my mother found out that she had breast cancer, which she was able to fight for two and half years before she finally lost the battle. By that time, my parents had been married for over forty years and had known each other for forty-six years. After my mother died, my father lost all will to live and, I often thought, died of a broken heart.

Theresa's parents have the kind of love that my parents had. They take care of me as if I were their own son. Whenever they came over, hot meals were always ready and the house was spotless from top to bottom. What more could one ask from their in-laws? However, I knew the real reason why they came over so much; they missed their daughter. Theresa was their only child and lived with them until we married seven years ago. They're lonely without her.

I leaned in and kissed Mama J on the cheek and then slapped five with Pops, who was already digging into the bacon. In his early sixties, Pops was a natural athlete who runs five miles a day and then bikes another twelve miles. His career in construction kept his arms strong and shoulders broad. The only thing that he wasn't able to fight was his grey hair, which he shaved bald. With his dark skin, he's often told that he looks like an older Michael Jordan.

Likewise, if there were a Senior Miss America, Mama J would be in the running. The years have been good to her, and the hourglass shape she had when she was twenty still existed today.

"Theresa upstairs?" I asked.

"Yep," Pops responded. "She's getting ready for her shift at the hospital."

"One coming, the other going," Mama J teased. "Guess that's why I haven't gotten any grandbabies yet." She winked.

"Keep your mind outta' the gutter," I responded with a playful smile.

"I'm just saying." She looked at her watch, "tick tock...tick tock."

"You need to tick tock that man right there. He's eating all my bacon."

"I'm still a growing man," Pops replied as he patted his stomach. "I need all the nutrients I can get."

"I'll show you some nutrients," I jokingly retorted.

I quickly reached for a piece of bacon in Pops' hand, but he moved quicker than I expected.

"Hey, hey, hold on now. Don't mess with my bacon. You may be a hotshot detective, but I was a Golden Gloves champ in 1968. I still got a mean jab now."

He began to bob and weave and threw quick jabs in the air. "I wouldn't want to connect two to your chin and knock you out."

I laughed. "Any time, old man. But first you'd have to catch me."

I quickly grabbed a piece of bacon from Pops' hand and darted from the kitchen and up the stairs.

"Imma remember that," Pops yelled.

"Good, and remember how good this bacon was, too," I laughed as I ran up the stairs.

<u>Four</u>

THE SHOWER WAS RUNNING when I walked into the bedroom. The en suite bathroom door was partially open, and I felt the steam from the shower. I took off my tie and quickly slipped out of my clothes until I was nude and entered the bathroom. Theresa still hadn't heard me. To my left was our white porcelain pedal sink with an oval mirror above it. To my right was the shower with a cream and brown colored shower curtain. I glanced at myself in the mirror before entering the shower, taking notice that the extra crunches I'd been doing were starting to show. I'm six feet three inches tall and weigh two hundred and twenty pounds. I'm a big guy, but light on my feet.

I leaned closer to the mirror and noticed a puffiness around my eyes. I needed to sleep for a few hours before I reconvened with Charlie, but I wasn't sure if I'd be able to. My facial hair was slightly overgrown, and Theresa kept telling me that she liked the look and how it made me look cool like TV detectives. I wear my hair close because I've been noticing that my hairline was starting to go in the opposite direction that I wanted it to. Fortunately, when my hair is close, my brown skin hides that fact that I'm slowly losing my hair.

I turned around and slipped into the shower where Theresa was facing the showerhead with a film of soap covering her curvy body. She looked great from behind, even though she was wearing an unattractive black shower cap. She began to hum a tune that I wasn't familiar with, but it didn't matter because I only had one thing on my mind. Theresa's back end instantly provoked a thought of lust. I always told her that if she hadn't gone to medical school and become a doctor, she could have easily made a career as a video vixen.

I reached for her waist, rubbed my hands over her flat stomach, and gently pulled her close. She jumped at first, but then turned around and smiled which made me jump back.

"What?" she asked.

"Didn't realize you had cream on your face."

Theresa's face was covered with a white cream that made her look like the Michelin Man.

"If I knew that a tall, gorgeous, chocolate brotha was going to be paying me a visit, I would have been a little more sexy." She giggled. "How long have you been home?"

"Just a few minutes. Your parents are making breakfast downstairs. Your dad wasn't too happy when I grabbed a strip of bacon from his hand."

Theresa shook her head. "You two. What am I going to do with you guys?"

"For starters, you can rinse that cream off your face." I raised my right eyebrow and gave her a look that I was ready.

She lightly nudged my chest. "Not with my parents downstairs."

"They're not going to hear us. Besides, when's the last time you had a quickie before work?"

Theresa raised her arms around my neck and pulled me closer. "You're a wild one, aren't you, Mr. Hayden."

"Only with you."

We kissed for a few seconds and I instantly felt myself become harder and more erect. Theresa pulled back and smiled.

"We can't."

"Why?"

"Sorry, babe, but I've got to get to the hospital. I'll just make it before eight o'clock rounds if I get out of here in the next fifteen minutes."

"I only need two, three tops."

"You're right about that," she giggled. "But I can't."

"Come on, babe, you can't leave me like this."

Theresa turned around and rinsed the mask off her face and the soap off her body. When she faced me again, she sensually squeezed her perky breasts and kissed me.

"Just think about this for the rest of the day and I promise I'll make it up to you tonight." She nibbled on my ear before slipping out of the shower.

"It's not that easy to turn off," I said through the shower curtain.

"Sure it is. Here, I'll make it easy for you."

She reached in and turned off the hot water and I screamed like a little girl.

"See, I'm sure it's turned off now." She laughed while I quickly found the hot water knob.

"So you've got jokes," I said.

"It's all in love, babe."

Five minutes later, I was out of the shower. Theresa was already dressed in her scrubs when my cell phone rang.

"Hello, this is Detective Hayden."

"Detective Hayden, this is Camille Johnson from last night."

"Yes, Ms. Johnson, how can I help you?"

Theresa leaned in and gave me a kiss on the cheek and mouthed that she'd call me later.

"I got a call this morning from a storage facility in Lanham, Maryland. They said they were calling because Melvin had missed two payments and that if he didn't pay his fees, his storage garage could go into auction."

"How long had he had the storage garage?" I asked.

"That's the thing. I didn't even know he had one."

Hmmm. My mind immediately asked two questions: why was Melvin hiding from his mother that he had a storage garage in Maryland? And more importantly, what was he hiding in the storage garage? If my suspicions were right and this was a professional hit, then whatever was in the storage garage could be the reason Melvin Johnson had been killed.

"Thank you, Ms. Johnson," I politely replied. "I'll definitely look into this."

Five

RUSH HOUR IN THE D.C. Metro area never really comes to an end, but traffic was generally lighter leaving the city than coming in at this time of the morning. At 10 a.m., I picked up Charlie from the station, and twenty-five minutes later, we were on Route 50 turning onto M.L.K. Jr. Highway in Lanham, Maryland, where the storage facility was located.

The sky was as blue as a tropical sea and the temperature climbed close to ninety degrees, unusually warm for that time of the morning in early June.

"So what do you think we're going to find?" Charlie asked. During his brief visit home, he'd changed to a pair of black khaki cargo pants and a short-sleeved white pullover collared shirt that had "Metro Police" stitched in yellow over the shirt pocket.

I, on the other hand, wore dark-colored blue jeans and a black button-up short-sleeved shirt. We both wore our detective shields on chains around our necks.

"It'd be great if we opened the door and the killer was strapped to a chair with the murder weapon on his lap and a written confession taped to his chest." I laughed, knowing how unrealistic that would be.

"I'll do you one better. The killer is tied to a chair, the murder weapon on his lap, a written confession taped to his chest, and the victim's blood is on his clothes."

"I'll do you one better than that," I teased. "Everything you just said plus an eyewitness to the shooting who unequivocally says that person shot Melvin Johnson."

We both laughed at our silliness, but the grim reality quickly settled in that this could be just a lead that got us nowhere. That kind of stuff happens all the time in police investigations, but it was better to check it out and make sure everything's crossed off the list before moving forward. There could be a hundred different reasons why Melvin had a storage facility and most of them could be legal. Maybe Melvin wasn't hiding this from his mother, but rather, he just never told her because he didn't think it was important enough for her to know.

I turned my black 2009 Chevy Impala into the parking lot of the Extra Space Storage. The inside lobby was stacked wall-to-wall with folded moving boxes, hanging moving tape and movers' gloves. We showed the young, dark-haired man behind the counter, who looked to be about twenty-two years old, our detective shields and asked for Melvin Johnson's storage space. The young man was about to say that he couldn't divulge that kind of information, but I handed him a search warrant, which quickly put an end to his chatter.

Minutes later, we were standing outside in front of a brown garage door. Rows upon rows of storage garages were lined up across from each other, spaced wide enough apart that someone could pull up a trailer and either load or unload their belongings. The clerk unlocked a padlock and pulled up the garage door to let us in.

I turned on a light switch. The lights flicked on and then we were able to see that there were three wooden crates along the far end of the wall, placed side by side. I immediately came to the conclusion that there were drugs in the crates and that whoever had killed Melvin Johnson had done so because of these crates.

"Looks like we may have found motive," I said.

"Jesus, what kind of dope was this kid selling?" Charlie asked.

"The kind that gets you killed."

I leaned over the farthest crate to the right and looked to see if there were any kinds of markings or writings on it. There were none. We exchanged glances with each other and then put on latex gloves before opening the crate.

"Here goes nothing," I said.

The crate's lid opened with ease and I was stunned to see what was inside. It wasn't drugs like I expected, but just as bad.

"We need to call the ATF," I said.

Six

GUNS. THE THREE CRATES each had their lids off and were filled with a combination of handguns, rifles and shotguns. I picked up a stainless steel handgun with a black handle and immediately recognized it as a 22 caliber Walther 10. I pulled out the clip and saw that it was full. I then pulled out a Browning shotgun with a long black barrel. I looked over at Charlie, who was already on the phone with the ATF, the Bureau of Alcohol, Tobacco and Firearms, and knew that we were in for a long day. Over the next thirty minutes, Charlie and I pulled out all of the guns and lined them up according to style and size. The guns covered the entire floor of the garage.

Melvin Johnson was a gunrunner. I knew that once the media got ahold of this that they were going to have a field day. Young black kids die every day in the city from gun violence, and unless there's a particular spin that the media can put on a kid's death, it usually doesn't get much airplay. But this was a whole different ballgame. In this storage garage in the suburbs of Maryland, there was enough firepower to stock a small army, and once Melvin's name was linked to gunrunning, the media would make a circus out of it. Which brought up another problem. Once this story hit the airwaves, whoever killed Melvin, if they weren't already in hiding, would go deeper in hiding and make it nearly impossible to catch them. And if, as I strongly believed based on the amount of fire power that was in front of me, the hit was done by a professional, the killer may be untraceable.

As I stared at the amount of weapons before me, my mind was searching for something, anything, that would help lead me to the killer. To move this much firepower, Melvin would have to have talked to someone or been working with others on the streets. I started thinking about the more organized criminals in the city and not the nickel-and-dime ones. The latter wouldn't have enough structure to push this kind of arsenal. Whoever Melvin was working with were professionals by the look of the weapons.

If I had to guess, I'd think that these weapons had never been used, which the ATF would be able to confirm. And if that's the case, then Melvin was definitely dealing with professionals all the way through. But who? The only name that continued to come into my head was that of the Gomez family, part of a crime family that had emigrated to the District from Mexico City, and who had been rumored to be into some heavy dealings of drugs, prostitution and even weapons smuggling. Every time the feds conducted a raid on a particular family member, they always came up empty, which led me to believe that they have people working on the inside of the FBI, D.C. Police and every other local government agency.

As I thought more about it, the name Hector Gomez had come up in briefings and meetings lately. He had migrated up from Mexico City about two years before and had numerous run-ins with the police. Nothing that resulted in jail time, but just enough that the department had been made aware of his presence and his reputation as a hothead. We had been advised to take caution if ever dealing with him.

"Anything off the top of your head on the Gomez family? I know a new family member recently came into town within the past couple of years," I asked Charlie.

"Hector. Yeah, his name's come up a few times. Street fights, cursing at cops. Someone said they saw him with a gun one time but it was never found."

"Think they could be involved in this? I mean, their family's been relatively quiet, but something like this would take some financial backing. And then you've got some hothead who thinks he's untouchable. We could be looking at a Scarface wannabe in our city."

Charlie formed guns with his fingers, pointed at me and, with his best Al Pacino impersonation, said, "Say hello to my little friend."

I shook my head, "Dude, good thing you became a cop, because your acting sucks."

"I wasn't believable?"

"Do I even have to answer that?"

"Point taken." Charlie's attention went to the crates before he spoke again. "But going back to your question, the Gomez family could be a good start. They have the resources and the history to be involved in something like this."

An hour later, after agents from the ATF had confiscated the weapons and talked to Charlie and me, we headed back to the city in hopes of finding Hector Gomez.

Seven

WHEN I FIRST MET Turtle, he was a thirteen-year-old kid selling weed out of his mother's basement. His mother worked two jobs and was never home, and like many of the kids in the city, his father had left the family before Turtle was old enough to walk. Also like many of the kids in the inner-city, money and food were sometimes hard to come by, so while the mothers worked two and three jobs to keep a place over their heads, a lot of the kids sold weed and dope to make ends meet. Turtle was no exception. He was an unfortunate product of his environment.

Turtle's real name was Malcolm Taylor, but as he'd explained to me, when he was a baby, he crawled so slowly that his father said a turtle could move faster than him, and thus the nickname Turtle had stuck with him. However, now the nickname's irrelevant because Turtle's one of the fastest people that I've ever met. If he'd kept his act together and stayed in school, I had no doubt that Turtle would be a track star competing for a world title in the two-hundred-yard dash. I know best because I had the luxury of trying to catch him that first day he got busted. I'm fast, but Turtle made me look like I was running in slow motion, even at thirteen years old. I only caught him because the kid ran into the street and was clipped by a moving car. Luckily, it didn't break his leg, but gave him a nasty enough bruise that he was limping for two weeks.

Over the years, I tried to mentor Turtle and tried to offer him some semblance of what a father could be. Sometimes, Turtle seemed like he would take a step forward, while other days he took two steps back. He never finished high school, didn't work and was twenty-one years old still living in his mother's house. I know that Turtle still sold weed, even though he denied it. How else does someone unemployed always have money? Nevertheless, Turtle's been a good informant for me over the years. He knows the streets and always seems to know what's happening. So when I called and asked if he knew anything about Melvin Johnson, I wasn't surprised with what he knew.

"Man, Gimmick was into some heavy shit," Turtle said.

"Yeah, I know. I came from his storage spot in Maryland."

"So you know about the guns?"

"You tell me what you know."

"I don't know much more than that. Gimmick didn't like to talk about it. He said that the people he worked for had eyes and ears everywhere. He always had stacks of paper on him and when I tried to get out of him how he was making the money, he seemed nervous."

"So how'd you know about the guns?"

"Didn't take long to put two and two together. I knew he wasn't selling dope. He wasn't pimping, robbing or stealing, so guns was the next logical thing. When I asked him about it, he said, yeah, he was running guns. But he didn't want me getting involved."

"What are you hearing about Hector Gomez?"

"That's one crazy son of a bitch. But if you're asking could Gimmick have been working for him, I'd have to say I doubt it."

"Maybe not for him, but for his family?"

Turtle paused before answering and I could almost feel his mind turning for the answer.

"Now that could be possible. Them Mexicans are starting to take over a lot of the guns and dope that come into the city. I mean my sales have—"

"What's that?" I quickly cut him off.

"Ah, naw, I was saying that I heard my man say that his sales have been declining ever since them Mexicans have been here."

"Turtle, don't make me come over there and raid your house. You're smarter than that."

"Of course, come on, man, I don't get down like that. It was my man, he's the one who told me."

"Uh huh, just remember who I am and how I can make your life miserable."

"For sure, for sure."

"You know what kind of car Hector Gomez drives?"

"I think it's a Mercedes."

I looked across the seat to Charlie and mouthed "Bingo."

"You've been a big help, man. What you got planned for the rest of the day? And don't say nothing because you need to be out looking for a job."

"In this economy? Come on, you know they ain't giving no jobs to brothas. Especially ones like me."

"Well that should tell you something then. Maybe you need to do something so you can get a job."

Suddenly, I started to hear static on the other end of the line. "...you're breaking up," Turtle said.

"Don't give me that bullshit, Turtle."

"What? I can't... hear you. I'll...keep my ears...open."

The line went dead.

Damn kids.

"What'd he say?" Charlie asked.

"He said that he thinks Hector Gomez owns a Mercedes."

"Ah ha," Charlie said, pointing his index finger in the air. "And the hunt begins."

Eight

HECTOR GOMEZ SAT AT a kitchen table in an apartment in the Adams Morgan neighborhood in D.C. In front of him on the table was a square mirror with white powder cocaine. He took a razor and separated the cocaine into five rows, then picked up a straw and put it in front of one of the rows, leaned over and sniffed. The cocaine hit his nose and the familiar burning was soon followed by a mild sense of euphoria, which soon turned into panic.

It wasn't warm in the apartment, but Hector was sweating profusely. His hands were shaking and he felt jittery and afraid. Hector's thoughts raced. Where's the bad man? He was there a few minutes ago standing behind the couch. Hector leaned down and took another snort from the second row of cocaine. When he lifted his head, white residue was on the tip of his nose.

He heard a man's voice laughing.

His eyes frantically shifted back and forth across the room, but no one was there.

Hector had been snorting coke off and on all day before the bad man came. How'd he get in here? Where'd he go? Next to the cocaine was a black .22 caliber Beretta. He was going to shoot the bad man when he first saw him, but the man vanished before Hector had a chance to shoot. Now all he heard was this insanely creepy laugh over and over again.

He leaned down again and took another snort. Then he heard the laughing again.

Hector lurched from his chair and grabbed the gun.

"Where are you, you fucker?"

The apartment was just a little over six hundred fifty square feet. The kitchen opened to the living room, where an L-shaped brown leather sofa sat in front of a wall-mounted forty-two-inch flat screen. Directly behind Hector was a glass sliding door that led to the back patio. The apartment was on the ground floor, and the large patio space was premium real estate for the city. The kitchen was modern, with sleek grey countertops, cherry wood cabinets and stainless steel appliances.

Hector had come to the apartment hours ago to meet up with a girl he'd been seeing who lived there. She left for work shortly after he arrived, and he'd been alone in the apartment ever since. So where'd the bad man come from? In his panicked state, his mind cleared just enough to realize that he must be hallucinating. But he still felt nervous. He started doubting himself and wondered if maybe there really was a bad man in the apartment.

Then the flat screen flicked on. Hector jumped because he hadn't turned it on. The channels began surfing by themselves until a channel came on that displayed the apartment. The flat screen showed him standing next to the kitchen table, looking at the TV.

"What the fuck is going on?" Hector was scared. The gun in his hand began to shake as sweat poured from every inch of his body.

He moved toward the flat screen and watched his own movements. Then the flat screen showed a man with his face blurred out wearing a dark trench coat standing next to him. Hector jumped back and looked to his right but no one was there.

"Who the fuck is here?" Hector yelled, looking around the room, aiming the gun in every direction.

Then the flat screen went blank again. With each second, Hector grew more paranoid that someone was in the apartment with him. Every creak of the floor or outside noise caused Hector to jump. He moved back to the kitchen table, looked down at the coke and wanted to sniff another row.

"This shit's got me trippin."

He started to see white spots dance across the apartment and he wasn't sure what was real anymore. Drenched in sweat, he walked to the couch and sat, his leg jumping up and down while his eyes continued darting over the room.

The laughing voice came back. Hector quickly raised the gun, stood and aimed it around the room. The room began to pulsate like the fast rhythmic beating of his heart. He felt like he was about to pop, but held back the vomit that quickly formed in his throat.

Air. He needed air. He rushed to the back door and opened it, allowing the night air to enter. The room suddenly stopped pulsating. He took a deep breath and began to control his nerves, but then the bad man showed up and this time he didn't leave. Standing near the kitchen table, his heart quickened and adrenaline rushed through his veins. The bad man with the blurred-out face took a step closer to him.

"What the fuck do you want?" Hector screamed.

He held up the shaking Beretta and was about to squeeze the trigger when a loud pounding came from the front door. Hector's eyes quickly glanced at the front door and then back to the bad man, but he was gone, disappeared like a ghost.

"Jesus."

Then an amplified voice called his name. "Hector." The voice didn't sound like the laughing voice, but was much louder. His name was being drawn out in slow motion as it was being called, H—e—c—t—o—r.

More pounding came from the front door, but this time, it came in loud, amplified succession, thunk, thunk, thunk.

Hector covered his ears with his hands to drown out the noise. Thunk, thunk, thunk.

"H—e—c—t—o—r G—o—m—e—z."

The bad man knows my name. He's going to knock down the door and take me away.

Thunk, thunk, thunk.

"Leave me alone!"

Hector couldn't take it anymore. He aimed the gun at the door and squeezed off three shots.

Nine

IT HAD TAKEN CHARLIE and me nearly all day to track down Hector Gomez. We finally found out that besides the Puerto Rican girlfriend he had who lived in the Columbia Heights neighborhood that bordered Adams Morgan, he also had another girl he was seeing who lived directly in Adams Morgan. We went to the girlfriend's apartment and learned he wasn't there, so we hoped that his trail ended at the second girlfriend's apartment. When we got there, we weren't expecting the kind of greeting we received.

I knocked on the door and thought that I heard movement coming from inside the apartment. I knocked again and called Hector's name.

Charlie stood to the left of the door and, instinctively, I stood to the right. We heard a man's voice scream "Leave me alone," and then, without warning, three shots hit the front door, leaving three tiny holes in the wood.

"Jesus Christ!" Charlie screamed.

"Shit!" I cursed.

Seconds later, we both had our guns drawn.

"Hector Gomez, this is D.C. Police!" I barked.

At the same time, Charlie reached for his radio and called in for backup.

"Fuck you!" Hector screamed. "You're not going to take me away!"

"Hector Gomez, put down your weapon. This is D.C. Police!" I yelled again.

Hector didn't scream back or shoot. Everything became silent.

"Hector Gomez, again, this is the police. Put your weapon down!"

No response.

Suddenly, I had an eerie feeling that Hector might try to shoot himself or his girlfriend if she were inside. I caught Charlie's eyes and motioned to the doorknob. Since I had the better angle, I reached for the knob and found that it wasn't locked. My heart was pounding a mile a minute. This kind of thing doesn't happen much, but when it does, we must be prepared.

I quickly twisted the knob and pushed the door open, and we moved back away from the door. No bullets came flying out.

"Hector," I yelled again.

I quickly moved closer and glanced inside. There was a straight view to the back of the apartment and I saw that the rear sliding glass door was open.

"Shit. I think he went out the back."

Just then, I heard a woman scream, which sounded like it had come from behind the apartment building.

"Go around the building, I'll cut through the apartment," I said in a hurried voice.

Charlie took off and I cautiously entered the apartment with my gun drawn and aimed in front of me. My eyes were wide open and I barely blinked as I looked around the room. My breaths came in short, quick intervals. I took silent steps across the living room and into the kitchen and finally out onto the back porch. The back porch was surrounded by a six-foot-high cement wall.

I quickly noticed that a green oval deck table had been slid to the far wall, which I assumed Hector used to climb the wall. I did the same. Once I was street level, to my right I saw that Charlie was a block down, sprinting across the street, and then I heard more screams from pedestrians.

I took off like a trained sprinter, extending my legs and arms as far as they would go to gain maximum speed. I caught up to Charlie in a matter of seconds and we ended up on 18th Street, Adams Morgan's main strip. The nightlife was in full effect. People were filling the sidewalks, hanging and talking. No doubt most were waiting to get into the bars and lounges. To my left, I heard more screams from pedestrians and saw Hector running down the middle of 18th Street towards Florida Avenue with a handgun in his hand.

Charlie and I took off after Hector and I could see that I was gaining ground with each step.

"Hector, police!" I yelled. "Stop."

Now I was running in the middle of 18th Street, passing slow-moving cars on either side of the yellow lines. Police sirens screamed in the distance and would be upon us in seconds. But I immediately saw a problem. The intersection of 18th Street and Florida Avenue was two blocks ahead, and the light for 18th Street was red. Hector wasn't showing any signs of slowing down for the light, nor was he moving to either side of the street. He continued running right down the middle yellow lines. I looked at the intersection and saw cars on Florida Avenue flowing in either direction, as their light was green.

"Shit, he's going to run right into the intersection and kill himself. Hector, stop!"

I tried to gain more speed, but my legs were extended to their fullest length. I continued pushing and pumping, hoping, praying that I could get to Hector before he dashed into the intersection.

We passed the final block before the intersection and Hector showed no signs of stopping.

"Goddammit, Hector, stop. It's the police for Christ's sake!"

Like a crazed man, Hector darted into the intersection and flew by one car that had to slam on its brakes and skid to a stop. But the next car, a black SUV, caught Hector square on and knocked him clear off his feet about twenty yards.

"Jesus Christ!" I yelled.

The black SUV skidded to a stop. I finally caught up to Hector, but quickly looked away, as part of his body was crushed beyond recognition.

"Shiiiitttt!" I screamed.

Charlie finally caught up and his eyes widened when he saw Hector.

"Dear God."

Within seconds, three squad cars stopped in the intersection and uniformed officers hopped out.

Later that night, I learned that Hector was high on cocaine, which probably caused him to see things and be in a state of panic. That would explain why he ran. As far as the Melvin Johnson case was concerned, I was now back to square one.

Just as Charlie and I finished searching the apartment, my cell phone rang. I looked at the caller ID and saw that it was Turtle.

"Not a good time, Turtle."

"Damn, Jacob, I heard what went down with Hector."

"News travels fast on the streets."

"So do other things. Look, we need to meet up. I've got some serious stuff to throw at you."

Part Two: The Sniper

Ten

The Next Day

THE SUN WAS BRIGHT in the middle of the afternoon. The sky couldn't have been any clearer, almost like an oil painting of a perfect hue of sapphire blue. The temperature was steady at eighty-eight degrees with very little humidity. A nearly perfect day to be outside.

I sat on a bench under a tree in Dupont Circle's park, eyeing my wristwatch every two minutes. I had agreed to meet Turtle in the park at 1 o'clock, but it was almost 1:30 and Turtle hadn't shown. The day was too nice to be annoyed, but that was the attitude I started to feel.

"Five more minutes."

When Turtle had called me the night before, I was tired and wasn't in the mood. Turtle said that he had something important to talk about, and implied that it could possibly be related to Melvin Johnson's murder. That was all he would say over the phone. No matter how hard I pushed him to talk, he wouldn't do it. He said that it was something we'd have to talk about face-to-face.

Reluctantly, I agreed to meet in Dupont Circle. There was more. Turtle sounded a little nervous. Whatever was on Turtle's mind must be important, and that was the only reason I'd been waiting as long as I had.

The Dupont Circle park connected Massachusetts Avenue, Connecticut Avenue, New Hampshire Avenue, P Street and 19th Street in a circle – in the middle of which was the park. In the middle of the park was a large fountain with a base was made up of three classical nudes, symbolizing the sea, stars and wind. The top of the fountain was an oval bowl where water streamed off into a surrounding pool around the fountain. I watched as people came up to the fountain and threw quarters into the pool, probably wishing for good luck.

The park was crowded around this time of day as people milled around during lunchtime. Some carried picnic baskets and blankets and found nice spots on the grass to eat. Others sat on the surrounding benches with carry-out food and Styrofoam cartons, trying not to get their business clothes messy. Then there were the homeless who walked around the park asking for spare change. I handed a bearded man who looked like he'd been living on the streets for years a five-dollar bill and wished him well. I wondered if the man was truly going to use the money for food like he said he would.

I looked at my watch again and noticed that five minutes had passed. I was about to get up and leave when I saw Turtle walking past the fountain with a look of "sorry, man" on his face.

I pointed to my watch, and Turtle double-stepped to reach me quicker.

"Sorry, man, it took a little longer for me to get away than I expected."

"Get away from where? It's not like you have a job."

"That's cold, man."

"No, it's called common courtesy. You don't make someone wait for you for a half an hour. Especially when I've got other things I could be doing." I was clearly annoyed and wanted him to know it.

Turtle lowered his head, apparently realizing his mistake.

The twenty-one-year old kept himself well groomed, even though he wore his pants halfway down his waist, like many of the young kids do. His goatee was freshly trimmed and his hair was short and neat. His dark brown skin hid any blemishes on his face. He was tall and lean and could have been a pretty good track runner had he kept his grades up.

I extended my hand and slapped him five. "Just trying to keep you on the up and up."

"Sorry, Jacob, I'll be on time next time."

We both took a seat on the bench.

"So what's this about anyways? Why couldn't you just talk to me on the phone last night?"

Turtle looked around like he was making sure no one was listening.

"Okay, what I'm about to tell you is big. I mean really big. I mean witness protection big."

"I'm listening."

"But you gotta promise me that if this gets out, I get protection."

"What kind of protection?"

"Protection protection. Federal protection. Like the government picking me up and sending me to Nevada or to one of them Midwest states."

"You know I can't make that guarantee."

He lowered his head a little and I could tell that my answer bothered him.

"But if what you tell me is true and credible, I'll do all I can to help you. But why would you need protection? And what does it have to do with Melvin Johnson?"

Turtle hesitated for a few seconds before speaking. He looked around the park again and then leaned closer.

"It's about a judge." Turtle didn't say anything else.

"Okay. And?"

Turtle sat back, apparently nervous. "Jacob, man, you've got to promise me that you'll protect me if this comes back to me, man."

"Okay, okay, you have my word. Now what's this about a judge?"

Eleven

ACROSS FROM DUPONT CIRCLE, on top of a nine-story white building, a sniper put the scope on a Parker-Hale M85 rifle with a firing range of about 900 meters or half a mile. Dressed in a janitor's uniform, he screwed on a silencer and set the rifle on a prong and aimed it at the park. Despite the warm weather, he wore a knit hat on top of his head with large dark sunglasses over his eyes, and his beard was slightly overgrown. He raised the sunglasses to his forehead and placed his right eye against the scope and carefully canvassed the park from left to right. A single bullet rested in the chamber, waiting to explode through the barrel and meet its target square between the eyes.

Large trees surrounded the perimeter of the park, so from his angle, he'd have to wait until his target was in the clear before taking the shot. All he needed was one shot. From this distance he had a more than ninety percent first-round-hit capability, and with his experience with sniper rifles, the percentage moved to ninety-eight percent.

The building was on Connecticut Avenue, near a crosswalk to the park, and which also provided an opening that was not covered by trees. When the target got in the clear, the shot would be taken; he'd leave the gun and nonchalantly exit the roof. Now all he had to do was wait. The target would cross through the park like he does every day to get to his office after lunch, only this time he wouldn't make it back.

Through the scope, the sniper watched as people casually walked back and forth without any knowledge that he held their lives in his hands. The simple pull of the trigger could kill anyone he wished, and yet they walked around without knowing the impending danger. Sometimes he wished he could be that naive and careless.

The summer's sun heated the top of the building, and he was beginning to feel like a sausage link frying in a skillet. He could feel sweat dripping inside the janitor's uniform that was trapping heat like a sauna. The hat on his head was damp and sweat surrounded the eyehole of the scope. Reluctance momentarily crossed his mind and he wondered if maybe he should have picked another spot to take the shot. Just then, he saw his target enter the scope. He steadied the rifle, took a deep breath and let his heartbeat slow. He waited until he could feel the rhythm of his heartbeat. Thump, thump, thump. Between the third and fourth thump, he squeezed the trigger.

Twelve

I SLOWLY WALKED WITH my hands in my front pockets as I carefully listened to Turtle dump a load of information on me. I immediately stood when Turtle laid out the allegations against one of the more prominent judges in the District. I like to walk while my brain processes complex information, so sitting on the hard park bench would have done no good. Turtle's words had flooded my mind with questions, but I was still skeptical.

"Don't get me wrong, Turtle, but something doesn't smell right. I don't like this one bit."

"Jacob, you know I'd never give you bad info. My source is airtight."

"Who's your source?"

"Not this time, man. I can't give him up right now."

"You haven't done wrong by me yet, but this...I don't know. This is even a stretch for you. I mean, how'd you come across this kind of information?"

"I told you, my source is airtight."

"So all of this can be proven, I assume?"

"Of course. Look, man, I wouldn't have risked my neck coming to you if it couldn't be."

"Sorry if I sound skeptical, Turtle, but look at it from my point of view. You don't have a job, and the people you hang around with are wannabe thugs who've got no shot at life. So when you come to me and say that Judge Frank Peters, one of the more prominent judges in the city, is into money laundering and weapons smuggling, I gotta take a step back and question it."

Turtle stopped walking, which took me a second to notice. I turned around and saw Turtle staring at me with a blank expression.

"What?" I asked.

"I came to you because I knew you'd be the only person who'd take me serious. And now it sounds like you're not."

I raised my hands to protest. "I'm not saying I don't believe you. But look at it from my point of view."

Turtle shook his head with obvious disappointment.

"Okay, let's assume that everything you're telling me is true. I personally know that Judge Peters and my lieutenant are good friends. He's also good friends with the Chief of Police, the Mayor and most of the politicians on Capitol Hill."

"So pretty much we should just turn a blind eye to this? Is that what you're telling me?"

"Not at all. What I'm saying is that there's a lot of loyalty in the judicial system, and trying to convince my superiors that Judge Peters is a crook won't be easy. I mean, the guy's been on the bench for over twenty years."

We started walking again and then stopped near the intersection of Connecticut Avenue. I looked to my right and saw my car parked along the curb. I dug in my pocket for the car keys and fiddled with them in my hand while giving one last thought to Turtle's accusation.

"Okay, here's what we're going to do." The tone of my voice lacked its usual confidence. "I'll do a little digging around and see what I can come up with. I don't want you doing anything or speaking to anyone about this until you hear back from me."

Turtle nodded his head in agreement.

"You may have just opened a huge can of worms that I suspect most would rather remain sealed shut."

"So you see why I mentioned the protection."

"Yeah, I think I can take that request a little more seriously."

"No doubt."

I lost the handle of my keys and they fell to the ground. As I bent down to pick them up, a man near me suddenly dropped to the ground, and a woman screamed in a high pitch like nothing I'd ever heard before.

Thirteen

THE VIBRATION OF THE gun lasted for a second once the shot was taken. Blood sprayed onto a woman standing near the target as his head rocked back from the blow, causing him to fall flat on his back. The target was a tall black man who was conversing with another man. The other man moved just enough for the sniper to get a clear shot to the head. The bulls-eye from the scope couldn't have been more centered to the forehead, so it was the perfect time to shoot.

And just as planned, the sniper set the gun down, lowered the sunglasses over his eyes and retreated back to the door. He reached in his pocket for a key and stuck it into the padlock, which immediately clicked open. He removed the lock from the door and casually entered the hallway that led to a set of metal stairs going downward. His plan of escape was simple; he'd rehearsed it two times the night before. The building's security system was elementary at best, only taking him thirty seconds to crack the code. He had spent just a couple of hours reviewing the building's floor plans and making sure that the janitor's closet on the ninth floor was the best place to make his change.

His work boots clanked against the metal stairs until he reached the bottom. He opened the door which led to a hallway and entered it as if nothing had happened. In the hallway, people passed him without incident. There were no frantic screams of bloody murder, nor did anyone know that a man had just been killed across the street. Business continued as normal despite the fact that a man lay dead nearly two blocks away.

The sniper turned the corner to a janitor's closet near the elevator. He pulled out a ring of keys from his pocket, quickly looked around before opening the door and then swiftly snuck inside. When the door closed, the room became dark as night. When the light came on, he began changing his clothes, paying no attention to the dead body propped along the back wall.

Fourteen

THE WOMAN'S SCREAMS RIPPED through my heart as I rushed to the man lying on the ground. No doubt that he was dead. A pool of bright red blood stained the concrete under his head and his eyes were wide open and lifeless. I knelt down and placed my fingers against the man's neck to see if I could feel a pulse, but didn't find one.

I reached for the BlackBerry on my hip and punched in 9-1-1.

"This is Detective Jacob Hayden," I said in a loud and rushed voice. "I need an ambulance at Connecticut Avenue in the park of Dupont Circle. I also need backup as shots were fired."

I re-clipped the BlackBerry to my hip and reached for my sidearm. I scanned the perimeter and saw the terrified faces of the people huddled around the body. Turtle was one of them.

"Turtle, I need you to stay here until the ambulance shows up. Make sure no one touches the body, understood?"

Turtle nodded, but his face was void of any expression except shock.

I jumped to my feet and faced the crosswalk. I quickly looked back at the dead man and then looked ahead again. I didn't recall hearing a shot, so that must mean the shooter had a silencer on the gun. No one in the streets had screamed or run for cover, so the shooter was not in the streets. He was on a roof. Seconds later, sirens from police cruisers blared into the Circle and three cars skidded to a stop. I pulled out my badge and quickly approached six uniformed officers.

"The shot came from that direction," I pointed north on Connecticut Avenue. "One deceased man down behind me." I looked at one of the officers and commanded him to stay with the body. "The rest, come with me."

We sprinted a block before stopping. I scanned the roofs of the nearby buildings and thought that the shot must have come from within the first two blocks.

"I want these buildings locked down," I demanded. "No one goes in or comes out until everyone is checked."

The five officers each took a building and entered it. Just then, more squad cars arrived and I gave the same commands to the arriving officers. I, on the other hand, took a second to gather my bearings. I looked around at the buildings again, studying the perimeter of the roofs and then looked back to where the victim had fallen. Across the street from where I was standing was the tallest building in the vicinity, a nine-story building. My gut instinct told me that the shot had come from that building. I gathered two officers and raced across the street.

"Radio your men and tell them we need this building locked down. I'm heading to the roof."

I exploded through dark tinted glass doors and was immediately met by a surprised security guard sitting behind a wooden desk. I raised my detective's shield.

"Stairs!"

The security guard pointed to his left.

I rushed to the door and stepped through, aiming my handgun. I took the steps two at a time, and at each floor, I raised my gun before proceeding to the next floor to make sure the stairway was clear. Halfway to the top, my lungs burned for air and I felt the fatigue in my calf muscles, but I didn't stop. Adrenaline drove me past the aching point that would make most quit.

I reached the top of the stairs gasping for air. I let my body rest for a few seconds before going through a grey metal door. The door opened to another set of metal stairs that led to the door on the roof. I slowly took the steps one at a time and then carefully opened the rooftop door. I wasn't sure what to expect, but I was ready for anything.

With my handgun aimed, I swept the roof, looking at every corner until I saw a rifle resting on prongs in the direction of the park. I made my way to the rifle and looked over the roof and saw an ambulance near the dead body. The police had already begun taping off the area.

The rooftop door opened and I swung around, aiming my Glock. Another uniformed officer stepped through the door with his handgun aimed.

"This is it," I said. "This is where the shot came from. Any luck downstairs?"

"No," the uniformed officer replied. "We're ordering the immediate evacuation of the building. No one leaves without getting checked."

"Good. Just make sure everyone is double-checked. The shooter may very well be in the building."

Fifteen

THE SNIPER STOOD IN a line with other businesspeople in the stairwell as police checked everyone's identification. The elevators had been shut down, so the only way out was through the stairwell. The police had locked down the area sooner than expected, which he thought meant that a cop must have been nearby when he took the shot. He was not worried because it was only a minor setback to getting out of the building unsuspected.

He was now dressed in a navy-blue pinstripe suit, and his fake driver's license said that his name was Harvey Lindenberg, from Minnesota. He was wearing dark-framed glasses and his brown hair was gelled back. His beard looked comfortably manicured, with no evidence that he just came from the roof's sweltering heat. A visitor's pass was connected to a silver chain around his neck, which everyone was wearing who had attended the IT Conference for the NuvoFone Corporation. If the police needed to, they could check his background and find out that he had been a systems engineer for twelve years, that he had been married for fifteen years and had two daughters. His criminal record was clear and he had never had a speeding ticket. His credit score was 710 and he had more than thirteen thousand dollars in his savings account. Everything about Harvey Lindenberg screamed that he was a boring suburbanite, which was precisely what the sniper wanted the cops to believe.

The stairwell felt stuffy. Its bleak grey walls and concrete stairs made the sniper feel like he was in a prison line waiting to go out to the yard. As the line slowly neared the bottom floor, he could hear the police telling everyone to have their IDs out, and if they were wearing jackets, to have them unbuttoned. Two lines formed at the bottom of the stairwell, one for men and the other for women. Police officers wearing white gloves searched the women's purses, asked the men to open their briefcases or bags, and then patted everyone down.

The sniper tapped the man in front of him, who he recognized from the conference.

"Does anyone know what's going on?" He disguised his voice by speaking in a lower register.

The man shook his head, "Nothing. There's a rumor that someone's been shot."

"Oh my. I hope he's not hurt too bad."

"From the looks of this, I'd say that he is."

"We should probably say a prayer for him, then."

The man strangely looked at the sniper before turning around. The line moved slowly, but he was now in the lobby and could finally see the doors leading outside. There were about fifteen people in front of him, and the pat down and search took about a minute each.

As he waited, a team of police dressed in SWAT gear rushed through the lobby; some entered the stairs while the rest headed into the service elevator. They had found the rifle on the roof and were probably searching the building floor by floor. He knew that it wouldn't be long until they found the body in the janitor's closet, so time really was starting to work against him. Nevertheless, in his estimation, by the time they found the body, he should be en route to his safe house, where he'd prepare for his next kill.

The line suddenly stopped. Something was wrong. The officers stopped checking people and gathered together like in a football huddle. One of the officers stepped aside and reached for his radio. He quickly spoke into it and then a voice replied, saying lock everything down.

The sniper became uneasy but didn't let his face show his concern. His eyes carefully looked to his right, where a nine-millimeter handgun was stashed behind a painting on the wall. He would only need a couple of steps to reach it and then he could use the man in front of him as a human shield. Patience, he thought. Patience. All he needed to do was get outside, where preparations would ensure that he'd be lost to the police. And he'd do it at all costs.

Sixteen

I WAS STANDING WITH a few other uniformed officers, going over details of the shooting when another uniformed officer quickly approached me with a man wearing a grey and blue cable uniform.

"This man says that he saw the shooter."

My eyes lit with excitement. I turned to the short, balding man who appeared to be of Latin American descent, and directed a precise question towards him.

"Are you sure?"

"Yes. Well, I didn't actually see him shoot. I heard frantic screams, and then a man caught the corner of my eyes when he stood up on the roof. I thought I saw a rifle, but I'm not sure."

"What's your name?"

"Manny."

"And, Manny, where were you when you saw the man?"

Manny turned around and pointed to the roof of the building behind us. The building was about three stories shorter than the white building. "Up there. I was working on a satellite dish when I heard the scream."

"Do you think you can ID the man if you saw him again?"

"I think so. He was wearing glasses and a hat, but I do remember that he had a beard. I think he may have been a janitor, because he was wearing a blue janitor's uniform."

"That's better than nothing."

I pulled out my radio and quickly spoke into it. "Lock everything down. We're coming in."

Only a handful of people had been let out of the building, so there was a good chance that the shooter was still inside. I remembered the faces of the people who had left and I hadn't seen anyone wearing a beard. Suddenly, I became excited about the chances of actually catching the shooter.

I was told by the building's management that ten companies occupied the building, and that each company had anywhere from twenty to seventy-five employees. Sifting through a few hundred people would be a daunting task, but one that I didn't mind doing. But there was another problem. One company was hosting a conference with close to another one hundred people from across the country in attendance. The shooter was smart in picking this day, which leads me to believe that we were dealing with a professional. Hopefully the eyewitness would be helpful.

I entered the building with Manny and another officer trailing close behind. The lobby was set up like a checkpoint at an airport, with officers frisking and waving metal detectors over each person. I felt the stares from the people in the lines. Some stared with anger that they were being forced to evacuate and wait in long lines, while others stared with intrigue.

I informed the officers that Manny was a possible witness and that he would be standing near the exit and looking at each person leaving the building. We'd be paying special attention to men wearing beards. I seriously doubted that the shooter was a janitor, and if he were wearing a janitor's uniform, it was just a means for him to enter the building.

The police started the line moving again. Already, I saw three men near the back of the line with beards, but they were dressed in suits and were wearing a tag around their necks, most likely from the conference. I wondered how long it would take for someone to change from a janitor's uniform to a suit. If he were wearing the suit under the janitor's uniform, then it wouldn't take long at all.

I leaned over to one of the officers and asked him to pull the three bearded men aside. I wanted to see how they would react to my questions. As a detective, I've dealt with liars of all types and like to think that I can spot a lie from a mile away. I study the person's overall posture.

Generally, when people lie, their bodies are stiff and they use fewer hand movements. Liars also tend to avoid eye contact and move their eyes around to avoid meeting the gaze of the person questioning them. Sometimes, if a person stares too long, that's another indication of a liar. They know eye movement may give them away, so they force themselves to keep their eyes fixated on the person questioning them. Liars also don't like to stand directly in front of the person questioning them, so they tend to turn their shoulders so that they're not squared.

If one of these men lies, I should be able to tell, and hopefully I can put this to bed before dinner.

Seventeen

THE SNIPER STOOD TO the right of the lines with two other men who were, curiously enough, wearing beards. Someone must have seen him on the roof and now the police were focusing on men with beards. He assumed it was the man wearing the cable uniform who was the eyewitness. No worries. The officer moved him right in front of the painting where the gun was stashed. He fought every urge to rip the painting off the wall and shoot his way free. He'd play along with their games as long as he needed, but if he got the feeling that they were on to him, the gun would be his means of escape.

Moving towards him was a man he recognized the instant he walked through the door. He had seen him through the scope as he canvassed the park, but didn't pin him as a cop. He was probably the reason the police arrived so soon. He was a tall African American man standing close to six feet three inches with a lean frame. He wore his hair close to his scalp with a shadow beard covering his face. His statuesque build wasn't intimidating by any means, but he carried an air of authority in his persona that begged to differ.

The man gracefully moved to them and looked them up and down before engaging in verbal communication. The sniper was the first of the three he passed.

"My name is Detective Hayden," he said, standing near the third man. "I just have a couple of quick questions to ask and then you're free to go. In case you haven't heard by now, someone's been shot a couple of blocks from here and we believe the shooter may have come from this building. All I ask is that you be straight up and honest with me and you'll be on your way."

The sniper's eyes followed the detective as he walked back and forth with his hands crossed behind his back. His body language seemed confident that he knew something the rest of them didn't, almost cocky. But the sniper sensed what he was doing. It's an interrogation method that's used to trick people into confessing to crimes by making it appear that the authority has the upper hand. Basically, they're looking for a reaction. If the one who committed the crime thinks that the police have evidence to substantiate a conviction, then maybe they'd confess without having to go through the hoopla of hours of interrogation. The sniper tried to hold back his smirk at the silliness of the whole charade, but nonetheless allowed a little one to form.

The detective asked the third bearded man where he was an hour ago and what he was doing. The man nervously answered and then the detective moved on. The same questions were asked to the second man, and then the detective moved to the sniper.

"So, what's your name?" The detective asked.

"Lindenberg, Harvey," the sniper replied with a cockiness of his own.

The detective didn't move his eyes away from the sniper's eyes.

"And, Lindenberg, Harvey, where were you an hour ago?"

"At a conference."

"Can anyone confirm you were there?"

"I'm sure someone could."

The sniper was taking a chance at his boldness, but he quickly sized up the detective and believed this to be the best way to answer the questions. In his opinion, the detective was looking for someone obviously trying to hide his guilt by pretending to be afraid and nervous, like he could never do anything as atrocious as what had been done.

The two shared stares for a few more seconds before the detective walked away.

"Thank you," he said.

The sniper nodded and followed the detective with his eyes as he headed back to the front door. Easy enough. A few more minutes and he should be out the door. Just then, he saw the detective speak in the ear of one of the officers, who gave the sniper a peculiar look. The detective then unlatched his sidearm and the sniper saw the officer do the same. Neither made a move, but the sniper suddenly knew this was going to end in a shoot-out. Acting on pure instinct, he spun around, knocking the painting off the wall, and reached for the nine-millimeter pistol. In the same movement, he grabbed the closest bearded man and took his first shot.

Eighteen

I FELL TO THE floor when I heard the echoing blast of the gun. I found cover next to the front desk and pulled my Glock free from its holster. Harvey Lindenberg was holding one of the other bearded men in front of him as a body shield as he sporadically shot around the room. The people in the lines screamed with fear. Some rushed the front, trying to break free, while others dropped to the ground.

"Don't shoot! He's got a hostage!" I yelled.

With the hostage as a body shield, I knew that none of the officers could get a clear shot. Harvey wasn't shooting at anyone; he was shooting at the room, trying to cause a distraction.

"Drop the weapon, Harvey!"

The shooting didn't cease. Harvey and the hostage rushed to the east side of the building, to the service elevator, and ducked inside. The doors closed with a ding.

"Anybody hurt?" I asked.

Everyone looked around the room and no one had been hit.

"Clear these people out of here on the double."

The lobby quickly emptied, with the exception of the police. I gathered the officers around me and barked orders.

"I need eyes on the outside and ears on the inside. Someone get me floor plans to the building. I want sharpshooters covering every angle of this place."

I reached for my radio, remembering that SWAT units were already scouring the floors.

"Tim, you read?"

A heavy voice came through the radio. "Whatcha got?"

"Our shooter is in the building. He's wearing a dark suit and a beard. He's got a hostage and he just entered the service elevator."

"10-4. I've got men on every floor. He won't get far."

Nineteen

BY NOW, THE SNIPER thought that he'd be at his safe house, preparing for the next kill. Instead, he was scaling a dark elevator shaft with a man who was crying his eyes out. The sniper stopped the elevator between the ground and first floors with the emergency button and then quickly climbed out through the escape door. Between the fourth and fifth floors, there's a ventilation shaft that leads to the building's maintenance room. The maintenance room is attached to the supply room where there's a window leading to the fire escape. The only problem was that the police would have all of the exits covered and sharpshooters aimed at the building. A metal ladder climbs the length of the elevator shaft, with the only light coming from the elevator. The one thing slowing him up was the hostage.

"Hurry up," the sniper repeated.

"Please, just let me go. I have a wife and family."

"And you'll see them again if you do as I say. Now hurry."

The sniper continued looking below, expecting to hear the voices of the police in the elevator's car. He pushed the hostage harder to reach the ventilation shaft, and once they did, they crawled in without incident. The ventilation shaft was three feet high and three feet wide. Without the dim light from the elevator's car, the shaft was completely dark.

"Keep going until you can't go anymore and then we'll make a right," the sniper said.

"I can't see anything," the hostage pleaded.

"Just keep moving."

It didn't take them long to reach the end and make the right. Ten feet down the shaft, light shined from the maintenance room. They shuffled on their hands and knees until they reached the vent. The sniper looked through the vent's openings and then pried it loose. He carefully lowered himself to the floor and then waited for the hostage to do the same. They went through a door to their left and entered a small supply room.

"Stand here. Don't move."

The sniper went to the edge of the window and looked out. They were now at the back of the building, facing an alley. Two squad cars were parked at either end of the alley and there were two sharpshooters on the roof across from them.

He looked back at the terrified hostage and smiled.

"Well, my friend, this is where we part ways."

Without another word, the sniper swung the butt of the gun and knocked the hostage out.

Twenty

WE ALL HAD OUR guns aimed at the service elevator on the ground floor. Two officers with crowbars in their hands were ready to pry the door open upon my command. I stood a few feet away, along with the rest of the officers, making sure that everyone was in position before giving the go-ahead.

SWAT leader Tim McDonald, a man built like a bull and who ran his squad as if he were still in the Marines, came down to the ground floor and confirmed that the elevator had not landed on any floor in the building. I instantly knew that Harvey was in the elevator shaft.

Once everyone was in position, I gave the command and the two officers pried the elevator door open. The empty elevator was between the lobby and first floor.

"Clear," one of the officers said.

I hurried to the elevator and looked inside and saw the trapdoor at the top of the elevator was open.

"He's in the shaft." I turned my attention to Tim. "Tell your men to open all of the elevator doors on each floor. We'll need all the light we can get."

I turned to one of the officers and asked him to boost me up so that I could climb inside the elevator. The opening between the elevator and the ceiling was wide enough that I could squeeze through. I reached up to the bottom of the elevator, and at the same time, the officer grabbed my leg and was about to push me up when Tim put his hand on my shoulder.

"You should wait until my men can make sure the shaft is clear."

"No time to wait. Floor plans show that there are ventilation ducts on each floor. He could be anywhere in the building by now. And who knows what he's done with the hostage."

Tim looked into the elevator and then back to me. "Ok, but I'll lead."

He radioed the rest of his men. "I want bodies in the elevator shaft now. Check all ventilation shafts between each floor. And remember, there's a hostage."

He turned to me, "Ready?"

"Always."

Twenty-one

AT THIS POINT, A reasonable person would say, I'm trapped, the building's surrounded with cops and the only way out is either in handcuffs or a body bag. Not to mention that by now, the police would have swarmed the elevator shaft and were inching ever so close to pinning him in a corner. All of this would make a reasonable person give up. The sniper wasn't that reasonable.

He still felt that he could walk out the front door unnoticed, but the plan had changed.

He stood with his ear pressed against the supply room's door and listened for any sounds of movement. Convinced the coast was clear, he slowly opened the door and peered out. Sterile white walls lined the empty hallway. He looked back into the supply room one more time, taking notice that the unconscious hostage was duct taped pretty well, should he regain consciousness in the next few minutes.

The sniper crept along the hallway, being careful not to make noise with his steps. His new plan called for a surprise attack, which was the only way he saw of making it out alive.

Four feet in front of him was a hallway which, he knew, by making a right would lead him to the service elevator at the end of the hall. As he suspected, the closer he got to the hallway, he heard voices.

He peeked around the corner and saw three SWAT police with their backs to him. The elevator door was open and the men were shining flashlights into the shaft. A thought came to mind, but he quickly dismissed it as it would only temporarily solve his problem. Rushing them and knocking them into the shaft would eliminate three officers, but he was sure that more would crawl out like ants in a anthill. By now, there were probably a dozen of them scaling the elevator shaft looking for him. He needed to draw them away from the shaft and deeper into the hallway for his plan to work.

Luckily, the break came just at the right time.

One of the SWAT officers climbed into the shaft, and while doing so, told the two others to sweep the floor again.

The sniper quickly backed away and returned to the supply room. The hostage was still unconscious.

He stood to the left of the door with his back against the wall, waiting for the door to open. Once the SWAT officer saw the unconscious hostage, the sniper would only have seconds to react. And then the plan would go into motion. But now he must wait.

When the waiting game began, seconds felt like minutes, and minutes like hours. The sniper started to feel antsy, but did a good job of calming his nerves by slowing his breathing and closing his eyes. He envisioned how the event would unfold in his mind.

The SWAT officer would slowly open the door, probably not expecting to see an unconscious man duct-taped on the floor. He should be alone because the other one would have taken the other side of the building. He would be surprised and then would rush to check the man's vitals. At that point, the sniper would come from behind the open door and take out the cop. He'd dress in the cop's uniform. Luckily, they're wearing black masks under their hardhats. Then he'd approach the second cop and take him out, too. Then he'd take the stairs, being careful not to look too rushed, and walk past the checkpoint where he'd be free.

The plan was nearly perfect, given the fact that he had come up with it when he realized that he wouldn't be able to go out of the fire escape. The only thing now was the execution.

Suddenly, he heard a door from across the hall close. He looked to his doorknob and watched as it slowly turned. Adrenaline rushed through his body as he balled his fists and waited for the cop to enter the room. And just as he thought, one of the SWAT officers rushed in and knelt down next to the hostage. And just as he imagined, he leaped from behind the door and attacked the first officer. What he didn't expect was that the second one was right behind him.

Twenty-two

TIM AND I CLIMBED to the fourth floor when we realized that the only ventilation shaft large enough for someone to fit in is between the fourth and fifth floor. Harvey's on this floor. Call it intuition, but it's the same feeling I felt when I sensed that the sniper shot came from this building.

I met Tim's eyes and confirmed the feeling without saying a word. Tim steadied his semi-automatic machine gun and I gripped my Glock.

"Where are your men?" I whispered.

Tim reached for his radio and quietly spoke into it. "Smith, Clayton, what's your position?"

Static filled the reception.

"Edwards," Tim said, "what's your position?"

"I'm on the fifth floor," came a husky reply. "I told Smith and Clayton to search the fourth floor one more time."

"Something's wrong." I said.

"We'll split up," Tim responded. "You check the right hallway and I'll check the left and then we'll meet back here in the middle."

I nodded and then turned left.

Five doors were on my side of the hallway: two offices, two bathrooms and one supply room. Management of the building contacted their security company and decoded all of the doors so that we wouldn't need security keys to open them.

The first door on the right was a glass door with the name Loventon & Smith, LLC, which I assumed was a law firm. I pushed the door open and entered a small lobby comprised of a reception desk and two leather couches in front of it. I passed through the reception area and entered the back offices and quickly made my rounds through each office. With everything clear, I returned to the hallway.

The second door on the right led to a men's bathroom. As I gripped the door handle, I heard movement coming from down the hall, which initially startled me. I released the door and aimed my gun in the direction of the sound and slowly moved towards it.

Harvey Lindenberg was all I could think about. The sound could be coming from the SWAT officers checking the rooms, but something told me it wasn't. It was Harvey Lindenberg.

I looked to the right to see if Tim was in sight, but he wasn't. I wanted to call for backup, but dared not as Harvey could hear the radio.

The sound became more pronounced the closer I got to the center of the hallway, and I knew it was coming from the middle door. With no backup, I took a chance on being one-on-one with a man who has no problem killing.

My heart was thumping in my chest as I reached for the door's handle. My eyes widened and I took a deep breath, ready for whatever was on the other side. I twisted the knob and exploded through the door with my gun aimed.

"Police!"

Twenty-three

I NEARLY DROPPED MY gun at the sight. If I weren't staring at it myself, I never would have believed it. Three people were lying on the floor, two of whom were unconscious. The one who was moving around and trying to unbind himself was the hostage. I reached for my radio, still shocked by what was before me.

"Tim, get down here fast, first door on the left!"

I hurried to the first man, a SWAT officer, who was both bound and nearly naked. He was alive. I stepped over to the next SWAT officer and saw that he was alive as well.

"Goddammit," I screamed.

Tim swiftly stepped into the room with his machine gun engaged, as if to shoot on sight.

"My God," he said.

He knelt down next to Smith, the nearly naked SWAT officer. He pulled the black duct tape from his mouth and unbound his wrists. Tim slapped Smith's face until he came around.

"What happened?" Tim asked.

Smith's eyes partly opened and then closed again.

"Smith!"

Tim rested Smith's head on the ground and then radioed the rest of his men.

"The shooter's still in the building, possibly wearing a SWAT uniform. Smith and Clayton are down. I repeat, Smith and Clayton are down. I need paramedics on the fourth floor, ASAP."

I jumped to my feet and started to leave the room.

"Stay with your men. I'm going back to the lobby."

I rushed down the hallway and found the stairwell, taking the stairs five at a time until I neared the bottom floors. The only way out of the building was through the front door, and the only way to catch Harvey Lindenberg was to beat him there.

I underestimated Harvey's skill. I figured the shooter had to be a professional for picking today to do the killing, while the building had a conference full of out-of-town people. But to be able to shoot his way out of a lobby full of cops and then take out two SWAT officers was unimaginable.

I reached the lobby and saw that it was full of uniformed cops and a few plainclothes detectives. I stood in the center of the lobby and raised my hands to get everyone's attention.

"Listen, the shooter's name is Harvey Lindenberg and he may be dressed in a SWAT uniform. Have any SWAT come down in the last few minutes?"

The officers shook their heads no.

"Be on full alert that no one wearing SWAT gear can leave the building until they are thoroughly checked."

Twenty-four

AN HOUR WENT BY, with no word from Harvey Lindenberg. The nail-biting suspense was killing me inside. I wanted to run through the building and check every room, but I also wanted to be in the lobby in case Harvey Lindenberg somehow made it down.

My last communication with Tim had been thirty minutes before, when he said that his men were scouring the building.

I didn't want to believe it, but I was beginning to think that Harvey Lindenberg somehow made it out of the building. How? I still held onto hope that Tim and his men would find him, but that hope was quickly slipping away.

"Jacob," Tim's voice came over the radio and brought me out of thought.

"Talk to me."

"We've got nothing."

I lowered my head as my fear was confirmed. Harvey had gotten away.

Part Three: The Judge

Twenty-five

The Next Day

AT NINE A.M. SHARP, the announcement was made for all to rise. Superior Court Judge Frank Peters entered the courtroom like royalty, wearing a sleek black robe. He stepped up to the bench and gracefully sat down. He scanned the courtroom and saw a couple dozen people scattered in the pews, all of them standing and waiting for his command.

"You may be seated," he said in a husky voice that sounded amplified in the quiet room.

Everyone took their seats.

He slipped a pair of wire-framed reading glasses over his eyes that nearly came down to the tip of his nose as he opened a case file. The caption for the first document read: The District of Columbia v. John Hayes, and under the caption, in bold letters, said: Decision. Judge Frank Peters glanced over the Decision and then raised his head, narrowing his eyes at the defendant.

"Will the defendant please rise."

The defendant, John Hayes, a slimy two-bit crook with tattoos covering his neck and a shaved head like a skinhead, slid his seat back and stood with his lawyer. He looked uncomfortable wearing a suit.

"Before I begin, I'd like to remind the defendant that you waived a trial by jury, which means that I'm the only one deciding your fate. Correct?"

Tim Johnson, a public defender who looked like he had just graduated from law school, acknowledged for the defendant, "Correct, Your Honor."

"Very well. As to the charge of felony aggravated assault with a deadly weapon, I find the defendant guilty and sentence him to the maximum time allowed, ten years."

Judge Peters slammed his gavel.

John Hayes looked to his lawyer with utter shock. Two uniformed court deputies stood behind the defendant and placed him in handcuffs.

Tim Johnson tentatively raised his hand and tried to speak up. "Your Honor?"

Judge Frank Peters yanked off his reading glasses and nearly growled. "Is there something you want, counselor?"

"It's just...I..."

The deputies took John Hayes out of the courtroom. He looked at Tim Johnson, confused, and then to the Judge, and then lowered his head as he exited the room.

Tim Johnson lowered his hand and dejectedly said, "Nothing, Your Honor."

"Very well."

The judge closed the file and moved on to the next one.

Twenty-six

"WAKE UP, SLEEPY HEAD."

I felt the tender touch of soft fingers rubbing my cheek. I slowly opened my eyes and then felt succulent moist lips gently press against mine.

"How's my tired detective doing this afternoon?"

I smiled as my body stretched to its full length.

"Afternoon?"

"It's just past one o'clock."

"Geeesh, I didn't mean to sleep this late."

"That's your body telling you it needs rest."

I nodded and then quickly grabbed Theresa and pulled her into bed. She playfully screamed, but willingly fell. I pulled her closer and wrapped my arms around her and laid my head in the center of her breasts. I loved this woman more than she knew. I closed my eyes and succumbed to the gentle massage that her fingers played against my scalp.

"You wanna talk about it?" she asked.

I exhaled as I moved my hand to her stomach and gently made circles around her belly button with my index finger.

"I had to finally call it a night. We searched for this guy for nearly ten hours after we left the building, with no luck. I've never experienced anything like it."

I turned my head and looked into her almond-colored eyes.

"It's like he just vanished off the face of the earth. How does that happen? I mean, how does a guy escape from a building swarmed with cops without being seen. It's a trick not even Houdini could pull off."

"Maybe Captain Kirk beamed him aboard The Enterprise with Spock and Bones."

"I wish that was the explanation. At least it would make sense. Although then I'd have to wonder why the Enterprise would have beamed him down in the first place."

Theresa kissed the top of my head and said, "Turn around."

She took off my shirt and motioned for me to lie on my stomach. When I was comfortable she straddled my backside.

"Take deep breaths."

I did. With the balls of her palms, she rubbed my lower back in circular motions and then slowly moved them up my spine and onto my shoulders. I felt like I was in Heaven. Once on my shoulders, she extended her fingers and rubbed deep into my muscles.

"How does that feel?"

"Great."

She laughed, "Okay, relax."

She then moved her hands to my neck, then wrapped them around the back of my head and chin. With a quick jerk, she jolted my head and cracked the bones in my neck.

"Hey."

"Feel better?"

I moved my head around from side to side. "Actually, I do."

She moved from my backside and laid next to me.

"You were stressed. Your muscles and joints were tight. By cracking the bones, I've relieved the tension."

"That's why I married a doctor. Now if you could only perform miracles and point me in the direction of my shooter."

"Let me pull out my crystal ball."

We laughed, but inside I couldn't help feeling the weight of not finding the shooter. To make things worse, we found out that the real Harvey Lindenberg died in April of 1947. So now I was faced with searching for a nameless suspect whose face was burned into my brain. Composite sketches had already been worked up and sent to every news outlet in the city, so now it's just a matter of patience. I'm also hoping that something about the victim will help point me in the right direction.

I kissed Theresa's hands and then rubbed my fingers through her hair.

"Thanks for everything."

Before she could respond, my BlackBerry chimed. I reached over to the nightstand and picked it up. A text message from Charlie Evans telling me that they had some information on the victim. Just what I was waiting for.

"Good news?" she asked.

"We'll see."

Twenty-seven

JUDGE FRANK PETERS COMFORTABLY sat in his chair as it leaned back, allowing his hands to rest on the edge of his desk with his fingers interlocked between one another. His face was expressionless as Tim Johnson, the public defender in the Hayes case, stood before his desk, nervous. They were in the judge's chamber because Tim had asked for a brief meeting to discuss the verdict against his client. Tim was of average height and build, with short-cropped hair, a long nose and bushy eyebrows. He'd only been out of law school for three years.

Frank curled his lips and then looked to his right. Nathan Hunt, a large Italian-looking man in a black suit sat on a leather couch with an open newspaper. Nathan appeared to be reading the paper and uninterested, but Frank knew that he was paying attention to every word. That's what he was paid to do.

Frank looked back at Tim.

"So you have a problem with the sentence, is that it?" Frank asked.

Tim gulped and, before responding, looked over to Nathan.

"It's not that, Your Honor. I just thought we had a different understanding."

"Understanding?"

Tim didn't respond, but his face screamed panic.

Frank slowly stood from his chair and casually walked around his large mahogany desk. Despite being sixty-two, he was in excellent shape, and if it weren't for his thinning grey hair, he would look like he was in his forties. He was wearing a blue collared shirt which accentuated his broad shoulders, strong pecs and bulging arms. When he was in his twenties, Frank had competed as an amateur body builder before he took to the bench. He knew he didn't have the physiology to go pro, but enjoyed the competition on the local level. Now his physique was likened to Sylvester Stallone's, who also didn't seem to age.

He motioned for Tim to sit in one of the empty chairs in front of the desk. Tim nodded and moved to sit, but before he could, Frank swung an open hand and smacked him in the face. Tim tumbled over the chair and fell on his back.

"Get up you, pencil-pushing coward! Do you know how much that idiot cost me?"

Tim stayed on the floor with a hand covering his cheek. He looked over at Nathan, who didn't bat an eye from the paper.

Just as casually as he had stood, Frank returned to his chair. He leaned back and placed his hands on the end of his desk, interlocking his fingers between one another.

"So what's our understanding now?"

Tim slowly stood and repositioned the chair to take a seat. The left side of his face was red as an apple.

"There's no misunderstanding, Your Honor."

A smile curled on Frank's face. "That's what I want to hear."

The phone on his desk beeped and a female voice came to life.

"Mayor Bradley's on the line, sir."

"Good. Tell him I'll be one minute."

Frank returned his attention to Tim. "Anything else?"

"No, Your Honor."

"Very well. Enjoy the rest of your day."

As Tim turned to leave, Frank picked up the phone. "Michael, good to hear from you, buddy."

Twenty-eight

"WHATCHA GOT FOR ME, Charlie?" I asked as I entered the back offices of the police station.

"We got an ID on the victim from the park yesterday." He shuffled some papers around and then pulled out a manila folder that had a picture of the dead victim. "Faraji Owusu. Originally from Kenya. Family emigrated here when he was ten years old."

Charlie handed the folder to me.

"Kenya?" I said as I sat at my desk.

"Yep. He used to be a prosecutor here in the city, but moved into private practice a few years ago."

I slumped in my chair and rolled my eyes. I knew my job of finding the shooter had just gotten harder. Prosecutors are known for receiving death threats from people they put behind bars, or from people who are close to the ones who were put behind bars. Depending on how long he had worked as a prosecutor, the list could be enormous.

"Do we know if he worked on any high-profile cases?"

"Not yet. We haven't gotten a chance to interview any of his present and former colleagues."

"Family?"

"I talked to his wife and she said that everything was normal. She doesn't know of anyone who'd want him dead."

I thought about the wife for a minute. General procedure in a murder investigation, although it's not written in stone, is to interview the family members or those closest to the victim. It's an unfortunate fact, but most murder victims are killed by people they know. Could the wife have put a hit out on the victim? Was he cheating on her? Beating her? Did he do something to her that was so bad that she had him killed? Did he have money? If it wasn't for that fact that a sniper shot him from the roof of a building, I would take those thoughts into serious consideration. This wasn't a typical murder and I believed that the man who called himself Harvey Lindenberg wasn't a typical killer. I thought I could go out on a limb and say that the wife wasn't involved.

So then why was he killed by a sniper? Who would possibly want him dead? Business associates? Greed could be a factor. All kinds of questions started to flood through my mind. The victim was from Kenya. Maybe he did something to someone over in Kenya and this was how he was repaid? Could the sniper be a contract killer? Or maybe a killer with a vendetta? The sniper attacks in

2002 in the D.C. area by Lee Boyd Malvo and John Allen Muhammad caused such a ruckus that people were terrified to leave their houses. Could this be a copycat killer trying to make a name for himself? I didn't think so, but the fact that a sniper had killed someone in the city nearly a decade after the 2002 sniper attacks would stay in the back of my mind until this was over.

The more I thought about it, the more I leaned on the fact that this was a professional hit. The sniper had stashed a gun behind a picture in the lobby just in case he had to use it, which showed that he was prepared for anything to happen. Also the fact that he was able to escape a building full of police showed that he's smarter than the average killer.

"Okay, we'll need to start at the beginning. Find out where he went to law school and who he clerked for. This was a professional hit, so somewhere down the line, he crossed paths with the wrong person."

"Actually, he clerked for Judge Peters from 1994 to 1996."

I sat up in my seat. With all the commotion of the sniper shooting, I had completely forgotten about my conversation with Turtle in the park.

"Judge Frank Peters?" I asked.

"Yep."

"Interested in taking a ride?"

Twenty-nine

WALKING DOWN THE HALLWAY to the judge's chambers reminded me of that long walk to the principal's office after I'd gotten in trouble in elementary school. I didn't know why I was nervous; I'd be the one asking the questions and the judge would be answering. Maybe it's the fact that a judge stands as the authority in the legal community; someone who's respected and feared, similar to a principal. Or maybe it's because in the back of my mind, I was thinking about the conversation with Turtle and how Judge Peters could possibly be involved in an illegal business.

After entering the D.C. Superior Courthouse, I found where the judge's chambers were held, pushed a button near the door and was let in after identifying myself as Detective Jacob Hayden. Charlie and I passed a few doors in the hallway until we reached the last one on the left. I slowly turned the handle and entered the room, met by a heavyset, grey-haired secretary sitting at her desk. Her gold nameplate read Sylvia Woodrow. With her hair wrapped in a bun and her eyeglasses attached to a chain around her neck, she reminded me of an elementary school teacher. The secretary was on the phone and raised her hand, letting us know that she'd be with us in a minute.

I smiled and stuffed my hands in my front pockets. Charlie did the same.

The reception area was small, not at all what I had expected to see. I'd never been in a judge's chambers before, so I could only go on what I had seen in the movies. The walls were stark white with no windows leading to the outside world. The room felt almost claustrophobic, just large enough to fit the secretary's desk and a few other office essentials. Finally, she set the phone down and smiled at us.

"Good afternoon, detectives. I'll let Judge Peters know you're here."

Moments later, she pointed at a side door behind her right shoulder and informed us to walk in.

Standing in front of a large mahogany desk, Judge Peters waited with his hand extended. His inviting smile wasn't at all what I was expecting, given what I had been told by Turtle the day earlier.

I shook his hand. "Detective Hayden, and this is Detective Evans."

"Take a seat, detectives."

We sat in the two leather-wrapped chairs in front of the desk. I glanced around the office and noticed the extensive amount of law books that filled the bookshelves behind the judge's desk. To my left was an empty leather sofa with a small coffee table. I noticed an open newspaper on top of the table with a recently put out cigarette in the cigarette holder. The smell of the smoke from the cigarette still remained in the air. Either the judge was sitting on the sofa smoking a cigarette or someone else had just recently left.

"So," Judge Peters said, "you wanted to talk to me about yesterday's shooting?"

"That's correct, Your Honor," I responded. "We found out that the victim was a former clerk of yours, a Mr. Faraji Owusu."

The judge's eyes widened with apparent shock. "Faraji? Oh, my. Are you sure?"

"Yes, next of kin identified him this morning."

Judge Peters exhaled and leaned back in his chair. He turned his head and faced the left wall, but didn't seem to be looking at anything in particular.

"I'm not sure how I can help," he said finally, turning back to us. "It's been more than ten years since he clerked for me, and the few times I've seen him since was when he's been before me in court."

"Do you know the last time he was before you?"

"I'd have to check the calendar, but it's probably been more than six months."

"And besides seeing him in court, you haven't been in contact with him?"

"No, although now I wish I had. Faraji was a brilliant lawyer. Wish he'd stayed with the DA's office instead of going into private practice. But I can understand. Money's better on that end, you know," he said with a smile.

"I can imagine. Do you know of any reason why someone would want him dead?"

"No, I don't."

Judge Peters opened a drawer from his desk and pulled out a handkerchief and dabbed his eyes.

"Excuse me," he says, "I'm normally not an emotional person, but this kinda caught me off guard."

"We're sorry you had to find out like this."

The judge put the handkerchief back in the drawer and directed his attention back to me.

"I know it's been a while, but do any cases stand out where someone could have made a threat either to you or him during the time he clerked for you?"

Judge Peters shook his head no, but there seemed to be a slight hesitation with his answer.

I studied the judge's facial expressions and body language and something didn't sit right. The judge didn't appear to be relaxed, and he was tapping his desk with his fingers like he was nervous. He didn't make eye contact with me when he was answering my questions, which raised a red flag. The warm smile that had greeted us when we first entered the room was no longer there, and I began to wonder what the judge was hiding.

I glanced over to Charlie and hoped that he was getting the same vibes, but he didn't show that he was.

"Is there anything else that I can help you gentlemen with?"

I wanted to ask him if he had ever heard of Melvin Johnson but figured this wasn't the time, so I simply responded, "No, not at this time, sir."

I pulled out my wallet, grabbed a business card and handed it to Judge Peters.

"If you can think of anything else, please don't hesitate to call."

Judge Peters smiled.

We left the room and smiled at the secretary as we passed her desk.

The judge closed his door.

"Excuse me, detectives," the secretary said.

We both turned around.

"The news this morning said that Faraji was the man who was shot in Dupont Circle yesterday. I suppose that's why you're here."

"I'm afraid so," Charlie responded.

The secretary's face started to crinkle and her eyes began to tear up.

"It's just that he was so nice," she continued. "He always commented on how beautiful my smile was whenever he visited."

Charlie and I looked at each other curiously.

"Had he visited the judge lately?" I asked.

"Just last week."

Thirty

"IS THERE ANYTHING THAT I need to be concerned with?" Frank asked Nathan Hunt, who returned to sitting on the leather couch.

"Nothing at all."

"Then explain to me why two detectives were just in here asking about Faraji?"

"Nothing can be linked back to you."

He slammed his fist against the top of his desk and his face turned bright red. "That's not what I asked you!"

Nathan didn't reply.

"Listen to me, dipshit, I want this taken care of. Find out who killed Faraji, and also what that detective knows." The color of his face returned to normal as he leaned back in his chair. "I didn't like the way he was looking at me."

Thirty-one

THE MORE I THOUGHT about it, the more I got the uneasy feeling that everything Turtle had told me about Judge Frank Peters was true. The judge had met me with a smile, shook my hand and then told a bold-faced lie right through the slits of his teeth. He'd seen Faraji Owusu a week earlier but told me that it had been at least six months. What was the reason for the lie? If the judge had been honest and said that he had met with Faraji a week earlier, I wouldn't have thought anything about it. Faraji had clerked for the judge and was also a prosecutor for the city, so a casual meeting wouldn't have raised any red flags. But now that I knew the judge had lied about something as innocent as a recent meeting, it made me also question if the judge was implicated in Faraji's murder in some way.

Hopefully, I could get some more answers from Faraji's partner at his law firm

Carter & Owusu, LLP, was the name on a silver nameplate next to a wooden front door. The law firm was only blocks away from the Dupont Circle park where Faraji had been killed. Brownstones lined a side street that had been refurbished into businesses, and the law firm sat in one of the middle brownstones.

Charlie and I walked up a couple of brick steps, and when we got to the front door, we saw a typed note on letterhead taped to the door that read that the office was closed due to the unfortunate events that had happened yesterday. I hesitated, but then reached for the front door and surprisingly found that it was unlocked. I looked at Charlie for confirmation before opening the door. Charlie shrugged his shoulders, I did the same, then I opened the door and stepped inside.

The lights were off on the first floor. We walked into a narrow foyer which led to an open reception area. A wooden desk with a computer and phone was at the back end of the room, while two sofas and a center table filled the other end of the room.

"Hello," I called out.

No one answered.

As tempting as it was to search the place while no one was there, I knew that anything we found would be useless because we didn't have a search warrant.

"Do we have a personal address on the partner?" I asked.

"Yeah, in the car," Charlie responded. "He lives in Maryland."

"How about a number? I'll call him and set something up for tomorrow when he's back in the office."

"Yeah, we have his number."

We turned to leave when we suddenly heard glass breaking from upstairs. Instinctively, we both pulled out our sidearms and looked around the room and then realized where the breaking glass was coming from. I found the stairs to the left of the foyer and rushed up them two at a time. Glass continued to break when we reached the second floor. We turned to the right and sprinted down a small hallway until we reached the last office. There we found a brown-haired Caucasian man with a thin beard sitting behind a desk slouching in his chair. His chair was facing the adjacent wall to his right. I looked over and saw broken wine bottles on the floor and spatters of alcohol covering the wall.

"Stephen Carter?" I asked.

Stephen didn't acknowledge me at first, but then slowly turned to me.

"Are you here to kill me too?" Stephen asked. His speech was slurred and his eyes were half-open.

"No," I quickly responded. "I'm Detective Hayden and this is Detective Evans."

Our tension eased and we put away our guns. I realized from the strong stench of alcohol and Stephen's slurred speech that he'd probably been here drinking for most of the afternoon.

"Why would you think that we're here to kill you?"

Stephen clumsily turned his chair towards me. His head slightly slouched towards his chest and his eyes tried to focus, but they looked down as soon as he spoke.

"Faraji's dead. I thought you were the men who killed him."

"Do you know why Faraji was killed?" I asked.

Stephen shrugged his shoulders. "Could be a number of things. We're all dirty, you know."

"When you say all, who do you mean?"

Stephen smirked. He was about to say something, but covered his mouth as if he were going to vomit.
"The guy's drunk out of his mind," Charlie said.

"Yeah, that's right," Stephen answered. "I'm drunk. Only because I know that I'm next."

I slowly sat in a chair in front of Stephen's desk. "What do you know about Faraji's death?"

Stephen shook his head. "It doesn't matter anyways. Either the person who killed Faraji's going to kill me or the other one will."

"What are you talking about? Which other one?"

Stephen raised his head and lifted his arm and pointed.

"The one behind you."

Before I could turn around, I heard a bang and then saw Charlie fall to the ground. I didn't have enough time to reach for my weapon before I got hit on the head and blacked out.

Thirty-two

FRANK ONCE AGAIN FOUND himself in the company of Tim Johnson, the defense attorney he had slapped in his chambers a few hours earlier. They were at the judge's private residence, and Tim sat in the living room chair like a whipped dog fearing its master. It was unusual for Frank to hold meetings at his house, but under the current circumstances, he felt it best to do so.

Frank paced the living room while talking into a prepaid cell phone. Agitation was in his voice as he held back the rage within him. He wanted to curse out the person he was speaking with. Rarely did he engage in these types of discussions anymore, but due to Faraji Owusu's death, he knew it was best for him to ensure that things would still go as planned.

"I know, I know, you'll have your shipments in two days...Look, no one planned for this. We're just as baffled as you are...I'm already on it. We're looking for the shooter as we speak...Two days. You have my word."

Frank hung up the phone and then tossed it to Tim Johnson. He walked to a wet bar at the back end of the living room and poured a glass of Scotch.

"You want a drink?"

Tim nervously shook his head no.

"How's the face?"

"It's okay, Your Honor."

"No hard feelings, huh? You've just gotta learn that what I say goes. Understand?"

"Yes, Your Honor."

"That son of a bitch could have cost us our livelihood. Never should have brought him on in the first place. You gotta be careful dealing with people you think you can trust."

Frank moved to the sofa across from Tim and casually sat. He crossed his legs as he took a sip of Scotch.

"You're being promoted."

"Promoted, Your Honor?"

"That's what I said." Frank placed the glass of Scotch on the coffee table. "Once Faraji's death blows over, you're going to leave the public defender's office and go work with Stephen."

Frank leaned forward in his seat and extended his hand. "Congratulations, Partner."

Tim seemed reluctant to reciprocate the handshake. He slowly rose and extended his hand. "Thank you, Your Honor. I don't know what to say."

Frank waved off the comment. "Just remember that with this new position comes greater responsibility.

And if you thought I was tough on you as a public defender, you haven't seen nothing yet. If you screw something up, I'll have my foot so far up your ass you'll be able to clip my toenails with your teeth, understood?"

"I understand."

"Don't make me regret this."

"I won't, Your Honor."

"I loved your father like he was my own blood, but if you fall out of line, with God as my witness, I'll kill ya."

Frank shrugged his shoulders before taking another sip of Scotch. "You're a bright kid and a smart lawyer, but you need to grow some balls. The sky's the limit in this business. Just be smart and do what I say, and you'll never have a problem with me."

Frank stood and moved to a side window. He slipped his hands through a set of sheer drapes and gazed outside.

"If I can only teach you one thing, let it be this: money always comes first. It comes before your family and your friends, your wife and your children. It comes before everything."

He turned around just enough that his eyes were able to pierce into Tim's soul. "Everything. Understood?"

"Yes, Your Honor."

He turned back around towards the window with an evil smirk on his face. He had made his point. He knew that he wouldn't have any problems with Tim after this. He was a puppet, just like the rest of them. Frank was the kind of man who needed to be in control. That's why the shooting of Faraji had been gnawing at him. It's not that he cared for Faraji; rather, the killing wasn't within his control. And as a result, it could possibly delay a big shipment worth hundreds of thousands of dollars that Faraji had been handling.

Frank began to turn from the window when he saw Nathan Hunt's car pull into his driveway. The driveway ran past the side of the house until it reached the garage at the back of the house.

"What's this idiot doing?"

He turned back to Tim.

"You see, this is what I mean. I've told this jerkoff a thousand times never to come here unless I tell him to."

The color of Frank's face reddened the longer he watched the car slowly move along the driveway. Frank squeezed the glass until the tips of his fingers turned pink. He threw the last ounce of Scotch down his throat and then stomped through the living room and past the kitchen until he reached the back door.

The back door flew open just as Nathan opened his car door.

"You'd better have a damn good reason for showing up here unannounced, you moron."

Nathan didn't say anything. He pushed the trunk release button on the driver's side door and stepped from the car. The trunk clicked and opened slightly.

"Oh, now you're ignoring me," Frank said as he stormed down three steps.

Nathan opened the trunk at the same time Frank reached the car. If he thought he was upset when he saw Nathan's car pull into his driveway, that was nothing compared to the way the blood in his veins boiled now.

"Oh what the hell is this!?"

Thirty-three

I FELT A THUMPING pulse from the back of my head that matched the rhythm of my heartbeat. Then a piercing pain shot through my skull. It felt like my head was tearing apart. My eyes partly opened and my vision was blurry. I blinked a few times, my vision became clearer, and I saw the intricate patterns of the Berber carpet right below my eyes.

My finger twitched as my senses regained control. I slowly lifted my head, which caused the piercing pain to shoot like scattered pellets throughout my brain. I grunted at the pain but slowly moved my arms to plant my palms against the floor, and then pushed myself up. Once on my knees, I touched the back of my head and flinched at the soreness. I pulled my hand away and saw blood on my fingertips.

It took me a few seconds to remember where I was or what happened, but seeing the desk right in front of me caused my senses to rush to high alert. My eyes widened and my heartbeat accelerated.

"Charlie," I whispered.

I turned around and saw Charlie lying on the ground. The wall next to him was covered with blood spatters, revealing the horrible truth. I crawled to Charlie's body and turned him around. I knew the instant I saw his eyes that he was dead.

"Oh no, Charlie."

I cradled Charlie in my arms and lightly sobbed over his body, ignoring the shooting pain that rushed through my head. I reached for my phone and punched 9-1-1, the second time that I'd had to do that in two days.

"This is Detective Jacob Hayden," I said in a desolate voice. "I have an officer down and need backup."

I hung up the phone after giving the address and sat against the bloodstained wall, cradling Charlie in my arms. My mind's eye started to play back the scenario of what had happened, when I realized that I never saw the shooter. Suddenly, I thought about the sniper and wondered if this was his work. But then I remembered that Stephen had said, "No, the other one."

What the hell's going on?

Sirens started to sound as I thought about the past two days. The two links to Faraji Owusu so far had been Judge Frank Peters and Stephen Carter. I knew that the Judge had lied about seeing Faraji, but I didn't know why. Stephen was drunk out of his mind when we entered his office because of Faraji's death. But I believe there's more.

While holding Charlie's lifeless body in my arms, my eyelids flickered and my eyebrows curled. I looked to

Stephen's desk and was surprised that I hadn't noticed the obvious.

Where's Stephen Carter?

Thirty-four

STEPHEN CARTER, WITH A blackish-blue swollen right eye, quietly sat in Frank's kitchen at an oval glass table with his head hanging low. Frank leaned against the center island with his arms folded on his chest, not taking his eyes off of Stephen. Nathan Hunt stood across from Frank, nonchalantly cutting into an apple with a sharp knife. Tim Johnson hadn't moved from the living room.

"You disappoint me, Stephen," Frank said. "We're supposed to be a family. Is this how you treat family?"

Stephen didn't respond at first, but then shook his head, no.

"So what, you were just going to spill the beans, is that it? Run your freaking mouth because of what happened to Faraji?"

Stephen shook his head again, "No, I would never do that."

"What then?"

"Come on, Frank, you know I'd never betray you. I was just...Faraji was just killed. How else was I supposed to act?"

"Like a fucking professional, numbnuts. That's how you're supposed to act. Not like some juvenile getting drunk because his partner's dead. Think, asshole."

"Frank, we're talking about Faraji here. He's been with us since the beginning."

"No, dipshit, he's been with you since the beginning. I've been in this game a lot longer and have seen a lot worse shit than this."

"He was one of my best friends, Frank."

"What'd you just say?"

"What?" Stephen replied.

"He was your friend?"

"Yeah, come on, Frank, we're all friends."

Frank turned around and grabbed a handful of red apples from the fruit bowl in the center of the island. One by one, he beaned Stephen with them, causing Stephen to cover his head and face with his arms.

"We don't make friends in this business, asshole. You and I aren't friends. You know better than that."

Stephen lowered his arms and looked up at Frank once the apples stopped flying.

"You were going to talk to the cops, weren't you? You're all fucked up inside because Faraji was your friend, and you were going to rat us out."

"No, Frank, no, I'd never do that."

Deep inside his core, Frank started to feel heat rise. He lowered his arms and clenched his fists as the heat became more prominent until it burst through his mouth.

"Then why the fuck did Nathan have to kill a cop just to shut you the fuck up?"

Both Stephen and Nathan flinched at Frank's outburst.

"I wasn't going to say anything," Stephen pleaded. "I swear to God, Frank."

Frank rushed to Stephen and grabbed his shirt with both hands and lifted him off the chair. His eyes bulged with anger. His face reddened with sheer rage. His lips were only inches away from Stephen's, causing spit to fly onto Stephen's face when he spoke. The years of bodybuilding paid off, as Stephen felt like a feather in his hands. He didn't yell; his threatening tone was surprisingly calm.

"You're goddamn right you're not going to say anything."

Frank jolted him one time, making sure their eyes locked with one another's.

"I'm only going to say this once. You do this again, you'll be tied up and forced to watch Nathan cut your wife and kid's heads off. Understood?"

Stephen nodded.

Frank released him and Stephen slumped back into the chair.

The room became deathly silent for a few seconds while Frank stood over Stephen. Finally, Frank turned around and went to the refrigerator and pulled out a carton of orange juice.

To Nathan, he said, "Get this drunk out of here and let him sober up. The cops are going to be looking for him and we need him sharp before they interrogate him."

He took a sip of juice from the carton and placed it back in the refrigerator.

"Oh, and take the other no·nuts pencil dick with you."

Thirty-five

TWO AMBULANCES PARALLEL PARKED in front of Stephen Carter's law firm. I sat in one holding an ice pack on the back of my head while the other ambulance waited for Charlie's body. The paramedics believed that I may have suffered a concussion and wanted to take me to the hospital, but I declined. Right now, the only thing on my mind was finding Stephen Carter because he knew who had killed Charlie.

With all of the commotion surrounding me: police questioning business tenants, squad car lights swirling around and inquisitive bystanders wondering what had happened, I didn't notice anything. I was in my own world and saw my own images. My mind continued replaying the altercation. I saw Stephen raise his hand and point to someone behind us, and then heard the gun pop and saw Charlie fall to the ground. I'm mad at myself for not turning around quicker when Stephen had said "The one behind you." If only I could have reacted, maybe Charlie would still be alive.

I raised my head and was startled to see my lieutenant, Robert Polenski, standing next to the ambulance. A handsome man in his mid-fifties, Lieutenant Polenski was tall and lean with a jagged chin and deep-set blue eyes. The mixture of grey in his short-cropped hair, along with wearing dark-framed glasses, made him look like a distinguished professor instead of a police lieutenant.

"How you doing, Jacob?"

"As good as I can be," I said as I took a step out from the back of the ambulance.

"Yeah," Lieutenant Polenski responded, lowering his head. "Look, I know this is difficult, but can you tell me a little bit about what happened?"

I removed the ice pack from my head and leaned against the ambulance.

"Just routine follow-up on the Faraji Owusu murder. We found the partner drunk in his office, and next thing I hear is a gun going off and then I'm hit on the head."

"Do you have any idea where the partner could be now?"

"Wish I did. He saw the shooter. He was babbling some things and I think he was getting ready to tell us something before Charlie was killed." I paused and shook my head. "It all just happened so fast I didn't have time to react."

"How's your head feeling now?"

I shrugged my shoulders. "It's okay. I'd rather start looking for Stephen Carter."

"We already have uniforms dispatched to his house."

I was getting ready to make a comment when the paramedics started bringing out Charlie's body in a black body bag. The area seemed to hush as the paramedics carried the body to the ambulance. The police who were questioning people stopped and stared, as I did, and Lieutenant Polenski. Normalcy didn't seem to pick up again until Charlie's body was in the ambulance and it started driving away.

I returned my attention to Lieutenant Polenski. "Look, Lieutenant, there's something I've got to talk to you about."

Lieutenant Polenski gave me his undivided attention.

"It's about Judge Peters. I don't know...call it a gut intuition, but I think he's somehow in the middle of this."

Lieutenant Polenski's eyes widened at the apparent shock of the allegation.

"Frank Peters, the Superior Court judge?"

Suddenly I realized how ludicrous that sounded and wished that I never brought it up. My voice lacked confidence when I continued with the allegations.

"I don't have any proof now, but I think the judge is connected to all of this. I even think he may know who killed Charlie."

Lieutenant Polenski leaned close.

"Jacob, you're a good and a bright detective, but you'd better have solid evidence before making allegations like that."

I raised my hands. "I know, I know." I looked around and lowered my voice before continuing. "I met with someone yesterday before the Owusu shooting who told me that the judge is mixed up in money laundering. I didn't want to believe it, but when I found out that Faraji Owusu had clerked for the judge a few years ago, I questioned Judge Peters about the last time he had seen Faraji, and he lied. Why would he do that?"

Lieutenant Polenski exhaled and rubbed his chin. "Who's your guy?"

"I don't want to reveal him just yet."

"Then there's nothing I can do. I can't ask for a search warrant based on speculation. Besides, I personally know Frank and I don't think he's mixed up in anything like that."

"Yeah, you're probably right."

"Let's concentrate on finding this partner and then let the chips fall after that."

I nodded.

Lieutenant Polenski patted me on the shoulder and then walked away. I realized then that if I wanted to get to the judge, I'd have to do it on my own. I returned the ice pack to the back of my head and looked around. I saw a man standing on the outer perimeter of the police tape wearing a Washington Nationals red and white baseball cap give me the thumbs up. I nodded at the man and then turned around and climbed back into the ambulance.

Thirty-six

FRANK DIDN'T LIKE WHAT WAS happening. The control that he required, that he needed to operate a business like his, was loosening just enough that it was making him nervous. Faraji's Owusu's death was a major blow. Totally unexpected. There had been no information on the shooter, either from the police or Nathan Hunt. Apparently, the police had someone contained in an office building, but that person had since escaped and there'd been no word of his whereabouts. Then there was Stephen Carter and his outburst, which, if Nathan Hunt hadn't been around, could have been disastrous, more than losing Faraji Owusu. Finally, there was the cop killing. Frank was not mad at Nathan for doing what needed to be done to protect the business, but it put him in a bind that he wished he weren't in.

To put it simply, Frank was stressed beyond measure. When that happened, he needed a stress reliever.

Frank sat back in a comfortable lounge chair with his hands folded behind his head and his eyes nearly rolled back into his eye sockets. Every now and again, his chest slightly rose and the muscles in his body tensed as Carmen's mouth worked magic on his penis. Every sensual stroke caused goose bumps to run along his skin and a tingle that tickled the back of his neck.

He unfolded his arms and moved his right hand to the back of Carmen's head.

"You got it, baby," he said.

Carmen looked up with big beautiful brown eyes and long eyelashes. She removed her mouth from his penis, wrapped her hand around it and continued stroking.

"I'm the stress reliever," she replied.

"You sure are, baby."

The young Hispanic woman smiled and returned to her duty. Frank moved her long brown hair away from her face so that he could see her lips slide up and down.

"Just keep it there. Daddy's got something good for you real soon."

Seconds later, his face tightened and his body stiffened as his stress released itself.

"No one does it better than you, baby," he said.

Carmen wiped her mouth and sat up. Her perky left breast hung out of her bra, while the other was firmly secured. She winked at the compliment.

"Only for you, Your Honor."

Frank smiled.

Carmen stood and placed her free breast into the bra. She turned around and bent down for her clothes. Frank stared at her thong and saw how it perfectly fit her hourglass frame. He began to get excited again.

"We've got another half an hour," he said. "Why don't we take this to the bed?"

Carmen slowly rose and stuck out her butt. "That'll be an extra hundred."

"Always business first."

"I learned from the best."

Frank stood and walked across the hotel room, where his wallet and keys lay on a nightstand. He pulled out a one hundred dollar bill and tossed it on the bed.

"I always come prepared."

Carmen dropped her clothes back on the floor and reached for her purse and pulled out a condom.

"So do I."

Thirty-seven

TWENTY MINUTES LATER, FRANK was lying on the plush king-sized bed naked, with his arms folded behind his head, relaxing after the intense sexual episode with Carmen. He was certain that some of the other hotel guests had heard their screams of enjoyment, but he didn't care. It had been over six months that he and Carmen had been in this relationship, and he had to admit that she'd gotten better with each appointment.

Rough sex was always a pleasure in Frank Peters' world. It was the only time that he didn't mind not being in control. He'd rather it be that way. So much of his time was spent trying to control everything else in his life that when a beautiful young woman wanted to control how and when she came, he was delighted to let her do it. Especially when she was as good as Carmen.

The hour they spent together flew by. Carmen was in the shower cleaning off while Frank's mind returned to the problems at hand. The cop being killed in the law firm would definitely bring heat upon Stephen, but Frank knew that when Stephen was not drunk, he was sharper than most. Another problem would be the law firm itself. No doubt that the cop killing would cause the police to do an investigation of the firm and would also bring unwanted media attention. Frank's connections in the police department were deep, but even he knew that he would have to walk a thin line with this one.

Then he still needed to find out who had killed Faraji Owusu. Could it have been the Africans? Mexicans? Maybe it wasn't related to the business at all? Frank shook the thoughts away. It had to be connected to the business. The media reported that the gun used to kill Faraji was a sniper rifle, so that meant he had been specifically targeted. Frank didn't think this was some random killing like what had happened in 2002 with the crazy snipers who went on a killing spree in the D.C. area. So that begged the question: why Faraji, and who killed him? Frank's contacts reassured him that none of their people had done this. So if it wasn't the Africans or the Mexicans, then who?

The shower stopped and Frank heard Carmen pull back the shower curtain. Seconds later, she appeared in the room with a towel wrapped around her body. Her skin was still wet and water dripped from her hair as she crawled onto the bed and straddled him.

"You know, Your Honor…" she said as she leaned forward and allowed the water from her hair to spill on Frank's face. She unwrapped the towel and lowered her body so Frank's nose was between her breasts. "I was just thinking that since you've been such a good boy, that maybe you deserve a freebie."

Frank felt himself rise again. Suddenly, his mind was clouded and he forgot what he had just been thinking.

"Freebie, huh," he said as he wrapped his arms around her body. "I could definitely use a freebie."

Carmen smiled and then lowered herself and kissed his lips. "Good. Let's just say that we'll do favors for each other."

"Anything you want is yours."

"That's what I wanted to hear."

Frank rolled over and was now on top of Carmen. They passionately kissed before he found himself inside of her once again.

Thirty-eight

NO ONE HAD BEEN able to locate Stephen Carter for the past two days. His wife and family hadn't seen him, nor had any of his coworkers. I was worried that the same person who killed Charlie had also killed Stephen and then dumped his body somewhere. All of the alleys and back-alleys across the city had been searched; the Potomac River and Anacostia River too, and Stephen hadn't been found.

I popped another Motrin in my mouth and gulped it down with a bottle of water. The blow to my head the other day had resulted in a concussion, which caused sporadic migraines. I wasn't going to go to the hospital, but on the insistence of my wife, I allowed her to check me out. My lieutenant wanted me to take a few days off, but I declined. Catching Charlie's killer was more important to me than my own health.

As I sat at my desk, I couldn't help but glance over at Charlie's desk. Throughout the day, police personnel had stopped by and placed roses on Charlie's desk, and then either hugged or chitchatted with me about Charlie. Police work was dangerous work, and this wasn't the first time that I had known an officer who had died in the line of duty. But Charlie was by far the closest. When Charlie had made detective, he was assigned to me and we instantly hit it off. We both loved police work and football, and when we weren't talking about police work we usually talked about football. I considered Charlie a friend and believed that he had a bright future with the department.

He shouldn't have died the way he did, I'd been thinking ever since it happened. Whoever had killed Charlie was a coward, sneaking up behind him and killing him like that. Hopefully, if the stars aligned in my favor, I would be able to confront the person who had killed Charlie and find out what makes a coward tick.

I leaned forward, placed my elbows on my desk and rubbed my temples. If someone would have told me a few days ago that I'd be thrown into a manhunt for a sniper, investigating a possible corrupt judge, while also searching for Charlie's killer, I'd have said they were crazy. Stuff like that just doesn't happen in real life.

So far, there hadn't been any leads in the sniper shooting. Forensics went through the building and dusted everywhere for prints and found no fingerprint match through the FBI's Integrated Automated Fingerprint Identification Systems or IAFIS. It's almost like he didn't exist. However, the more reliable theory was that he has never been printed before.

In the middle of my thought, my phone rang.

"Detective Hayden."

"Detective Hayden, this is Stephen Carter."

My eyes widened and I instantly sat up in my seat. It took my mind a few seconds to register the name, but when it finally did, I quickly asked, "Where are you?"

"I'll tell you, but you've got to come alone."

"Alone, why? I can have uniforms pick you up in a few minutes and safely bring you in."

"No. It has to be you."

"Are you injured?"

"I'm fine. Look, are you coming or not?"

I paused. The detective in me wanted to rush to wherever Stephen was, but my gut also told me that something was not right. I quickly rationalized this in my brain. Stephen Carter was the only link to the person who killed Charlie. He saw who had done it and possibly knew him. The answer was simple.

"Of course I'll come. Where are you?"

"In your living room."

My eyes widened again. I dropped the phone and raced out of the office.

Thirty-nine

I QUICKLY DUG INTO my pocket for my house keys as I raced up to the front porch. Once the key was in the lock, I rushed through the front door and found Stephen sitting on my brown living room sofa. His right eye was bruised.

"What the hell are you doing in my house?"

"This is the only place I could think of where I'd be safe."

I looked around the room. Nothing appeared to have been disturbed. The front door was locked, as were all of the windows, and I presumed that the back door was locked as well. I knew because I had checked them before I left the house that morning.

"How'd you get in here?"

Stephen devilishly smiled, "I wasn't always a lawyer."

"How'd you know where I lived? You were drunk off your ass the last time I saw you."

"Really? With today's technology, you're asking how I found out where you live?"

I relaxed a little and made my way to the couch across from him.

"Do you know that we've been looking for you for the past two days?"

Stephen nodded.

"Where have you been?"

He momentarily looked away as if debating whether to answer, but before he did, I asked, "And what happened to your eye?"

"I can't answer either question."

I pursed my lips. I quickly stood up and motioned with my hands.

"Get up. We're going to the station."

Stephen didn't move. "I can't."

My brows curled and I could tell that my face lightly reddened. The muscles in my body became tense.

"Look, a good cop died," I said, pointing my finger. "You obviously know who did it."

Stephen shook his head. "Jacob...may I call you that?"

"No."

Stephen hesitated. "I'm sorry about your partner. I really am. I wasn't even supposed to be there that day."

"Who killed Charlie?"

"I can't tell you that. I only came here to warn you not to get involved in this. It's bigger than you could possibly imagine."

I clenched my teeth as the words burned through my mouth, "I'm already involved."

I reached for my sidearm and unlatched the safety strap. "There's two ways we can do this."

Stephen raised his hands in protest. "Detective Hayden, you don't want to do this."

"You give me no choice. Now turn around and place your hands behind your head."

"If I go to the police station, I'm as good as dead."

I grabbed ahold of the Glock and aimed it at Stephen. "You could say the same about being here. You broke into my house. I could shoot you dead right here."

Stephen slowly stood. "Okay...okay. Just point that thing somewhere else." He sighed, "I'll talk to you, but we can't go to the station."

"And why not?"

"Did you tell anyone that I was here?"

"No, I came right over."

"Okay, good."

"Why can't you come to the station?"

"Because," he said. Then he paused and sat back down.

"What?" I was getting frustrated.

He looked up at me and the silence of his words pierced through my heart. I could tell this wasn't going to be good.

"You've got dirty cops."

And there it was.

Forty

LIEUTENANT ROBERT POLENSKI SAT at a center table in a busy food court, biting into a steak and cheese sandwich. Before he was able to put the sandwich back down, Nathan Hunt approached the table. Lieutenant Polenski leaned back in his chair and wiped his mouth with a napkin.

"Nathan."

"Lieutenant."

Nathan pulled a chair out and sat down. He reached into the inside pocket of his blazer and pulled out a thick envelope.

"Sorry to hear about your detective."

"Yeah, Charlie was a good kid."

He placed the envelope on the table and slid it halfway. Lieutenant Polenski reached for the envelope and placed it into his blazer's inside pocket.

"How's the family?" Lieutenant Polenski asked.

"As good as it can be," Nathan responded. "My father wasn't doing so well the other day, but he's doing better now."

Lieutenant Polenski nodded. "Tell your dad I wish him the best."

"Will do. I'm sure he'll be happy to know that you're thinking of him."

Lieutenant Polenski grabbed the steak and cheese sandwich and brought it to his mouth.

"Tell him that I'll come and see him sometime soon. We haven't played checkers together in quite some time."

Nathan nodded and then stood up.

"Lieutenant."

"Nathan."

He walked away just as quickly as he had approached. Lieutenant Polenski took a bite of the sandwich, wiped his hands and then stood from the table and walked away in the opposite direction.

Forty-one

A SMALL LAMP ON his desk provided just enough light that Frank didn't need the overhead light to read his newest case file. The day had ended for most in the courthouse, but the Judge was staying late to catch up on some work that he'd put off over the past couple of days. The only problem was that his mind was somewhere else.

His eyes glossed over the words in the pleading, but he wasn't really reading it. He glanced at his watch and realized that the drop off was less than thirty minutes away and neither he nor Nathan had heard from Stephen Carter. He had sent Nathan in Stephen's place to make sure that everything went according to plan. Thirty minutes from now, Frank should be receiving a call saying that everything was okay. Until then, the only thing he could do was worry.

And think. Stephen's unusual actions the last few days had caused Frank to realize that Stephen had become more of a liability than an asset. Frank had already informed Nathan that after he received the package from the drop off, he was to find Stephen and put a bullet in his head. The police would be led to believe that the same person who had killed Faraji also killed Stephen. The law firm could operate without Stephen; as a matter of fact, Frank was the real brains behind the operation, so he only needed more puppets to act as the face of the firm.

The more he thought about Stephen, the warmer his skin began to feel. He clenched his fists and shook his head. How dare someone like that betray me? All that he'd done for Stephen over the years; the cars, the house, the supermodel-looking wife, and the countless vacations to the Caribbean. That was all because of Frank. And this was how Stephen repaid him, by not contacting him for a day and a half and possibly blowing hundreds of thousands of dollars.

Frank slammed his fist against the desk. He took his reading glasses off and sat back in his chair. This was the first time in his twenty-year career that he'd been this unnerved.

His phone rang, which brought his mind out of thought. Frank looked at his watch and realized that it should be Nathan calling.

"Frank Peters."

"It's done," Nathan said on the other end of the line.

"Good, good," he said with a slight smirk on his face. "Now follow up on what we discussed."

Frank hung up the phone.

A partial weight felt lifted off of his shoulders. Part of his worry was done. Now he hoped that Nathan could finish the rest. Once that was taken care of, Nathan's next project would be to find Faraji's killer and bring him straight to Frank.

Part Four: The Thirst

Forty-two

NIGHT FELL UPON THE city, and I was in a quandary that I hadn't felt in over a year. I was thirsting for alcohol again. Specifically, vodka, the drink that had changed my life a few years ago and had almost cost me my wife. I knew that I could never touch it again, and if I did, everything that I worked so hard to obtain would be lost. Still, that didn't stop the craving.

The thirst had started to come back after I lost the sniper, and then became more intense after Charlie was killed. Now, with Stephen's accusation of crooked cops in my precinct, the only thing keeping me from drowning a bottle was the fact that there weren't any in the house.

A couple of hours had passed since Stephen had made the accusation. He told me that he would tell me everything if I could guarantee federal witness protection. How ironic, I thought. In my ten-year career, I'd never been asked about federal protection, however in the past few days, I had been asked that question twice. I told Stephen the same thing I told Turtle, that I couldn't guarantee it. I saw the same sparkle leave Stephen's eyes, but the urgency never left.

Now I had a tough question to answer. Should I believe Stephen or call my lieutenant?

The past couple of hours, I had tried to read into Stephen's allegations. If Stephen was lying, then why would he have shown up at my house in the first place? If he was telling the truth, then I didn't know who I could call for help. I wanted to call my lieutenant, but Stephen said that he didn't know who was on the take. He was never told, for obvious reasons: he could all of a sudden get a change of heart and reveal to the media which officers were crooked. When I tried to press harder, Stephen backed off. He wouldn't tell me who he worked for, only that his boss was very powerful and influential.

"Stephen," I said, "I want to help you, but you've got to give me something, anything."

"Like I said," Stephen replied, "I'll tell you all you want to know, but first I need a guarantee that I'll be protected." He shifted in his seat. "I mean, if they can kill a cop without worry, then they'll have no problems coming after me."

I shook my head. I was about to speak again when I heard the lock on the front door turn. Theresa was home. I quickly looked at Stephen.

"That's my wife. Not a word about this."

Theresa entered the living room wearing her hospital scrubs and carrying a brown paper bag. She smiled when she saw us and leaned down to kiss my cheek.

"This is a nice surprise. Didn't think you'd be home."

"Took off a little early today."

"You should have told me we were having company. I would have brought home more food."

We awkwardly smiled. I stood up and gently took the paper bag from Theresa.

"Sorry, this is Stephen."

Stephen stood up and extended his hand.

"Nice to meet you, Mrs. Hayden."

"Call me Theresa," she said. "Are you staying for dinner?"

Stephen quickly glanced at me and before he could respond, I cut in. "Ah...he actually may be staying the night with us."

"Oh?" Theresa said curiously.

"Yeah, problems at home," I replied.

Theresa smiled. "Okay, I'll make sure the guest room has some fresh sheets. Dinner will be ready shortly."

She headed into the kitchen while Stephen and I returned to our seats.

"I'll give you until morning," I said. "After that, I'll have to contact my lieutenant."

Forty-three

THE MEDIA HADN'T RUN a story on Faraji Owusu's death in two days. The papers pushed the search for his killer to the back pages. The killing of the detective in the law firm stormed the headlines, both on the local news channels and in the newspapers. What did all of this mean? For the sniper, it was a good thing. It meant that the crowded metropolis which was inundated with crime had already forgotten about the murder of Faraji Owusu. The city and its citizens returned to their normal operations, depending on what normal was.

If normal was kicking back in a La-Z-Boy and watching one's favorite television show while drifting off to sleep, then the sniper would never be normal again. At least not until the job was finished. Even then, normalcy would never be the same. How could it when such a tragedy had changed the sniper's life in more ways than anyone could understand.

From the sniper's perspective, normalcy was chaos. Normalcy was anger. Normalcy was revenge.

The sniper's eyes felt heavy while he laid in bed on top of the blanket, partially falling asleep. Above the bed, a ceiling fan slowly swirled around, offering little relief from the night's muggy heat. The air-conditioner unit in the small studio apartment had finally given out, so the only airflow was from the ceiling fan and an open window next to the bed.

The pale moonlight shined through the darkness of the apartment and touched the corner of the sniper's face. A film of sweat was along the sniper's skin, which made the pillowcase underneath his head feel like he was lying on soiled linen. It didn't bother him much as his eyes became heavier and he drifted off for a second, but then they shot open again when he thought he heard something. He lifted his head and looked around the room, and then returned it to the pillow, where his eyes became heavy again.

This was how the sniper fell asleep every night. If and when he was able to sleep.

At one time, sleep used to mean simply closing his eyes and allowing his mind and body to relax and then drift off into a peaceful unknown land. Now the only thing sleep brought were bad dreams. Tormenting dreams. Dreams that, on occasion, caused the sniper to jump out of bed, crying and screaming. Hopefully tonight's wouldn't be one of those kinds of dreams.

Just as he finally fell asleep, his cell phone rang. He reached for it on the windowsill and his eyes perked open when he recognized the number. He quickly pushed the talk button and raised the phone to his ear.

"You alone," he said.

"Yes, but not for long," a soft female voice responded.

"I hope you have good news."

"I found him."

"Through his cell phone?"

"Yes, he finally used it."

The sniper sat up and stepped out of bed. He headed to a small desk across the room and clicked on the desk lamp.

"Give me the address," he said as he lifted a pen and pulled out a sheet of paper from a drawer.

"This won't be easy."

"It never is."

"No, I mean he's with a cop."

"A cop?"

"The house was listed to a Jacob and Theresa Hayden."

The sniper paused before responding. The name instantly rang through his mind and the sniper realized that it was the same detective from the office building. Disappointment settled in, but the sniper didn't reveal it through his voice.

"What's the address?"

"Are you sure about this?" The woman's voice sounded concerned.

"I'm sure. Now what's the address?"

"2145 Kalmia Street, Northwest."

"Thanks."

The sniper hung up the phone after writing down the address. He returned to the bed and laid back down. This time his eyes didn't feel heavy and he knew that sleep wouldn't come for a couple of hours. There were questions in his head that he needed to figure out, starting with why a scumbag like Stephen Carter would be with a detective like Jacob Hayden. He knew the question would eventually be moot, because by this time tomorrow, Stephen Carter would be dead.

Forty-four

DARK GRAY CLOUDS BLANKETED the early morning sky and unleashed a torrential rain over the city. Lieutenant Polenski stood at the corner of P and 14th Street, Northwest, holding a large black umbrella over his head which only kept three-fourths of his body dry. His lower pants and shoes were drenched.

The city's streetlights would be turning off soon, which would make the streets dark under the gloomy sky.

Lieutenant Polenski checked his watch again as he waited for Detective Hayden, who should be arriving within a matter of minutes to pick him up. In his twenty-five years of being on the force, he'd seen and heard a lot of things which made it extremely difficult for anything to surprise him. However, when his phone rang at 4 a.m. and Jacob was on the other end of the line, saying that Stephen Carter was at his house, he admitted to himself that this was nearly the surprise of his lifetime. He immediately instructed Jacob to pick him up, saying that he had a safe place for Stephen to hide out until they could get the okay from the Justice Department to get him into the witness protection program.

After hanging up with Jacob, he made a call to Nathan Hunt, who was just as surprised. The two quickly devised a plan that they believed would work.

Three minutes later, the sound of tires splashing through water caused the lieutenant to look to his right. When the vehicle stopped in front of him, he saw Stephen Carter sitting in the front passenger seat. He quickly opened the rear passenger door, shook his umbrella and got in.

The vehicle made a right onto 14th Street and pulled away. However, not far behind, a black sedan with its lights off also made a right onto 14th Street. The car kept its distance, far enough behind so as not to be noticed, but close enough that it didn't lose sight of its target.

Forty-five

THE WINDSHIELD WIPERS SWAYED back and forth on the fastest speed, yet visibility through the front windshield was near zero. I kept the pace of my car at twenty-five miles per hour, sometimes needing to drive slower when I was unable see in front of me. Despite the fact that there was an eyewitness to Charlie's murder in the car and a lieutenant who had arranged for witness protection, the drive to the safe house was somber and no one had said a word since the initial greeting.

Maybe it was the heavy rain. Rain has a way of keeping people quiet, especially this early in the morning. In my rearview mirror, I saw Lieutenant Polenski staring out of his passenger door window, not appearing to be looking at anything in particular. Stephen Carter rested his head against the headrest with his eyes closed. Something about the silence in the car made me feel uneasy. Also, the fact that I didn't know where I was going bothered me as well.

Hours before I called Lieutenant Polenski, I had tossed and turned in my bed, debating whether to call my commander or not. Stephen's accusation of dirty cops bothered me more than I thought, but I believed in my heart that if there were dirty cops, Polenski was not one of them. I'd known him for as long as I'd been on the force, and the lieutenant had always been a stand-up guy. I had to trust someone, and with Charlie dead, the lieutenant was the only other person I trusted.

Thomas Circle on 14th Street began to approach when Lieutenant Polenski finally spoke. "Go around the circle and continue on 14th Street."

I nodded and then continued around the circle to 14th Street.

I looked in the rearview mirror again and saw that Polenski was still looking out the window, expressionless. What could he be thinking about? Is he leading us to a safe house or a trap? I couldn't shake Stephen's comments and I was starting to wonder if calling Polenski had been the right thing to do. It was 4 a.m. and Stephen still hadn't talked. Calling my lieutenant was the logical thing to do, especially since Stephen knew who had killed Charlie.

The lieutenant didn't appear to be himself. He had never been much of a conversationalist, but I'd never seen him that distant and distracted. As I looked through the rearview mirror, I caught the sight of a car I had noticed behind us when we picked up Lieutenant Polenski. The car had been behind us ever since, and was keeping its distance.

The longer we drove, the more tense I became. The car continued to keep its distance, even when I took my foot off the gas and allowed the vehicle to slow.

"Sir, I think we've got a tail."

Lieutenant Polenski turned around. "Are you sure?"

"Pretty sure. A dark sedan has been behind us ever since we picked you up."

Stephen finally opened his eyes and looked to his side-door mirror. After seeing the dark sedan, he turned to me. "Remember what I said yesterday."

I quickly gave him a look that told him not to say another word.

"Sir," I said, looking in the rearview mirror, "what do you think?"

"Besides me, does anyone else know that he's with you?"

"No."

"Then let's be patient with this. It could be nothing. Just keep driving a little longer."

I switched to the driver's-side mirror and saw the car continue its pace. Something hadn't felt right the entire ride, and the way the car cautiously trailed behind almost confirmed my suspicions.

"Sorry, sir," I said. I didn't take my eyes away from the driver's-side mirror. "But it's best that we take care of this now."

Forty-six

THE VEHICLE THAT HE was following stopped in the middle of the road. The sudden stop surprised the sniper, who thought he'd done a good job trailing at a distance that wouldn't be alarming. What surprised him even more was that the driver's door opened and Detective Hayden stepped out into the pouring rain, staring him down. The sniper didn't look the same as when the detective had first seen him, so he wasn't worried that he'd be recognized. His beard was gone, his hair was lighter, his nose was longer and he was wearing glasses.

The sniper didn't stop his car, but slowed down. He quickly placed his free hand on the Beretta attached to the holster inside his jacket and made a quick and precise decision. The rain fell harder, which made visibility much more difficult. He slowly changed lanes and decided to drive past the vehicle without looking at the detective and bringing any more unwanted attention to himself. As he passed, he felt the cold stare of the detective on him, and fought the urge to stop the car and go out in a gunfight. That wouldn't solve the ensuing problem.

Stephen Carter was the target, not the detective. And within the hour, Stephen Carter would be dead.

The sniper wouldn't be able to follow the cruiser any longer, but he would still be able to find its location with the tracking device he had attached hours earlier. When he was a safe distance from the detective's vehicle, he released his hand from the Beretta and reached for a cell phone on the passenger seat. He pushed the "on" button and the GPS tracking system loaded. Instantly, he saw the police cruiser on the screen. He turned right off of 14th Street and then to another side street before he pulled over. The detective's vehicle hadn't moved yet, and he wondered how far he would have to travel before he would be able to kill Stephen Carter.

Forty-seven

MY HEARTBEAT SLOWED A little when the car passed. The move was bold, but it was something I felt that I needed to do to be safe. The car drove by without incident, but that didn't mean that it hadn't been following us; just that the driver could have decided to wait until another time to make his move. Still, I breathed easier knowing that the possible threat was over.

I waited to get back in the car until I couldn't see the rear lights of the vehicle any longer. Now drenched from head to toe, I eased back into the driver's seat, closed the door and shifted the gear into drive. I pulled to a side road and placed the gear in park, turned around and faced my lieutenant and unapologetically directed a bold question to him.

"Sir, I'm going to ask you to be straight with me. Are you on the take?"

Lieutenant Polenski, apparently surprised by the question, rapidly blinked his eyes and hesitated before answering.

"Are you serious?"

"Yes, very."

"Let me remind you, Jacob, that I was there when you went through your rehab for alcohol." His face reddened a little. "I was the one who spoke up for you when the chief recommended that I suspend you." His voice escalated the longer he spoke. "Remember that when Theresa almost left you, it was me who talked her into staying."

Suddenly I felt embarrassed and I wished I had never asked the question. My lieutenant had been by my side for many years and never showed any signs of being corrupt. He'd been my mentor ever since I came into the detective's squad, so why would I even have considered accusing him of this?

"So just remember who you're talking to before you ask a stupid question like that," Lieutenant Polenski sharply responded.

I turned around like a defeated puppy with my tail between my legs.

"Sorry, sir. I just got carried away."

"Why would you even ask me a question like that?"

My eyes shifted to Stephen Carter and then back to the front windshield. I exhaled before responding.

"Doesn't matter. We should probably get moving."

"Look," Lieutenant Polenski said, his voice had calmed, "sorry about the reaction, but you caught me off guard. I've never been accused of being dirty."

I nodded but didn't respond. The silence that had engulfed the drive earlier returned, and this time I invited it to stay.

"Just so you know, we're heading to a church," Lieutenant Polenski said. "That'll be the safest place for him for now."

Forty-eight

I PULLED TO THE left side of the road on 10th Street, a one-way road where Saint Patrick's Catholic Church was located at the corner of 10th and G Streets. The large, historic stone church founded in 1794 sat between modern office buildings and took up half of the block. Large brown doors ten feet in height were at the front of the church. I parked the car directly in front of the steps leading to the church. There were only a couple of other cars parked on the street, but that would change within the hour as the early birds begin arriving for work.

"Father Jefferson will be expecting us," Lieutenant Polenski said.

"And you didn't tell him the nature of why we're here?" I asked, trying not to sound too untrusting.

"Of course not. He and I go way back and I've done some favors for him in the past. All he knows is that he'll be taking in a boarder for a day or two until we get clearance from the government. Trust me, this is the safest place for him in the city right now."

Lieutenant Polenski grabbed his umbrella and then reached for the door. Before opening it, he tapped me on the shoulder with an approving nod.

"Listen, you did good by calling me."

"Yeah," I replied, turning my head and acknowledging the compliment.

"I'll give Father Jefferson the heads up that we're here."

Lieutenant Polenski quickly opened the door and raised the umbrella over his head. The sound of the thundering rain loudly entered the car for a few seconds until the door closed. Lieutenant Polenski rushed up the steps and entered the church.

"I never would have tapped you for being an alcoholic," Stephen said.

"That was a long time ago," I said, still looking out the window.

"Once you're an alcoholic you're always an alcoholic."

I sharply turned my head, "You've got some nerve."

"I'm not throwing stones. I'm one too. I was sober for three years. All the way up until Faraji's death."

"Well, I'm not an alcoholic." I turned around and faced the window again. "Not anymore, at least."

"How'd you become one in the first place?"

"That's none of your business."

"I suspect it was the job."

I didn't answer. The car became silent and I found that I was no longer looking at the church's door, but at the blur of rain that was fiercely falling around us. Stephen's questions annoyed me, but only because I had started thinking about drinking again. And Stephen was right, it was the job. Before a few years ago, I could count on my hand the amount of times I'd actually had a drink. But everything changed after that one evening I was heading home.

My mind drifted back to the countless hours I'd spent plastered on a barstool, drinking as if my life depended on it. My mouth watered a little as if I could taste the vodka dancing on my tongue before it gently slid down my throat. I thought of the intoxicating feeling I'd get when my face started to tingle a little before the buzz kicked in. The addiction kept this recurring pattern night after night until there came a time when all I wanted to do was live to drink.

The question that Stephen had asked was how'd I become one in the first place? The thing about addiction is that it makes you forget what actually brought you to it.

My mind would have kept me looking into that open door if it weren't for Stephen's voice in the background.

"Detective Hayden," Stephen said as he tapped me on the shoulder.

I blinked my eyes and looked at Stephen.

Stephen pointed out the window and up at the church. "Your lieutenant's been trying to get your attention."

I looked over and saw Lieutenant Polenski waving me on.

"Let's go."

Forty-nine

A BLOCK AWAY ON 10th Street, the sniper sat in his car and watched Detective Hayden and Stephen Carter quickly enter the church. Things hadn't gone exactly as planned and the sniper sensed that his chances of killing Stephen Carter were becoming slimmer by the minute. He believed that if he were to kill Stephen Carter, he'd have to do it inside the church. How ironic. The church was supposed to be a symbol of forgiveness, yet killing Stephen Carter would be anything but forgiving. It'd be restitution.

Now, how to get inside?

The simple approach would be to go through the front door, but that almost guaranteed that he'd be seen. The detective had seen his new face and would recognize him within an instant. The back and side doors likely would be locked this early in the morning and there was no way to scale any of the windows without bringing attention to himself.

As the sniper pondered his options, he saw a black hearse in his rearview mirror slowly approach and pass his car, turn left onto G Street and pull to the side of the church. Two men in black suits stepped out of either side of the hearse, opened large umbrellas and walked to the back where they lifted open the hatch. Suddenly an ingenious thought popped into his head.

The sniper opened his door, stepped out and found close to a half of an inch of water under his feet as he quickly walked towards the hearse. He was wearing a black raincoat, black slacks and shoes that added about two inches to his height.

The two men appeared to struggle with holding their umbrellas while also trying to maneuver a dark brown casket onto a metal gurney.

"Looks like you gentlemen could use a hand," the sniper said as he leaned forward and assisted with the casket.

"That would be great," one of the men said.

The casket slid onto the metal legs and the men locked it in place.

"Thanks, friend."

"Why don't you let me hold your umbrella while you push? I'll hold it over your head to keep you dry."

The two men smiled and one of them handed over the umbrella. They pushed the casket onto the sidewalk and made their way to the side of the church.

"What a day for a funeral," one of the men said.

"Yes," replied the sniper, "what a day indeed."

Fifty

FATHER JEFFERSON STIFFLY STOOD in the foyer as he waited for us on the other side of the front door. He was dressed in a black priestly suit with a white collar around his neck. His greying hair was neatly brushed back and a lightly grown beard covered his face. His jawline was rigid and his eyes were set back in his head. Behind Father Jefferson were a glass wall and doors that led to the sanctuary

Lieutenant Polenski ushered us through the front door and greeted Father Jefferson with a firm handshake.

"Alex," Lieutenant Polenski said, "I'd like you to meet one of my detectives, Jacob Hayden, and the man you'll be keeping for a couple of days, Stephen Carter."

We exchanged pleasant handshakes, but there was an absence of personality that I found odd in a man whose job it was to serve the people.

"Gentlemen, if you'll follow me, I'll show Mr. Carter to his quarters," Father Jefferson said in a displeasing tone.

As he turned around, I tapped Lieutenant Polenski on the shoulder and eyed him with a look of concern. The lieutenant shook it off and then turned to follow Father Jefferson.

Before we got too far inside the church, Stephen cleared his throat and asked a question.

"Do you think we can go to the sanctuary first?"

The three of us turned around and looked at Stephen inquisitively.

"I just feel the need to say a prayer."

"I didn't know you were a praying man," I said.

"I'm not, but something tells me that I should start."

Father Jefferson and Lieutenant Polenski shared an exchange before Father Jefferson addressed Stephen.

"They're setting up for a 10 a.m. funeral this morning."

"It'll only take a minute," Stephen replied.

"I don't see any problem with it. Matter of fact, I should probably say a few prayers myself," I said with a touch of humor, although no one smiled at the comment.

"If it's only for a minute," Father Jefferson responded. "We really shouldn't interrupt those men when they're setting up."

"Thank you," Stephen replied. "I'll be quick."

Father Jefferson turned around and led us through the glass doors. He made the sign of the cross in the air before entering the sanctuary.

The sanctuary was grand, with high, arching ceilings and rows upon rows of wooden pews. Stained glass décor of Biblical characters filled the ceiling-high windows above the pulpit in the back of the church.

Bouquets of flowers lay on the marble floor in front of the pulpit, with a large picture stand nearby holding a black-and-white picture of an elderly Caucasian man.

Stephen and I sat in the front pew while Lieutenant Polenski and Father Jefferson sat a few rows behind us. Stephen leaned forward and rested his forearms on his thighs and lowered his head as if deep in thought.

"Detective Hayden," he whispered.

I leaned forward, "Yeah."

"I don't really want to say a prayer. There's something I need to tell you."

I slightly glanced behind me to see where the other two men were.

"I'm listening."

"Something's not right. I don't trust your lieutenant. In case anything happens to me, I have a safety deposit box at the Bank of America on I Street." Stephen paused a second before continuing. "The firm is a front. Look at the firm. In the safety deposit box, there's a disk with every illegal transaction that it has been involved in over the past six years."

"What do you mean a front? A front for what?"

Father Jefferson cleared his throat. "We really should get moving."

Just then, to the left of the sanctuary, a side door opened and two men in black suits slowly pushed in a casket.

"Gentlemen, our time is up. The dead deserve our respect," Father Jefferson said.

I looked over at Stephen and he silently mouthed the name, "Judge Peters."

My eyes widened with surprise. I was about to say something else, but then heard what I thought sounded like a gun cocking.

Fifty-one

I WASN'T PREPARED FOR what happened next. No one could have been. The blast was instant and deafening. Blood sprayed onto my face, and before I realized what had happened, Stephen Carter slumped forward. He didn't make a sound. The bullet pierced his skull before he had a chance to react.

Stephen's body fell onto my lap. A large hole cratered the back of his head. I couldn't move. I was dazed. It felt like a fog had covered my brain and paralyzed my limbs. My eyes widened and my heart was beating quickly. The only inkling of a movement I mustered was a simple gasp. "Stephen."

"I can't go through with this," a nervous and distraught voice said behind me.

I recognized the voice as Father Jefferson's.

"Get down!" Lieutenant Polenski yelled.

A simple thought zipped through my head in the split second before my body was able to move again: is he talking to the priest or to me?

"Shoot!" Lieutenant Polenski screamed.

I finally shook off the shock and reached for my Glock. I quickly slid off of the bench, and as I did, Stephen's limp body fell to the floor, making a thud sound. My sidearm was in my hand within seconds and I immediately looked for Lieutenant Polenski. I saw the top of his head three rows behind.

"Shoot now!" Lieutenant Polenski yelled again.

By now, I had the strong suspicion that Polenski wasn't talking to me, but to whoever had killed Stephen.

I quickly scanned the room and wasn't able to find the shooter. Sweat dripped into my eyes, but I didn't wipe it away for fear of losing my aim. Suddenly, just as a tear of sweat crossed in front of my left eye, I saw a blurry vision of a rifle aimed at me from the upper balcony.

I knew that I didn't have enough time to aim and shoot before the shooter took his shot, but I tried anyway. I moved my weapon towards the rifle, but then heard the riveting blast of a gun go off. I expected to feel the fiery burn of the bullet pierce my head, but instead realized that the shot hadn't come from in front of me, but from behind.

I quickly spun around and saw one of the men who pushed in the casket holding a gun in his hand, aiming at the balcony. The man looked at me and I instantly recognized him as the man who had been following us a few minutes earlier in the rain. But there was something else. As I stared longer, I realized that this was also the same man wanted in the death of Faraji Owusu. The man who told me that his name was Harvey Lindenberg.

Fifty-two

THE SNIPER WASN'T TRYING to save anyone's life today, rather he wanted to end one. He was just as surprised as everyone else in the room when he heard the gun go off and then saw blood spray from the back of Stephen Carter's head. His first reaction was to duck, and then he pulled out the Beretta 9 millimeter he had used to knock out one of the two men that he had helped with the casket just minutes earlier. He had told the second man that as long as he followed along, his life would be spared. The man had obviously believed him.

The sniper just happened to be facing the balcony and saw the spark from the rifle as the bullet left the chamber. His eyes widened with disbelief when he saw Stephen's body slump forward, and then after the initial shock ended, his blood began to boil. The previous two years of his life had been consumed with thinking about this day; the way Stephen and Faraji would look when one of his bullets pierced their skulls. He wanted to consume the gratification of what it felt like to bask in revenge's glory, but now that feeling would never come. His moment was stolen forever.

When he saw the shooter, he instantly recognized him as Nathan Hunt. He saw his rifle aimed at the detective and quickly realized that both men had been set up to die. When the sniper took the shot, he wasn't trying to save the detective's life, rather, in that split second, revenge took on a new face.

Unfortunately, the shot missed and the sniper became the next target. Multiple bullets sprayed across the room, which caused the sniper to leap to his left and take cover behind the pulpit. As he laid on the ground, bullets crashed around him, causing bits of stone and wood from the podium to break off. To his left, he saw Detective Hayden taking cover between the pews. The two made eye contact and the way the detective looked at him, with shock and disbelief, the sniper knew that the detective had recognized him from the Dupont Circle shooting.

He carefully held the Beretta in his hand and, for the shortest of seconds, questioned who he should aim it at when the bullets stopped flying. He sensed that the detective was feeling the same way. Then, suddenly, the clapping of the gun stopped and the sanctuary became quiet, with the exception of the shooter shuffling through the balcony in an apparent escape attempt.

The sniper's eyes darted from the detective to the door from which he had entered, and then back to the detective. He knew that it would only be a matter of minutes before cops from all over the city swarmed into the church. He took a quick peek around the podium, glanced to where the shooter had been and saw that he wasn't there. With one movement, he hopped to his feet and made a dash towards the door.

Fifty-three

I WATCHED AS HARVEY Lindenberg made a break for the rear door. The bullets had stopped flying, so I assumed that the first shooter wasn't at his position any longer, given that Harvey was able to run without being shot at. I needed to make a decision and make one fast: should I go after Harvey or the first shooter? I heard Lieutenant Polenski saying something, but it wasn't coherent, possibly because my mind was focused on something else. Then I made the decision I thought was best: go after Lindenberg. He's the one who started all of this. I jumped to my feet and rushed after him, yelling to Polenski that I was going after Lindenberg.

I glanced around the door and then ran through a long, narrow hallway that led to another door with a red and white exit sign over top of it. Lying on the ground was an unconscious man wearing a black suit. I quickly knelt down and placed two fingers against the man's neck to feel for a pulse. There was one. Good. The police would be here in a minute, so I decided to continue my pursuit.

I cautiously pushed through the side door and pointed my gun in every direction before stepping outside. Now standing in the pouring rain on the G Street side of the church, Harvey Lindenberg was nowhere to be found. I jogged to the corner of G & 10th Street and looked to my left and saw the tail end of someone dashing into a parking garage next to the church.

I sprinted along the sidewalk; my feet splashed against the soaked pavement with each long stride until I reached the opening of the parking garage where I cautiously came to a complete stop. At the entrance of the garage was a street-level sign that read "Early Bird Special - $13 all day." Past the sign, the garage darkened and descended into the lower depths of the city. Heavy wet footprints led straight past the cashier's booth, and the deeper they descended, the lighter the prints became until they faded altogether.

I pulled out my badge and stopped at the cashier's booth where an Ethiopian-looking woman with short hair and full lips was reading a magazine.

"Did you see a man just run through here?"

The woman nodded and pointed down into the garage. "He ran right past me."

"Call the police," I quickly responded, "and tell them that Detective Hayden is in pursuit of a shooter, and then leave the garage."

I cautiously descended down the throat of the garage with my firearm aimed. I came to the first turn, which was a left, leaned against the wall and took the

[187]

turn without a sound. I was on the first lower level where parked cars were scattered in various parking spaces. As quiet as I was, the thumping sound of my heart seemed to echo throughout the large space. I took deep breaths to try and calm my nerves, but I was finding it nearly impossible to do. The man who had killed Faraji Owusu in cold blood a few days earlier was somewhere close by, and I knew that if I weren't careful I could be the next casualty.

I walked along the wall, making myself as little as possible so as not to be an open target. With each car I passed, I waved my gun towards it, almost expecting Harvey Lindenberg to jump out at me. But nothing happened.

I came to the next left where the garage led to the second lower level. I took the left and made sure that each step was a whisper of itself. The second level had fewer cars than the first. I continued walking along the wall until I reached a car where the ceiling light above it was busted and shattered glass was on its roof. I steadied my aim towards the busted light and carefully approached it. Could Harvey be hiding behind the car?

The sound of a click behind my head quickly answered that question. I stopped and felt the heaviness of my legs as they struggled to hold me up. It wasn't every day that a killer held a gun to one's head and one lived to tell about it.

"Slowly open your hands and drop your gun," a familiar voice firmly whispered from behind.

I didn't hesitate. I slowly opened my hands and allowed the gun to fall next to my feet.

"Now kick it behind you."

I kicked the gun behind me.

Harvey Lindenberg didn't immediately speak again, but I heard him bend down for the gun and pick it up.

"You won't get away with this," I finally summoned the courage to say.

"Raise your hands above your head."

As I raised my hands, I felt Harvey reach for the handcuffs that were strapped to the back of my belt.

"Put these on."

Harvey raised the handcuffs to my hands.

"You need to just turn yourself in," I said. He placed the cuffs around my wrists and snapped them together.

"You were a target, too, you know," Harvey said.

"How do you know that?"

"I bet you weren't supposed to leave there alive."

"What are you talking about?"

"I saw the shooter. He was about to put a bullet right between your eyes."

I didn't respond.

"I have one more job to do and then I'll be out of your city forever."

"I can't let you do that."

"You have no choice. This is my revenge."

Police sirens began to scream in the background.

"The garage will soon be surrounded," I said, hoping that he would understand the gravity of the situation. "Give up now and—"

Without warning, I was hit on the back of my head. My knees buckled and I fell to the ground. Before I passed out, Harvey bent down and looked me in the face. My vision was blurry, but I remembered Harvey's deep blue eyes piercing into mine.

"Stay away from this one."

Then I saw Harvey start to run away, and everything around me soon faded into a sea of blackness.

Fifty-four

JUDGE FRANK PETERS ENJOYED getting his head massaged, especially after an invigorating sexual escapade with Carmen once again. Their weekly meeting went without a hiccup, and Carmen continued to prove why she was worth the three hundred fifty dollars he paid for the hour.

With their bodies totally nude and a light film of sweat along their skin, Frank laid with his back against her belly and was partially propped up as Carmen gently massaged his temples, and then moved her fingers around his skull. Occasionally, she'd inhale deeply through her nose and let her breath escape past her lips. When her breath touched Frank's skin momentarily, it got him excited. However, unlike last week's multiple orgasm, this week he decided that one was enough.

He was content for now, enjoying the trance-like feeling that the massage had put him in. If he didn't know any better he'd think that she was purposely trying to put him to sleep with the magic that her fingers were making.

His eyelids became heavier with each passing second, and his body felt like it was floating on a cloud.

"You're the best," he managed to say.

Carmen chuckled, "No, Your Honor, you're the best."

He slightly smirked, "You know, I've never heard you call me by my name."

"I thought that we'd keep it professional."

Frank exhaled and opened his eyes. Professional, he thought. This indeed was a business arrangement, but being with Carmen the past few months had changed something inside of him.

"What would you say if I wanted it to be more than just professional?"

Carmen stopped rubbing his head. "What are you saying?"

The tough guy with near-limitless power in Washington, D.C., turned around with puppy dog eyes and lovingly gazed at Carmen.

"You know what I mean. We've been going at this for quite a while and...maybe it's time you put this business to a halt and let me take care of you."

"You want to take care of me?"

Frank leaned forward and gently kissed her.

"Of course I do. You don't need to live this kind of life anymore."

Carmen didn't immediately respond. Her eyes gazed back into Frank's with the same emotion and intent that his did hers.

[192]

"I don't know what to say."

Before he was able to respond, his cell phone rang from inside his pants, which were spread across the floor. He rolled across the bed and reached for his phone. It was Nathan calling.

"Yeah."

Within a matter of seconds, the skin on his face reddened, his jaws clenched together and his free hand balled into a fist. The anger that he constantly struggled with nearly unleashed itself in a way that wouldn't have been good for anyone. He couldn't help it. When things failed that were outside of his control, the devil, as he calls it, that lives deep within him, wanted to be freed. If Carmen wasn't in his presence, he would have exploded through the phone, but instead, he kept his tone peaceful, yet threatening.

"The two of you, at my house in one hour!"

He clicked off the phone and managed his temper before turning around.

"I've got to go," he calmly said. "But think about what I've said.

"I will."

Fifty-five

LIEUTENANT POLENSKI WAS THE highest-ranking officer with the Metropolitan Police Department who knew of Judge Frank Peters' business. He knew everything about his business: who the important contacts were and how much money it made. For his part, Polenski got a generous monthly stipend to make sure the police department turned a blind eye if something fishy ever popped up. For the most part, he'd done his job; steered investigations in the opposite direction they should be going, sometimes caused evidence to disappear, and the list went on and on. Everything was going the way it should until Jacob decided to poke his nose where it shouldn't be.

Jacob should be dead right now, Polenski thought. His corpse should be lying next to Stephen Carter's. One bullet and that's all it should have taken. The quickly-devised plan between Nathan Hunt and him shortly after Jacob had contacted him about Stephen should have been foolproof, and yet it wasn't; assumedly spoiled by Faraji

Owusu's killer. Which brought Polenski's mind to another question: what was the killer doing here in the first place? Who was he after? The only conclusion was that he was after Stephen Carter. He'd killed Faraji and was now after his partner. Did they do something to him? Was it related to the business? It took either a crazed lunatic, someone extremely desperate or highly skilled, to try and kill someone in the custody of two police officers. Perhaps he was all three. If this was tied to the business, then there was a whole bigger problem on the lieutenant's hands than what he had originally thought.

He had heard Jacob and Stephen Carter talking shortly before Stephen was killed, and although he hadn't heard what was said, he had the hunch that Stephen had told him some important information. Possibly about Judge Peters.

His pocket radio came to life and he heard the dispatcher call for officer assistance at the parking garage next to the church. Standing outside at the back of the church, Lieutenant Polenski saw Nathan Hunt duck into the driver's seat of a late-model black vehicle a block away and drive off. He turned around and headed back inside the church, where he quickly made his way through the halls until he was met by Father Jefferson near the church's lobby.

"When the police get here, tell them exactly what I told you. That Detective Hayden and I brought a witness here and then we were ambushed by a shooter in the

[195]

balcony. I'll lead them to believe that it was the shooter from a few weeks ago. Understood?"

Father Jefferson nodded, but the way he shifted his eyes away from Lieutenant Polenski and slouched his shoulders led Polenski to believe that Father Jefferson might not fully cooperate.

He leaned in closer to Father Jefferson and patted him on the shoulder.

"You okay? You're not getting cold feet on me, are you?"

Father Jefferson looked up and shook his head, "No."

"Good. I'd hate to have to remind you of why you're helping me in the first place."

"That won't be necessary," Father Jefferson softy replied. "It'll go down exactly as you say it did."

Two years earlier, after Mass, Polenski had caught Father Jefferson inappropriately touching an altar boy in the back of the church. Polenski never turned him in, but told him that from time to time he might be called upon if his services were ever needed. If Father Jefferson didn't oblige, the lieutenant made it clear that he'd do a full investigation and would talk to all of the altar boys in the church and find out how many he'd actually molested. Polenski had never had a problem from Father Jefferson in the past two years.

"That's my man," Lieutenant Polenski said with a smile on his face. "Now wait here for the police and make sure you look very scared."

"That won't be hard to do."

Lieutenant Polenski turned and headed out the front door, taking the front steps two at a time, and then quickly jogged to the parking garage.

When he got there, he saw that the parking garage attendant wasn't at the work station. He looked around and saw wet footprints leading down into the garage. He pulled out his Glock and cautiously followed the prints until they dried out, and then he continued down into the garage. On the second lower level, he saw scattered parked cars, and then one with broken glass covering it. As he neared it, he saw a body lying motionless on the ground. His palm tightly griped the handle of the gun as he got closer to the body, until he recognized that it was Jacob.

His eyes opened wide as he walked towards Jacob's unconscious body. He placed two fingers on his neck and felt his pulse. He looked around and saw that his hands were handcuffed behind his back. Immediately, a thought popped into his head as he looked at his gun. He would tell his peers that the shooter ran out of the church and into the garage. Jacob came after him and somehow was overtaken by him and then was shot in the head after being handcuffed. The only problem was that ballistics would be able to trace the bullet back to the lieutenant's gun if ever an inquiry came up.

He quickly looked around the garage for anything that could be used as a weapon and then noticed all of the broken glass on the ground around the car. He reached over and grabbed the largest piece. A long, sharp edge pointed out between his thumb and index finger. He looked down at Jacob's neck and thought that one slice should put him out of his misery.

The lieutenant brought the broken glass close to Jacob's neck and then hesitated. Could he really do it; cut the neck of a man he'd known for more than ten years and then watch him bleed to death? Shooting him from a distance would be hard enough, but he wasn't sure if he could really kill Jacob this close and intimately. He imagined that once the glass cut into Jacob's skin that his eyes would shoot open and Polenski would be forced to hold Jacob down and watch him struggle to breathe. If that happened, Jacob would fight as much as he could until the life left his body.

He came to the conclusion that it had to be done; that this was the only way. He lowered the shattered piece of glass to Jacob's neck and watched as the tip touched his skin. Polenski told himself that he wouldn't look when the tip pierced the flesh, and that all he had to do from there was just hold Jacob down until he stopped moving. He readied his thoughts and tensed his arm. At the count of three, he would swipe the neck. Just then, as he was mentally prepared to end Jacob's life, he heard a scurry of footsteps coming down the garage. He quickly opened his eyes and tossed the piece of glass to the side. He breathed. He turned around and saw three uniformed police officers nearing. Relief and despair came across him at the same time. The tug of war that he fought within himself would have to wait for another time.

He stood up and raised his badge. "Officer down! Officer down!"

Fifty-six

Two Hours Later

THREE ICE CUBES FELL into a glass and rolled around a bit before being covered with Scotch. Frank picked up the glass and gently shook it before taking a sip. The tart alcohol momentarily cooled his nerves as he sat on his living room sofa listening to Nathan Hunt and Lieutenant Polenski describe their partially-failed plan.

He leaned back and crossed his legs. His face was void of expression, but that wouldn't last long because he could already feel the anger swelling in his body as if it were an alien trying to gain control of him. He took another sip and let the alcohol sit on his tongue before swallowing.

"Frank, the plan was foolproof," Lieutenant Polenski said.

"Obviously not. The two of you fools didn't get the job done. Without me even knowing, mind you."

"Stephen was going to spill his guts to Jacob if we hadn't interrupted things. You, the business, everything you worked for would have been in jeopardy."

"And how do you know that Stephen hasn't already told your detective everything?"

"He hasn't."

"How do you know for sure?"

"Because," Lieutenant Polenski paused, "I just know. You work with a guy for ten years and you know him pretty well. If Stephen had told him anything, I would have known."

Frank took another sip of his Scotch and then set the glass on the table. The tension in the room was thick enough to slice with a butter knife. Frank wanted to do his normal "fly off the handle" act, but decided to take a different approach.

He motioned with his head for Lieutenant Polenski to come closer. The lieutenant didn't move at first.

"Come here for a minute," Frank said calmly. "Sit next to me."

"Frank," Lieutenant Polenski apologetically gestured, "I'm not sure what..."

Frank smiled. "Just come here."

Lieutenant Polenski slowly stood from his chair and moved next to the judge. Frank raised his arm and placed it over Polenski's shoulders as if they were old buddies, sipping on a beer, telling jokes about the girls they'd conquered.

"So you think that just because you've known someone for a long time that you know them pretty well. Is that it?"

"Frank, I'm just saying..."

"No, you listen to me, dipshit," Frank said without raising his voice. "I don't care how long you've known this prick, he and Stephen were alone for a period of time. He needs to be dead."

Lieutenant Polenski was about to speak again, but Frank cut him off.

"If not him, then it'll be you. Do I make myself clear?"

Lieutenant Polenski nodded.

"Good," Frank replied. "Now, on another note, are you sure the man who shot at Nathan was the same one who killed Faraji?"

"We think so," Lieutenant Polenski softly replied.

"Well, now you've got two problems on your hands. I want the detective dead tonight and the shooter in custody by tomorrow."

"We're doing all we can to find this guy."

"Well, do some more. Obviously there's some connection as to why he'd be after Faraji and Stephen. Find it."

"I'll do my best."

"I hope so. For your sake."

Polenski stood to leave and Nathan started to follow until Frank stopped him.

"Not so fast, Nathan. Sit down."

Nathan sat.

"Since you're the other conspirator to fuck this up, you've got a little job to do to earn my trust back. I want you to charter a flight to Houston and come right back."

"Houston?"

"That's right. Seems like one of our guys got a little ahead of himself and managed to hide twenty grand from the books. Go down there, take care of business and come right back."

"Sure thing."

"And Nathan?"

"Yeah?"

"Don't fuck this up."

Fifty-seven

THE ANSWER TO THE question was more troubling than the question itself. I now knew why the sniper had killed Faraji Owusu. I knew why the sniper had been at the church and why he wanted to kill Stephen Carter. Revenge. That's why he came to the city. That's why he risked his life trying to get away from the police after they had him trapped in the building. Revenge. And that's why he'd do almost anything to kill his next victim, which made him even more dangerous than I had initially anticipated. I'm not religious, but I know the reason why the Good Book says "Vengeance is mine, says the Lord." Because revenge, once embedded in the heart and mind of a person, takes over that person like a fatal disease and won't let them go until the revenge has been satisfied.

I've seen it before, the look of a madman whose eyes and mind were fixated on revenge. The circumstances were different, but the mentality of the young man with the semi-automatic handgun was the same. Revenge.

It happened four years ago in a rough part of the city. I had just made detective and was heading home from a party when I heard the call over the radio. I was just two blocks away from the address and decided to respond. Evening had just turned into night when I turned into the parking lot of the apartment community. I pulled in front of the apartment building that had requested assistance when a mid-twenties Hispanic man came flying out the front door with a look of terror on his face. He was wearing only a white tank-top T-shirt and blue boxers. His hair was cut close and his body was of medium build. I quickly stepped out of the car and flashed my badge, when seconds later, another Hispanic man came out of the same door wielding a handgun. The second man was bigger and muscled up, wearing a blue mechanic's uniform.

My heart immediately started pounding as I reached for my sidearm and stepped back behind the driver's side door.

"Police!" I screamed. "Put the gun down."

The young man acted as if he didn't see or hear me. He continued pursuing the first man.

"I said put the gun down!" I yelled again. "Or I'll shoot."

The first man finally reached the back of my car and ducked down. The second man stopped in front of the car.

"I'm not going to tell you again," I said. "Put the gun down."

"Or what?" the young man surprisingly replied. "You'll shoot me? Go ahead. But I'm going to kill that punk-ass bitch for what he did."

"You don't want to do that, son," I said, trying to control the situation.

"What are you talking about?" The young man's voice rose an octave. He aimed his gun at the back of my car.

Then, within a matter of seconds, I realized what had just happened. An attractive young Hispanic woman with long curly hair came from the same front door wearing only a small bathrobe.

"I just caught that *puto* in bed with my girl!"

"Jorge," the girl called, "please, don't do this."

"Shut up, bitch," Jorge said, "I'll deal with you later."

"Jorge," I tried to say calmingly, even though my nerves were through the roof. "You need to put that gun down. I can't let you come out here flashing it around like that. Now if you put it down, we can try to settle this like adults."

"Fuck you, *pendejo*, I'm not afraid of you. Just because you got that badge don't mean shit to me."

Jorge removed one hand from his gun and began unbuttoning his blue mechanic's shirt. When the shirt was finally unbuttoned he shook his shoulders and allowed the shirt to slip off of his body. I instantly recognized the many tattoos along Jorge's torso and realized that he was part of the famous Hispanic gang MS-13.

"I gangbang with kids who have more heart than you, puto."

I gripped the handle of my gun a little tighter as I realized by Jorge's demeanor that this wasn't going to end well. The young man wasn't intimidated by my presence or the gun aimed at him.

"Jorge, I can't let you do this. Backup will be here soon, and if you don't drop your gun, things won't go so well for you."

"Think I care? I change oil for a living at a local gas station and live in this hellhole. The only thing I had going for me was my girl, and now that bitch took that from me."

Jorge's voice started to crack, but the intensity of rage in his face grew stronger. I sensed that the more Jorge talked, the angrier he became.

"Jorge, I'm only going to say this one more time," I said with a stern voice, hoping that Jorge would get the point. "Drop your weapon."

Jorge moved the target of the gun from the back of the car to me. "Or what?"

In the distance, I heard what sounded like a lawnmower engine slowly moving towards our direction. I looked to my left and saw a kid on a bicycle riding along the sidewalk and realized that he must have a playing card taped to the spokes of his wheels that makes the sound of an engine when the bike is moving. At the same time, I heard police sirens, multiple police sirens quickly getting louder.

I looked at the kid again and hoped that he saw what was going on and would stop, but he didn't.

"Hey, kid, stay back."

The kid didn't stop. The police sirens grew louder and would be in the parking lot in a couple of seconds. Apparently, the man behind the car thought that it was a good time to break away. He stood up and took off in the direction of the kid riding the bike.

"Hey," Jorge yelled.

I turned and saw the first man making a move for it, and that's when I heard the gun blast, two, three, four times. I quickly ducked, thinking the bullets were meant for me, but then immediately froze when I realized where the bullets were flying to. From my bent position, I saw that the bike the kid was riding wasn't upright any longer. My heart sank to the bottom of my stomach when I saw the kid lying next to the bike, not moving.

Then, as I was about to stand and return fire, I heard a roar of guns popping from behind me and then heard the young lady in the bathrobe scream Jorge's name. Four cops from two squad cars opened fire, and without looking, I knew that Jorge was dead.

When the loud crackling of gunfire had stopped, I stood up and ran to the kid on the bike and saw that he had headphones covering his ears. I didn't need to feel his pulse because I knew, from the lifeless void in his eyes, that the kid was dead.

Fifty-eight

A DAY DOESN'T GO by that I don't think of that kid. I learned that his name was Mark Turner and that he was coming home from the community recreation center where a science fair was being held for the neighborhood youth. Mark was in the ninth grade and was there to receive an award for his part in a science project that had somehow reached the eyes and ears of NASA. Apparently, the kid was one of the brightest in his science class.

It didn't take me long from that point to fall into depression. I kept thinking that if I'd just shot Jorge, Mark would still be alive. He'd be a freshman in college now, with his whole life ahead of him. Instead, well, now Mark's mother can only visit him at the cemetery.

My depression led to drinking which led to Theresa nearly leaving me and disciplinary action from my superiors. Had it not been for Lieutenant Polenski, I probably would be a divorced security guard somewhere, guarding someone's warehouse. Nearly half of the past four years had been spent at O'Malley's bar on 18th Street, downing drink after drink, hoping that the alcohol would somehow wash away the memories of seeing Mark Turner lying on the ground lifeless. It didn't. How ironic was it that I now found myself sitting on the same barstool at O'Malley's, trying to figure out a killer whose motive was the same as Jorge's.

O'Malley's was a small, dark pub with a single bar in the back end of the room and a few round tables filling the rest of the bar area. After the confrontation with Harvey Lindenberg in the garage, I couldn't stop thinking about O'Malley's. The stress was getting to me. The more I couldn't figure this thing out, the more I wanted to drink. But I knew I couldn't. Yet, I found myself sitting at the bar, inhaling the scents of past drinks that had been poured throughout the day.

The man who called himself Harvey Lindenberg said that there was one more that he had to kill and then he'd be gone. Who was it that Harvey wanted to kill? And why? What was the connection between Stephen Carter and Faraji Owusu for Lindenberg? Were they former associates? Had they wronged Lindenberg in some way? I remembered that Stephen told me when we first met that "we're all dirty." What were they into?

The answer to many of my questions lay in a safety deposit box in the Bank of America on I Street. I knew in order to get access to that safety deposit box, I'd need a search warrant. The problem was that I didn't know who to trust in the department. If I went to a judge requesting a search warrant, Lieutenant Polenski would surely find out. If he was dirty, working with whomever killed Stephen, then he could be linked to the firm and likely confiscate the evidence.

As I continued pondering, I heard a familiar friendly voice from behind.

"Didn't think I'd see you here again."

I turned around and saw Nadine, a mildly attractive middle-aged woman, take the seat next to me. Her hair was longer than I remembered, dark and curly. Her skin was pale white and her eyes were the color of a clear sky.

"Didn't think I'd see myself here again either."

"You know that I'm supposed to call your wife or your lieutenant if you were to come in here again."

I knew. I knew that Nadine, along with the rest of the bartenders, had been given numbers to call if I ever tried to drink in here again.

"Yeah," I pointed to the bar, "but as you can see, I'm not drinking."

"So what are you doing here then?"

I sensed a concern in Nadine's voice.

"Just thinking about things. This place...I don't know...for some reason, it clears my head."

Nadine didn't immediately respond. She looked into my eyes and leaned forward.

"Are you drinking again?"

"No."

"Jacob, I've been around for a long time and have poured a lot of drinks. I can tell when someone's about to fall off. And you, my friend, are about to fall off."

"That's not true," I responded defensively, although I knew she was right. "I've just been under a lot of stress lately."

"Go home, Jacob, and take some friendly advice: clear your head some other way. You don't want to pick up a bottle again. Believe me, you don't want to go through that hell again."

"I'm fine."

"Well then I guess you won't mind me letting your wife know that you're here?" She reached for her cell phone from her purse and flipped it open.

I raised my hands in defeat, "Okay, I get it."

I turned around and stood from the barstool, leaned over and kissed Nadine on the cheek.

"Thanks."

"Don't mention it."

"No, really, thanks."

I turned and walked out of O'Malley's forever.

Fifty-Nine

Houston, Texas

Greg Bines, a short, stocky African American, was behind a counter, locking the counter cases. Cliff Akers, a tall, thin, pale-skinned man with shoulder-length hair and a thick mustache stood behind another counter of the Houston Premier Gun Shop, clipping together the receipts for the day. The counters were across from each other and held various handguns on display. On the walls were different kinds of machine guns and framed pictures of various guns. The shop was getting ready to close and there hadn't been a customer in nearly an hour.

"What you getting into tonight?" Cliff asked.

"Same thing I always get into, my sloppy wife."

They both laughed.

"I don't even need to guess what you're doing," Greg said. "Hitting up that nasty strip club with those two-dollar strippers and one-dollar hookers."

"Hey, you know my motto, once the lights are off, we all look the same."

"You couldn't pay me to go into that disease‐infested hole."

"Ain't that bad. I only caught crabs once."

"You need help."

"Come on man, it ain't that bad. You just need to shave your pubic hairs and wash them off. Good as new once they're gone."

"Okay, you really need some help."

"No, I need some ones. It's going to be packed tonight and I plan on getting some good head."

"Should feel good. Most of them don't have teeth."

They laughed again.

"What time is Raul coming for the pickup?" Greg asked.

"Should be here within a half an hour."

Just then, the front door opened and a bell chimed. Greg looked up and was surprised to see the large man standing in their shop.

"Nathan," Cliff said. He stopped clipping the receipts together and walked around the counter. "What are you doing here?"

Nathan looked around the gun shop. "The judge asked me to come."

Greg suddenly felt very unnerved. Nathan's reputation preceded him, and Greg knew that whenever the judge asked him to pay someone a visit, things usually didn't end well. Greg looked at Nathan's hands and noticed that he was wearing gloves.

"To what do we owe this honor?" Cliff asked. He tried to smile, but Greg saw that it was forced.

"This isn't an honor visit," Nathan said. "I think you know why I'm here."

"I honestly don't. Our guy is about a half an hour away from making a pickup. He's even picking up two Armalite assault rifles, which go for ten grand each. Apparently, that's the cartel's weapon of choice these days."

"I know what he's picking up."

The room fell silent. Greg thought he heard a roach skitter across the floor, but he wasn't sure.

Nathan backed towards the door and turned the lock. He looked around the room and Greg saw that Nathan's eyes had landed on the camera propped against the rear wall in the corner.

"The judge wants his twenty grand back."

"Twenty grand?" Cliff asked.

"Don't play stupid. Twenty grand and I leave."

"I don't have twenty grand."

"Too bad for you."

Nathan whipped out a handgun and shot off two rounds to Cliff's chest. Greg jumped back and bent down behind the counter.

"Stand up, Greg. Don't be such a pussy."

"I...I...I don't know anything about twenty grand," Greg said.

"I know that. If you knew, you'd be dead as well."

Nathan put his gun away and stepped over Cliff's body.

"He thought he could hide money from us. Big mistake."

"What are you going to do with me?"

"Nothing. After your guy makes the pickup, call the police and tell them you've been robbed."

Nathan walked to the cash register, punched in a code and the register opened.

"Go to the back and bring me the disk for the camera and whatever money's in the safe."

Greg left and returned minutes later holding a bag of cash and a CD.

"You're our new front man. Take a good look at him. Double-cross us and I'll be paying you a visit."

Nathan grabbed the bag of cash and the CD.

"Hopefully I won't be seeing you again."

Part Five: Havoc

Sixty

FOUR DAYS HAVE GONE by since Stephen Carter was murdered. Whoever was hiding in the balcony of the church that fateful morning made a clean getaway and hadn't been heard from since. How'd he get up there in the first place without anyone seeing him? Lieutenant Polenski and I questioned Father Jefferson for more than four hours and his story never changed. He'd gotten to the church an hour earlier and started his day, beginning with his devotional scripture reading. Two funerals had been planned for the day, which was confirmed by the church's secretary. The priest claimed that he had been in his office right up until we arrived at the church that morning.

Even if the priest had nothing to do with the shooter, how'd the shooter know that we were bringing Stephen to the church in the first place? The only other person who knew where Stephen was going was Lieutenant Polenski. In fact, Lieutenant Polenski hadn't told me where we were going until we were a few miles away from the church. Was it a setup?

The second problem that I faced was how to handle Harvey Lindenberg. Harvey's trail had gone cold again, just like the first time. It's like he hopped in and out of existence without leaving so much as a fingerprint behind. He had told me that there would be one more killing and then he would leave the city. How long did I have before he killed again? The most obvious link would be someone within Stephen and Faraji's inner circle. Harvey had killed Faraji and was coming after Stephen, so the third person must somehow be connected to the law firm. I placed police watch with the staff of the law firm, hoping that Harvey would reveal himself sometime soon.

I interviewed the two witnesses who had been overtaken by Harvey and they both told the same story: that a man had approached them and offered to help in the rain. Once they opened the back door, the man had pulled out a gun and hit one of them over of the head, and then had the other man lead him to the sanctuary. The two men's criminal records were clean and they had no prior history of violence, arrest or terrorism. Their employer vouched for them and said that they were stand-up men, so I had no reason to think they were any more involved than what they told me.

The whole thing sucked.

The one positive about the slow past few days was that I was able to catch up on paperwork and spend time with my wife. A lot of people don't realize how much paperwork is involved in police work. I don't mind the paperwork, but I'd rather be on the heels of the two shooters I was trying to catch.

Little did I know that my slow week was about to come to an end.

Sixty-one

STEPHEN CARTER'S FUNERAL WAS filled with former colleagues, friends and family. The mid-sized church on Rte. 450 in Bowie, Maryland, was moderately filled. I came in late, as the procession had already begun, and sat in the back row. There were at least five rows between me and the closest mourners. In the front of the church, I saw Stephen's dark brown casket with a large bouquet of colorful flowers sitting on top. A short, pudgy, balding minister stood on a small stage, over top of the casket, behind a wooden podium, speaking a prayer from the Book of Psalms. In the front row, I saw Stephen's wife wearing a black dress, with two children next to her. From time to time, she'd lower her head, and her shoulders shook just enough that I knew she was crying.

I scanned the room and recognized some people I'd seen at the Superior Courthouse in D.C. There were a few public defenders, district attorneys and judges. They all were sitting with each other on the right side of the church with the man I was hoping would be here as well, Judge Frank Peters.

My hands began to sweat, and suddenly I felt very antsy. Judge Frank Peters was the last name that Stephen had said before he took a bullet to the head. He was the key. Stephen worked for him. I was sure of it. I had started a preliminary investigation of the law firm and found no ties between it and the judge, but I knew that he was somehow involved with it.

Another thirty minutes passed. Various people took to the podium and described the good person that Stephen had been. Even though I had no proof, I knew that Stephen and Faraji Owusu were definitely into something foul, and that he wasn't the good person who was being described.

Finally, the minister said a prayer and then an organ began to play softly while people stood from their seats. My anxiety level grew just a hair, as I planned on confronting the judge. People started to file out of the church. Some gathered in groups and talked while others shook hands. I stepped into the aisle and waited for the judge.

Judge Peters spoke with a few people before making his way to the exit. A tall, burly man with dark hair walked behind him, scoping the room as if he were the judge's bodyguard. I waited for the judge to finish his conversations before stepping in.

"Judge Peters? I'm Detective Hayden. I spoke with you a few weeks ago about Faraji Owusu."

The judge seemed to have been caught off guard, but tried not to show it, putting on a fake smile.

"Yes, I remember. How's the case coming?"

"Kind of hit a stall, sir."

"That kind of thing happens from time to time."

The judge started walking down the aisle as if he had finished his conversation with me.

"Sir, if you don't mind, I'd like to ask you some questions about Stephen Carter."

The judge paused and then looked around the room. "You do realize that we're at a funeral here."

"Yes, sir, I do."

"This type of behavior shouldn't be carried on at a funeral. I would have expected more professionalism from you, detective."

"Yes, sir, I understand, but I was one of the last people to speak with Stephen before he died and he had some interesting things to say about you."

Judge Peters cocked his head slightly to the left and I saw a thick vein bulge from his neck. His skin began to redden and when he looked at me, his eyes squinted as if he were a tiger who had just found his prey. When he spoke again, his voice deepened and the words barely passed through his pressed lips.

"Is there something you want to say to me?"

At that moment, the large man standing behind the judge took a step closer and peered down at me. I'm six-three, so it felt a little weird having a man look down at me. I momentarily forgot that I was a police detective and felt like a schoolboy about to take a beating from a bully.

"Actually, I do. Right before Stephen died, he told me that he worked for you. Now, I found that a little interesting, because he was supposed to be a partner of his own law firm."

Judge Peters took a step closer. "Look here, detective, I don't know who you think you are, but I'd warn you to be careful what you're about to accuse me of."

"It sounds like you're about to threaten me, Your Honor."

Judge Peters looked me up and down and then dismissively waved his hand in the air. "This conversation is over."

Sixty-two

JUDGE PETERS SLIPPED A pair of sunglasses over his eyes upon exiting the church. His pulse was racing but he managed to contain himself and not make a scene as he slowly strode to his car. Nathan Hunt followed close behind and said a word or two, but Frank wasn't paying attention. The detective had gotten too far under his skin to let anything that Nathan said be of any relevance. The only thing that was on Frank's mind was killing the detective. It has to be done.

The detective was beginning to put little bits of pieces together, and given the opportunity to do a complete investigation, he might find out that the law firm was really a front. There was no way Frank could be implicated in the firm, but the business would take a huge hit and millions would be lost.

"Goddammit," he muttered under his breath.

He reached his car and handed the keys over to Nathan so that he could sit and think without having to drive. He opened the passenger-side door and sat down.

When the door closed, the mirror caught the reflection of Detective Hayden standing in the doorway of the church, looking at Frank's car.

Frank stared back at the mirror for what felt like hours, absorbing the hatred that he was starting to feel toward the detective. His eyes couldn't look away, even when Nathan said something else to him again.

"Call Polenski," he said. "I need to see him right away."

"The detective?" Nathan responded.

"That son of a bitch just caused his death sentence."

"I can handle it."

"Not this time. I don't want any heat coming down on you. We'll let Polenski take care of it."

Nathan shifted the car into reverse and slowly backed out of the parking lot. When the vehicle began to move forward, Frank looked to his right and saw Detective Hayden still standing in front of the church, looking at him as if to say "Come on and try me." Frank balled his fists so hard that the tips of his fingernails nearly pierced the flesh of his palms.

"You're one dead son of a bitch."

Sixty-three

LATER THAT NIGHT I tossed and turned in my bed for hours. My mind was not allowing me to rest. It was good that Theresa was working the midnight shift at the hospital. She would have thrown me off the bed for causing such a commotion with my back and forth flip-flopping. In all fairness, the floor might have been more comfortable.

Truth be told, it wasn't the bed that was causing the discomfort, it was the judge. Ever since the killing of Faraji Owusu, I had witnessed two people murdered inches from me and I believe that Judge Frank Peters was connected in some way. But that's not what was causing my insomnia. During my tenure with the police department, I had studied lip reading in case I was ever on a stakeout and a person wasn't wired—I wanted to be able to read the lips of the individuals involved in the sting. My lip-reading training had paid off a couple of times, but never did I think I would need it to read the lips of a judge who said, "You're one dead son of a bitch."

At first, I was shocked. I didn't move off the church's steps for over five minutes as my mind wrestled to understand what I had seen. Did the judge really say that? It wasn't until the pastor tapped my shoulder and asked me if everything was okay that I finally walked to my car.

The rest of the day was a blur. Nothing new came up on the murders of Faraji Owusu or Stephen Carter, and no new leads on the sniper. I made a few phone calls to the IRS about the law firm, and was told that nothing stood out in their tax filings despite some large settlement statements that the firm had filed. After some additional administrative paperwork, I called it a day and headed home.

I hadn't slept much over the past few weeks, and figured that since Theresa was going to be working at night, I would be able to get to bed early for a long and overdue good night's sleep. I couldn't have been more wrong. I kept thinking about the judge and what he had said. Did he really want me dead? Would he go after a cop? If he was behind Charlie's death, then yes, he would.

I decided to sit up. If lying in bed couldn't put me to sleep, maybe a hot bath would. In no time, I was in the bathroom, watching steam rise from the hot water. I undressed and was about to step in the soaking tub when the phone rang.

2:17 a.m. is what the clock read. No one calls at that hour, not even Theresa, unless she knew that I had just gotten home from work. I quickly reached for the phone and saw that it was Lieutenant Polenski's phone number.

"Lieutenant, is everything ok?" I asked without saying hello.

"Sorry to call you this late, Jacob, but a raid is about to go down at a house on East Beach Drive and I need you there."

"East Beach Drive? A raid? That's a pretty affluent area of the city. I wasn't informed of anything. Shouldn't we already have people in place?"

"This just came in. I'm assembling a team now to meet you en route. You'll be debriefed by Johnson and Duncan."

"With all due respect, sir—"

"Jacob," Lieutenant Polenski cut me off, "this isn't a request. You're the best I've got. I need you there ASAP."

I hesitated before answering. "Sure, OK, I'll be there in ten minutes."

Sixty-four

TWO TEAMS HEADED BY Scott Johnson and Anthony Duncan had canvassed the large house on East Beach Drive, and their informant told them that there were three adult males and two females inside. Weapons and drugs had been confirmed. Not the kind of stuff that people living in this upscale Northwest, D.C., neighborhood were usually known for.

About two miles down the road, SWAT leader Scott Johnson, a big beefy man and thirteen-year vet of the force, debriefed me about the situation. As far as they knew, their undercover buyer had confirmed that three of the men were armed with semi-automatic machine guns and were high on coke and heroin.

"So they're going to be hallucinating as well? Great," I responded.

"Gets better," Scott said. "Our informant believes that the two girls inside are underage prostitutes."

Scott opened a manila folder which held the three men's mug shots, with rap sheets attached. Two of the men were African American, bald-headed with necks thick as a woman's thighs and utterly mean looking. The third man was Caucasian, leaner, with short-cropped dark hair and a long scar across his cheek.

"These men are known for violent crimes and, from what we've gathered, won't hesitate on shooting at us."

"This is all good Scott, but why do I need to be here? Seems like you guys have everything under control?"

"Lieutenant said that he wanted you on this because it may have something to do with Charlie's death."

My eyes widened with shock. "You gotta be kiddin' me. How could these thugs be involved with Charlie's murder? Lieutenant didn't mention anything about this over the phone."

"Ballistics from the bullet pulled from Charlie's head matched another bullet found in a dead guy a few days ago that allegedly came from one of the guns inside the house."

"Why wasn't I informed of this?" My voice started to rise.

Scott shrugged his shoulders. "Don't know, man. Word on the street was that this guy," Scott pointed to the Caucasian man, "bragged that he capped our dead guy Francis 'Little Man' Hayes, a few days ago."

"Christ!" I backed away and rubbed my hands over my head. Anger and excitement flushed through me at the same time. This could be the break I had been waiting on that could tie the judge to Charlie's murder.

I gathered myself and turned to Scott Johnson. "What are we waiting for?"

Sixty-five

THE HOUSE SAT ON a steep hill on the right side of East Beach Drive. The left side was full of woods. Every house on the right side had neatly-trimmed manicured yards with long driveways leading up to the houses. Two SWAT teams secured the perimeter of the house, covering the back sliding glass door and side door on the right of the house.

On the front porch, four SWAT officers stood in front of the door; the first one was holding a long battering ram. Scott Johnson stood at the bottom of the hill with me and another SWAT officer. Scott raised his hand and gave the command to breach the front door. The first officer with the battering ram looked to his colleagues and they all nodded. Then, with one forceful movement, the battering ram slammed into the front door and it flew open with great force. Seconds later, a flash bang went off in the front foyer, which was meant to daze and confuse anyone in the house. SWAT officers yelled at the top of their lungs, "Police."

They stampeded through the front door one after another. From where I stood, I could hear the back door break and SWAT officers yelling at the top of their lungs. An arsenal of shots rang throughout the house and I could only hold my breath that the perpetrators hadn't been killed. Finally, the shooting died down and a SWAT officer radioed Scott Johnson that all was clear.

When I entered the house, I looked around and saw to my left a set of stairs leading to the lower level. In front of me was a foyer, and past the foyer was the great room with three steps that led to the next level. To the right of the foyer was the kitchen. I walked to the great room, where two of the perpetrators were dead on the floor with handguns in their hands. The third perpetrator, the Caucasian man, was lying on the floor on his belly with his hands cuffed behind his back.

"Where are the girls?" I asked.

"In the back rooms," one of the SWAT officers responded. "They didn't have weapons on them and didn't resist arrest."

I looked around the room; drugs and weapons were scattered across the floor and on top of the center table. I made my way to the handcuffed perpetrator on the floor and knelt beside him.

"Where's the gun that killed Little Man?"

"Don't know what you're talking about," the man replied, not looking at me.

"Did you use it to kill a cop, too?"

"Fuck you. I ain't no cop killer."

"Is that right? Let's hope so, for your sake."

I stood up and walked around the house. I made my way down the stairs, where I found myself in a long hallway. To my right was an open door that I saw was the laundry room. To my left, the hall led to what appeared to be a family room. I took the laundry room first.

A lightbulb hung from a chain that provided the only light in the room. The laundry room was large and also doubled as a storage room for the house. A washing machine and dryer rested against the left wall, while a hot water heater rested against the wall in front of me. The room was dingy and looked abandoned compared to the rest of the house. The walls and floor were concrete. I stood in the middle of the room directly under the hanging lightbulb and took a spin around, making sure my eyes landed on everything in sight. When I looked to the far right of the room, I noticed that the back wall wasn't completely built to the ceiling; it looked partially done. I raised my flashlight and saw dark empty space past the wall, almost like a cellar was further back. Just as I was about to investigate further, two bullets from the darkness slammed into my chest, knocking me against the washing machine.

Sixty-six

IT HAPPENED SO FAST that I didn't have a chance to react. Two small torpedoes with the impact of ten Mike Tyson punches knocked me against the washing machine, but remarkably, I didn't fall to the ground. Just as quickly, someone stepped from the dark wearing a black hood with its eyes cut out and pulled the trigger two more times, causing two more bullets to pound into my chest. The gun had a silencer, so the only two people who heard the shooting were the gunman and me. The man didn't wait around to see if he had finished the job.

He exited the room quicker than he had appeared from the dark, leaving me lying on the ground, barely able to breathe from the four gun shots. I gasped for air, but every time I inhaled, sharp pains pierced through my lungs.

It took less than three seconds for four bullets to interrupt my life, but in those three seconds, I saw all the way back to my childhood. I saw my mother and father smiling and congratulating me when I brought home my first straight-A report card in the sixth grade. The next vision was when my father and I were in my high school's parking lot and my father was teaching me how to drive a stick shift. The next vision came was my first kiss at prom. I was a late bloomer, and Kelly Thompson, the girl I had had a crush on since junior high, agreed to be my date to the prom. It was during a slow song that we looked into each other's eyes and the mood overtook us. The kiss only lasted a few seconds, but it was a moment that I cherished my entire life.

The final vision was when I had met Theresa. She was in her second year of medical school at Howard University and I had just finished with the academy. I'd like to think that our chance meeting was romantic, but in reality, it was my clumsiness that caused us to speak in the first place.

The often-crowded McDonald's across from Howard University was where our love affair began. I bumped into her after I'd ordered my food, causing both of our meals to fall on the floor. What was supposed to be just a quick run in and out ended up being an hour conversation with my future wife. In that hour, I'd already fallen in love with her. Three seconds and four bullets caused my mind to swim through a lifetime of memories.

I slowly turned to my side, feeling like my ribs were cracking with the slightest movement. I glided my hands over my chest where the bullets had hit. The Kevlar bulletproof vest I wore under my shirt had stopped the bullets from penetrating my flesh. Thank God for technology.

Seconds later, a SWAT officer who was probably just passing by the room yelled at the top of his lungs, "Jacob!"

The SWAT officer quickly kneeled next to me and told me not to move. I obliged without hesitation. Seconds later, more officers started filling the room, and even though I was in pain, my mind kept saying, "You know who did this, right?"

·   I sure did.

Sixty-seven

TWO HOURS LATER, A phone rang. It took three rings before Frank Peters slowly opened his eyes to his dark bedroom.

"Damn," he tirelessly muttered.

He slowly turned around to face the nightstand where his phone and clock rested. With a lazy hand, he reached for the phone and slowly spoke into the receiver.

"This better be damn well important, whoever this is."

"It's me."

Frank instantly recognized Nathan Hunt's voice. He rolled his eyes because he knew the only reason Nathan would be calling him at his hour was because something had gone wrong.

"Don't even tell me. One of you fucked up. Is that why you're goddamn calling me at 4:30 in the goddamn morning?"

"Sorry, Frank, he was wearing a vest. Our guy hit him four times in the chest."

Frank rubbed his eyes, too tired to strain his voice, even though the inner man in him was screaming at the top of his lungs.

"So you mean to tell me that you dickheads brought someone in who wasn't smart enough to think that a cop would be wearing a vest to a raid?" He waved his hand in the air. "Unbelievable."

"Well, he won't be around to make that mistake again," Nathan reassured. "Let me take care of it," Nathan's voice pleaded for another chance.

"Where is he now?"

"At Georgetown University Hospital."

"Fine. He's all yours." Frank took a deep breath before continuing. "And Nathan?"

"Yeah."

"Don't disappoint me."

Frank set the phone receiver down and then swung his legs out of bed and sat up. He rubbed his face with his palms before his body caused his arms to swing out wide in a forced stretch. He turned around and looked at the woman lying next to him. As if she knew he was looking at her, Carmen turned around and smiled. The blanket lay partially across her chest, and Frank could make out the perkiness of her left breast.

"Is everything okay?" she asked with a soft and sensual voice.

Frank's lips curled to a smile and he leaned over and kissed her on the forehead.

"Everything's fine," he responded. "You should go back to sleep."

Carmen turned to her side and Frank could still smell the perfume that she wore when she had arrived earlier in the night.

"You know I don't make it a habit of sleeping over."

"You should."

"Well...for the right price, maybe I will," she said, smiling.

"I told you before, name your price. The world is yours as far as I'm concerned."

"Hmm," she raised her pointer finger to her lips. "If the world is mine, how about showing it to me then."

"What, the world?" Frank excitedly responded, climbing back in bed. "Where would you like to go? France, Sweden, the Caribbean? Name the place and I'll take you there in a heartbeat."

Carmen looked into his eyes and Frank gazed back into hers. Even in the dark, he could see how beautiful they were. He was falling in love with her, harder than he ever had with anyone else.

"Would you really take me anywhere I wanted to go?" she sincerely asked.

"Of course." He leaned in and gently kissed her lips. "You act as if you don't know that..." he paused before he said it, "I love you."

They gazed into each other's eyes again and Frank could tell that Carmen was searching for something, anything that would tell her any different. Finally, she reached out and pulled him close with a hug. She kissed his ear and said, "I love you too." Frank embraced her tighter, but the lovingness that he heard with his ear didn't match the blank expression that Carmen had on her face.

Sixty-eight

IF THERESA WEREN'T AN ER doctor at Georgetown University Hospital, I would have gone to the Washington Hospital Center which was closer to the raided house. I didn't think that my ribs were broken, but they sure felt that way. Dark bruises covered my upper torso where the bullets had struck the vest. I was sitting up on the examining bed in one of the ER rooms when Theresa brought X-ray sheets for me to review. She was wearing green ER scrubs and a white lab coat which had her name, Theresa Hayden, MD, stitched above her left breast.

"Nothing's broken," she said, concern filling her voice.

"That's a relief."

Theresa sat next to me and kissed my cheek. "I'm worried about you. Maybe you should take some time off. I'm sure the department would understand."

I slowly raised my left arm, winced at the pain and wrapped it around Theresa's shoulders. Our heads leaned against each other, which nearly caused me to sob. I loved her too much to tell her about my suspicions of Polenski and the judge. I also knew that if I didn't do something soon, the attempted attacks on my life would eventually be successful. I couldn't imagine leaving Theresa alone, having to live the rest of her life without me.

"You know," I said, "I wish I could take time off. Actually, I wish you and I could just get up and leave forever. But the way this case is going, I owe it to the people who've been killed to solve their murders."

"I know, babe," Theresa sighed. "Just wishful thinking. But you need to get to the bottom of how that guy was left alone without being spotted. I mean, if it wasn't for the vest, you'd be dead right now."

"I've gone through it in my head a hundred times. SWAT was supposed to have cleared the house, meaning that every room should have been checked."

"You don't think..." Theresa quickly sat up, her expression near panic, "that they meant for this to happen?"

I wanted to tell her of my suspicions, but thought better to keep it to myself. I didn't want her to worry. "No, I don't think so. The guy was hiding in the dark. There were only supposed to be five people in the house. I'm not sure how he didn't get accounted for."

I was relaxed when I spoke, which calmed her down. Theresa leaned in and hugged me and then kissed my forehead.

"I worry about you so much. Please promise me that you'll be careful."

"I promise," I said, gingerly wrapping my arms around her. "I always do."

Sixty-nine

LATER THAT MORNING, THE front door closed louder than usual, which caused me to jerk up from a deep sleep. When I did, I winced at the soreness my chest felt from the sudden movement. Realizing that it was Theresa coming home from her shift, I plopped back down, allowing my head to snuggle against the soft pillow that it had just been on.

Sunlight filled the room and when I looked at the time, I saw that it was a few minutes past eleven in the morning. Theresa should have been home hours ago, I thought. Why is she just getting home now? Her shift had ended at eight and the hospital was only a ten-minute drive from our house. Maybe there was an emergency at the hospital and she had to stay later.

"Honey?" I called. "Can you bring up some painkillers when you come up?"

The 800 milligram prescription painkillers worked wonders for my soreness, but since it'd been more than four hours since I had taken a dose, the aches were starting to return.

A few minutes went by and I realized that Theresa hadn't responded.

"Theresa?"

Still no answer. That wasn't like her.

I slowly sat up and listened to the house to see if I could hear her moving around downstairs, but not a sound was made. I didn't want to jump to conclusions, but after the near-death experience I had had the night before, anything was possible. Then a sudden thought popped into my mind. Maybe whoever tried to kill me last night was back to finish the job.

I threw the blanket off my body and grabbed my Glock that I kept in the nightstand. I ignored the piercing pain that shot through my chest as I checked to make sure the gun was loaded. I wanted to call out to Theresa again, but decided against it. I didn't want to give away my position in case the intruder hadn't heard me the first time.

Each step down the stairs seemed to creak louder than the last. Within seconds, I was on the lower level, carefully looking around the house before I made another move. Just then, I heard a whimper coming from the kitchen. I straightened my aim as my nerves swam uncontrollably through my body. My chest didn't seem to hurt anymore because of the adrenaline rush I was feeling. Before I knew it, I'd taken three steps through the living room when I heard the whimper again.

I imagined someone holding Theresa in the kitchen with their hand covering her mouth, just waiting for me to show my head around the corner before they tried to blow it off. The whimpering came quicker this time. I was about to sneak around the corner when tiny little footsteps stammered against the hardwood floor. I saw a little furball of an animal race towards me.

Giggling uncontrollably, Theresa came from around the corner of the kitchen only to be caught by surprise that I was aiming my gun.

"Jacob? What are you doing?"

I quickly lowered the gun, feeling the relief of a thousand weights fall off my shoulders. The little brown monster raced to me and started licking my toes.

"What's this?" I asked as I knelt down and picked up the little puppy.

"A chocolate Lab," Theresa replied. "He's just eight weeks old."

"How...where'd he come from?"

"I've been wanting to surprise you for a few weeks now. I picked him out a couple of weeks ago from a woman who breeds Labs out in Maryland, but had to wait until he was at least eight weeks old before I could bring him home."

I turned the puppy around and looked into its eyes.

"Aw, you shouldn't have. What am I going to do with a puppy?" I asked as I made silly faces.

Theresa stepped next to me and wrapped her arms around me and stood on her tippy-toes to kiss my cheek.

"Hopefully he'll be able to keep you company on those days when I do double shifts. Besides, I know how much you've been wanting a dog. And after what you've been through, you deserve him."

I brought the puppy close and rubbed noses with him.

"So what's the deal with the gun?" Theresa finally asked.

I smiled. "Next time when I call you, just answer. It'd make things a lot easier."

I hugged the little puppy as if I were a proud new father just seeing his baby son for the first time.

"So, whatcha gonna name him?"

I shrugged my shoulders, cocked my head and furrowed my eyebrows in thought.

"Let's call him Henry."

Seventy

A FEW HOURS INTO the afternoon, Lieutenant Polenski sat at a table on the far end of a Five Guys Burgers restaurant on Connecticut Avenue. He bit into his double-patty cheeseburger when Nathan Hunt entered the restaurant. They exchanged a glance before Nathan went to the front counter and ordered his meal. Three minutes later, Nathan brought his tray of food and sat with Polenski at his table.

Nathan reached inside his jacket pocket and pulled out a small envelope filled with crisp hundred dollar bills and handed it to Lieutenant Polenski.

"I don't have to tell you what kind of hot water we're in if this doesn't go right tonight," Nathan said.

Lieutenant Polenski nodded as he stuffed the envelope inside his inner jacket pocket. "There won't be any more complications," Polenski assured.

"We've been paying you good money throughout the years, Robbie." Nathan pointed towards the envelope.

"Too much to let some dickhead detective, who's under your watch, for Christ's sake, ruin it for us."

"Yeah, I know," his voice trailed off as he looked down at his plate. He'd known Jacob for ten years; watched him transition from a beat cop to a detective, a fine one at that, and now he had to witness the man get killed. Polenski wasn't sure that he could go through with it. Just like in the parking garage, when he had held Jacob's life in his hands, he knew he couldn't kill him.

When he raised his eyes, Nathan was looking at him inquisitively, as though he had been reading his thoughts and heard what his inner voice was saying.

"You fucking pussy," Nathan said.

The comment caught Polenski off guard.

Nathan leaned in closer, "What the fuck? You getting cold feet or something?"

Lieutenant Polenski took a sip of his soda before responding. "Look, this isn't just some nobody from the streets, all right. I happen to have known the guy for a long time so--"

"Let's get one thing straight, Robbie," Nathan said cutting him off. "I don't give a fuck how long you've known this guy. He's getting too close. And I'll be damned if I'm going to let that motherfucker take us down. Now, is this going to be a problem?"

"How's it gonna look, Nathan?" Polenski fired back. "He was there when Stephen got killed. He was there when Faraji got killed. He was there when Charlie got killed. Jesus, he was shot in the chest four times last night. If we go after him tonight, the department is gonna want answers."

"That's what we pay you for."

"Yeah, but if we go after him like this, I don't think this is something that even I can cover up."

Nathan leaned back in his seat and relaxed. "Well, I suggest that you find a way."

Lieutenant Polenski smirked and rolled his eyes. "I'm not going down for this shit, Nathan."

"None of us are. Just be at the spot at ten o'clock. We'll be in and out in no time."

Nathan took a big bite of his burger and then wiped his mouth with a napkin.

"And by the way," Nathan said with a mouth full of food, "I'll keep this conversation between us. I wouldn't want the judge thinking that you're having cold feet."

"Yeah, I'll be there," Polenski responded.

Nathan took another huge bite. "Damn, this is a good burger."

Seventy-one

I PLAYED WITH HENRY as best I could on the floor for most of the day. When the little puppy wanted to tumble, I winced at the soreness of my chest, but tumbled with him. When Henry barked, I barked back, causing him to twist his head at the odd sound. And when Henry got hungry, I fed him puppy food that Theresa had bought, and I ate as well. Of course, no puppy would be a puppy without the occasional bathroom breaks that he did on the floor. Good thing for hardwood floors. The cleanups were quick and easy. My little furry surprise was quickly becoming my best friend in the few short hours that we'd spent together.

Evening came quickly without me even noticing. Theresa had been out most of the day shopping and running errands, and when she got home, she smiled at seeing Henry and me on the floor, with Henry resting on my chest, licking the bottom of my chin.

"I see the two of you have gotten pretty close," she said as she closed the front door.

"Yeah, Henry just can't seem to get enough of me," I responded, and smiled at the tickling sensation the little pup was making by licking my chin.

"How are you feeling otherwise?"

"Better. Maybe instead of prescribing medicine, you should prescribe puppies to your patients. It's amazing how they can take the pain away."

"I'll remember that the next time someone complains of chest pains." She placed her bags on the floor and knelt down to kiss my forehead before she sat on the couch.

I looked out the window, finally realizing that it was nearly dark outside. "Aren't you going back to the hospital tonight?"

"Nope. Told them that I had to tend to you, so another doctor is covering for me." She slid off of the couch and sat next to me on the floor and rubbed Henry's back.

"You like him?" she asked.

"Best gift I've ever gotten. Well, except for you."

"That's why I love you so much," she said and leaned over to kiss my lips.

The softness of her touch immediately caused me to get aroused. I gently grabbed the back of her head and kissed more sensually than she probably anticipated. When she pulled away, there was a look in her eyes that screamed desire and lust.

"You and me have a date tonight upstairs," she softly said.

"Once the kiddie is asleep," I responded.

Theresa rubbed Henry's back again. "Yes, let's hope he goes to sleep soon."

Seventy-two

THE REMAINDER OF THE evening couldn't have been more perfect in my eyes. Theresa baked a honey-glazed salmon and whipped up some cream potatoes and broccoli. After we ate, we watched James Cameron's latest movie, *Avatar*. When the movie was over, it was a little past ten o'clock and little Henry was unconscious to the world on his doggy bed.

Theresa grabbed my hand and escorted me upstairs. We took a hot shower together, making love in between washing. The bathroom was full of steam from the hot water, but I whispered in Theresa's ear that it was her who was causing the shower to steam so much. After our passionate affair in the shower, we found our way onto the bed, where Theresa climbed on top of me and reached climax after climax. We were both exhausted when we finished, and fell asleep within minutes.

Three hours later, I woke up. Henry was in the bed, licking my bare chest. I patted Henry on the head and looked to where Theresa should have been and saw that she wasn't in the bed.

"How'd you get up here?"

Henry barked and then moved closer to lick my chin.

"Theresa?" I called, but she didn't respond.

Then I heard a sound coming from downstairs. Theresa must be getting something to drink from the kitchen, I thought. I petted Henry a little longer before I heard what sounded like glass breaking.

"Theresa, you okay?" I called again.

Still no response.

I got out of bed and put on a pair of sweatpants and walked downstairs. The first floor lights were off. I went to hit the light switch and the house still remained dark.

"Theresa?"

Another sound came from the kitchen. I was about to get nervous, but then I remembered the joke Theresa had played on me earlier in the day. She must have taken silly pills again.

"You're not going to get me again," I said, rounding the corner wall that led to the kitchen.

"What's going on with the lights?"

My eyes were adjusted to the dark, but I didn't see that Theresa was lying on the floor until I tripped over her.

"What the hell?" I gathered myself and then realized that I'd tripped over Theresa.

"Theresa!" I yelled.

I quickly grabbed her and turned her over. I leaned over and put my right ear next to her face and realized that she wasn't breathing.

"Theresa! Baby!"

I was about to stand up and reach for the phone to call 911 when a dark figure stood over me. I didn't have time to react. The dark image swung his arm and something hard hit me over the head. I was instantly out cold.

Seventy-three

WHEN I OPENED MY eyes again, everything was blurry and the right side of my face stung from where I had been hit. Slowly, my vision came into focus, and as it did, I heard male voices near me. As my eyesight became clearer, I looked around and realized that I wasn't at home any longer, but on a boat. The smell of the salty sea suddenly entered my nostrils.

"Theresa," I moaned.

"Hey," I heard someone say, "he's awake."

Then one of the men kneeled down, close enough for me to see who it was. I immediately recognized him as the large man who had been with Judge Peters the day of Stephen Carter's funeral. The man took a long drag of a cigarette and blew the smoke in my face.

"He is, isn't he." He turned around and spoke to two men. "Stand him up."

Within seconds, two pair of strong hands grabbed me by either arm and slung me to my feet. My legs weren't strong enough to hold me up at first and I almost fell back down. The two men supported me until my legs were under me and then they let me go. I still had a hard time supporting myself due to the swaying of the boat, but I managed not to fall.

I looked around and saw that I was on a small yacht. The front part of the yacht was indoors while the part where I was standing was outdoors. To my left and right there was nothing but darkness, and I figured that I must be somewhere in the Chesapeake Bay.

The large man took a step closer to me and puffed on his cigarette again.

"My wife," I said through a raspy voice. "Where is she?"

The large man blew out smoke into my face again.

"The judge offers his condolences," he said matter-of-factly.

I dropped my head and wept. I couldn't believe what I had just heard.

"But look at it this way," he said, "she went peacefully. Her neck snapped with one twist. I didn't even have to struggle with it."

I felt rage sweep through me and I lashed out. "Imma kill you, you bastard!"

The two men grabbed me before I could touch him, and one of them punched me square in the back. I dropped to my knees and all of the air in my lungs felt like it escaped with the powerful blow. I coughed and inhaled deeply to catch my breath.

Between inhaling, I nearly choked from crying. Snot seeped from my nose and spit hung from my lips.

"Why, you fucking bastard?" I tried to reach for the man again but one of the other men kicked me from behind, causing me to fall flat on my chest. I didn't try and get up.

"Why?" the man repeated. "You wanna know why, asshole? Because you started poking that black nose of yours into our business." He took another drag from his cigarette. "I should have just killed you in Stephen's office like I did your partner, and your wife would probably be alive right now."

"Fuck you!" I screamed.

"No, fuck you!" he screamed back. "Because of you I've had to kill a cop, a wife and now another cop. This is all your fucking fault, you prick."

"You'll never get away with this. Someone will find out," I responded.

"Of course I'll get away with it and you wanna know why? Because your little buddy Polenski has the whole thing set up."

The man motioned for the two other men to stand me up. They quickly grabbed me and brought me to my feet.

"Bring him over here."

I was dragged to where the yacht became covered and looked inside. Lights inside the yacht revealed two dead men on a sofa, shot in the head.

"You see, Polenski's been thinking for a while that you're a dirty cop," the man started to say. "He believes that you're mixed up with the Gomez drug family and have been taking bribes."

"That's bullshit."

"Is it?" he responded. "Then why are you on their boat? And why are slugs from your gun in those men's heads right there?" He pointed to the two dead men. "And what's worse, Theresa found out about it. You see, she called Polenski and told him about a huge stash of money and drugs she found on your side of the closet. Polenski told her not to confront you about it, but she did anyway. That's when you killed her. And to cover up everything, you made an appointment to see these two assholes and figured you'd kill them so no one would find out. So an argument started and then a gunfight broke out. You killed them but in the gunfight you got killed yourself."

"If they're dead, who's going to kill me?" I asked.

He looked at one of the men to my left. "That's Javier. He's one of the other brothers. He's a heartless prick who doesn't care about anyone except himself. So to see his brothers dead doesn't even phase him. But more than that, he's wanted to get back at you for getting his younger brother Hector killed. Hector was the only one he cared about."

"Hector died because he ran from us and was high on coke."

I looked to my left and Javier, with a rigid jawline and shoulder-length dark hair, just stared at me without an expression.

"You see," he continued, "during the gun battle, Javier was able to put two in your chest before taking a flesh wound to the arm. And the judge in the case will take sympathy on him, calling your death self-defense and will only give him the minimum sentence required by law."

Javier took two steps towards the large man and was handed a handgun. The man raised the gun and aimed it at my chest, and then moved it to my head. My eyes widened and all of the pores on my body seemed to have opened at once. I glanced at the large man, who had a smirk on his face. I wanted to plead for my life but knew it was worthless. I was in the middle of nowhere with a stone-cold killer who had masterminded a plan that would make me look crooked and dirty.

I gulped and stared at the man pointing the gun and then closed my eyes. I didn't want to see him pull the trigger; I was just hoping that my death wouldn't be painful. I heard the man release the safety, and then expected to hear the blast of the gun, but instead, a bright light lit up the area.

Seventy-four

THE BRIGHT LIGHT SURPRISED everyone, including Nathan Hunt. The bright light also caused Javier to shoot prematurely, striking Jacob, which caused him to fall overboard.

Nathan quickly turned around towards the bright light and saw that another boat, smaller than the yacht, was to its right.

"This is the Coast Guard," came a loud and booming voice. "Drop your weapon."

Javier quickly turned the gun around and started shooting at the Coast Guard's boat. Nathan ducked inside the yacht, grabbed a machine gun and rushed back outside to the deck. He aimed the gun at the Coast Guard's boat and started firing. The third man pulled a handgun from the back of his pants and commenced to firing as well.

The Coast Guard's boat quickly veered away from the rapid firing, but not before bullets shot back to the yacht. The man with the handgun was hit in the chest and fell backwards. When the Coast Guard's boat veered, the bright light wasn't shining in Nathan's eyes and he was better able to aim the gun at his target. He saw that there were three men on the boat. He aimed the gun and took out one of the shooters.

He reached in his back pocket and pulled out a CB radio. He pressed the talk button and yelled into the CB.

"Get your ass over in a hurry!"

He put the CB radio back into his rear pocket and continued firing the machine gun. The Coast Guard's boat didn't attempt to turn around and exchange fire, and Nathan knew that within minutes, reinforcements would be upon the yacht, ready to take out anyone and anything shooting back.

Minutes later, a speed boat came upon the yacht from the other direction. When the speed boat was next to the yacht, Nathan quickly tossed the machine gun into the speed boat and then jumped in. Javier was about to do the same, but Nathan grabbed the machine gun and turned it on him.

"What are you doing?" Javier asked through a thick Hispanic accent.

"What I always do," Nathan quickly retorted. Then he squeezed the trigger and Javier was hit with a flurry of bullets. His body slumped and fell overboard.

Nathan turned to Polenski, who was driving the speed boat, and was about to aim the machine gun at him.

"What the fuck was that!?" Nathan screamed.

"Don't look at me," Polenski quickly responded. "I didn't call them."

"Fuck!" Nathan yelled at the top of his lungs.

"What about Jacob?" Polenski asked.

"He got hit. He's somewhere in the water."

"Is he dead?"

"Don't ask such a stupid question. They'll find his body when they do a sweep of the area. Now turn this thing around and let's get the hell out of here."

Polenski turned the steering wheel and pushed the throttle up. The boat revved and made a hard left and, within seconds, disappeared into the darkness of the Bay.

Seventy-five

WHEN THE BRIGHT LIGHT hit the boat, I immediately opened my eyes and, for a split second, thought I had a chance of making it out of there alive. But then I heard a loud bang and then felt searing heat slice the left side of my cheek. The pain was immense and I fell backwards off the boat and into the Bay. I heard the rattle of gunfire before I started sinking into the dark water. I felt semi-lifeless, worn down and beaten. I didn't want to live anymore, so all I needed to do was wait and death would take me like it had taken Theresa. Just wait and relax. Soon it would come.

I thought about swimming to the surface, but fought against it. They won. They had beaten me. There was nothing left to fight for now that Theresa was gone. My lungs burned as buoyancy started to carry my body back to the surface. That's okay, I thought. I'll be dead by the time I reach the top.

Just then, I saw another light above, touching various angles of the water before it hit me. They found me. But it's too late. Here I come, Theresa. I hope you'll be waiting for me. Just as I opened my mouth and inhaled, someone crashed into the water and grabbed my arm.

Part Six:
The Sniper Returns

Seventy-six

WHEN I OPENED MY EYES, I immediately felt a soreness throbbing from my left cheek. Instinctively, I raised my hand to the left side of my face and touched what felt like stitches penetrated into my skin in the form of a long line that went from the front of my cheek to the back of my jawline.

What happened?

The room was dark and the bed that I was lying on was firm, similar to my bed at home. But I sensed that this wasn't my room.

"Theresa?" I called out. My voice was low and hoarse.

Theresa didn't respond. I heard Henry's baby bark to my left. I turned, and immediately Henry was licking my lips and chin.

The licking tickled a little, which made me smile. But soon the pressure on the left side of my face grew more intense, which forced me to turn my head.

Just then, as if a Mack truck crashed into my brain, I suddenly remembered tripping over Theresa' dead body, the gun aimed at me on the boat, being shot in the face, and then drowning in the Bay. But I hadn't drowned. I was alive.

Theresa! Oh God, my Theresa.

I quickly sat up in bed, looking around the dark room. Where am I? If I'm not home, how did Henry get in bed with me?

I threw the blanket off my body and realized that I was naked. Where are my clothes? I swung my legs to the right and let them hang off the bed until they touched what felt like a wood floor.

"Hello?" I called out. Immediately, I felt a sharp pain shoot from my left cheek. I winced and covered the sore spot of my face with my left palm. In doing so, I felt something pinch the inside of my arm. I ran my fingers near the middle of my arm and felt what I believed to be a catheter.

"What the hell?"

I needed to find the light switch. I stood up and stretched my arms out in the dark and made my way to the nearest wall and started feeling for the light switch. I bumped into a desk and found a small lamp. I turned on the lamp, which lit the room dimly. What I saw next made me gasp and raise my hand to my mouth in disbelief.

I was in a studio apartment that couldn't have been any larger than five hundred square feet. To my right was the double bed that I had recently been in and where

Henry was comfortably cuddled next to a pillow. The bed sat about a foot away from a window that had a navy blue blanket taped to the wall, covering it completely. On the opposite end of the apartment was a small makeshift kitchen with small white cabinets, a two-burner stove, a sink and small refrigerator. Next to the kitchen was the entrance door to the apartment. What I found shocking was what was on the wooden desk.

Wigs, fake mustaches and beards, different style hats stacked upon one another, fake noses and a tray full of makeup. To the left of the desk was a body suit, propped against the desk on the floor, that when worn made a person appear slightly heavier than what they really were.

Over top of the desk, taped to the wall, were large pictures of Faraji Owusu, Stephen Carter, Judge Frank Peters and the man who had killed Theresa. There were five pictures of each of them in different settings. Two pictures captured both Faraji and Stephen walking together through Dupont Circle. Two other pictures captured both the judge and Theresa's killer walking in front of the courthouse.

I walked to the desk, not caring that I was naked, and examined what else was there. I saw a couple of IDs that bore the same face, but wearing different disguises with different names and different states of residence. I immediately recognized the face as Harvey Lindenberg.

I looked around the room again and saw that my clothes were neatly folded and sitting on the floor at the end of the bed. I quickly got dressed, and as I finished, I heard keys enter the door knob.

Seventy-seven

THE SNIPER STOOD IN the doorway and slowly closed the door behind him. One hand held two plastic grocery bags, which the sniper placed on the kitchen counter. He wore a red Washington Redskins baseball cap and black-rimmed glasses. A fake goatee covered his upper lip and chin. After placing the bags on the counter, he turned to Jacob and through the dim light, they stared at each other for a few seconds before the sniper spoke the first word.

The sniper wasn't sure how Jacob would react upon seeing him, but he had believed, when he pulled him out of the Bay, that this was the safest place for Jacob to be. They shared a common enemy who had taken away someone close to them. Jacob would now have to see things through the sniper's eyes.

"You must be hungry," the sniper said. "You haven't eaten in two days."

"I haven't thought about it," Jacob solemnly responded.

"Well, soon you will be. I got us some food." The sniper motioned to the two grocery bags.

"So you pulled me from the water?"

The sniper nodded.

"Why?"

"You didn't deserve to die like that. I saw what they did to your wife, and I couldn't allow them to kill you as well."

Jacob's head sunk and he staggered to find the bed. "You saw...Theresa?" His words were partially covered by sobs.

The sniper nodded again. He felt Jacob's pain. He knew how it felt to lose someone close at the hands of another person.

"Where are we? Jacob asked.

"In Silver Spring, Maryland."

Jacob rubbed his eyes and looked up at the sniper. "What happened to her? Where's her body?"

"Listen," the sniper said, "you can't go back. They think you're dead. Your name has been smeared all through the media."

"What are you talking about?"

"You've been here for nineteen hours. I kept you unconscious with a drug called Diprivan so that your body could rest from the wound."

"Are you a doctor?"

"I used to be a nurse."

Jacob rubbed his left cheek again and realized that he was feeling stitches.

"For the past nineteen hours, the Coast Guard has been scouring the Bay for your body. Your name has been linked to the Gomez drug family and they're saying that you were one of the men that opened fire on the Coast Guard before you were shot and killed. They're also saying that there's strong evidence that you killed your wife. The media has made a circus of all of this."

"How did you know where to find me?"

"I have someone on the inside who told me what was going down. I knew they were going to try and set you up on the boat. " The sniper lowered his head. "They've done this before," he softly said.

"What do you mean?" Jacob asked.

The sniper raised his head, "My brother...they killed my brother."

Seventy-eight

I WASN'T SURE HOW I felt at the moment. The life that I had once known was gone. The beautiful wife that I had loved since the day we met was dead. My career as a police officer was over, and if I showed my face in public, I'd more than likely be arrested and charged with murder, drug trafficking and a host of other offenses.

What complicated things more was the fact that I was now face-to-face with Harvey Lindenberg, who had killed Faraji Owusu in cold blood. But he was also the single reason why I was alive. If it wasn't for Harvey, I would have been shot in the church or drowned in the Bay.

"Why did they kill your brother?"

The sniper took a step back, leaned against the kitchen counter and stuffed his hands into his front pockets.

"He used to work for the law firm of Owusu and Carter. His official title was paralegal, but unofficially, he helped them smuggle weapons in and out of the country.

Before working for the firm, he was in the military; worked for the Army as a sniper and could shoot a fly off a cow's nose from a thousand yards away. After he got out of the military, he met a guy named Mac Truck."

"Mac Truck?"

"From what I understood, Mac was a big black guy, about six-four, and over three hundred pounds, hence the name Mac Truck. He was small time compared to the law firm. He fenced stolen weapons across the city and brought my brother in as a partner. He thought that my brother could help him attract a broader clientele."

I sat on the edge of the bed, trying to picture in my head what Mac Truck would have looked like. Washington, D.C., was no stranger to its gun problems, but it was making a valiant effort at gun control and getting guns off the streets.

"The name doesn't ring a bell," I replied. "We've busted dozens of weapons smugglers in the city but none of them fit that description."

"It helps when you have connections from the inside," the sniper responded. "Which leads me to the law firm."

"Stephen and Faraji?"

The sniper nodded. "Stephen worked with Mac a few times, helping him out with some," the sniper formed quotation marks with his fingers, "legal matters. Mac introduced Stephen to my brother, and within a short period of time, my brother had proven his worth and then was introduced to the firm. Because of his military background and good understanding of weapons, my brother was a perfect fit. He was dumb, willing and able."

"So what happened to get himself killed?"

"The bastard finally got a heart. He had just come back from a trip to Africa and he told me how he witnessed a boy, no older than twelve, shoot down a family with an AK-47 machine gun he'd gotten from the judge's weapons. He told Mac what he witnessed and said that he couldn't be a part of the operation anymore. He made the mistake of telling Mac that he was going to go to the Feds to turn himself in and bring down the whole operation. Two days later, my brother and Mac were found shot to death in an apartment."

A thought suddenly popped off in my head. Nearly two years ago, I remembered two men that had been murdered in an apartment, execution style, with their arms tied behind their backs, shot in the head. The case was thought to have been a drug deal gone bad, as cocaine and marijuana were found throughout the house.

"I think I remember the shooting. A big black male and a white male were shot execution-style about two years ago."

I stood up and paced in front of the bed as I recalled the investigation.

"The black male victim's name was Reginald Johnson, and the white male's name was Scott Duffy."

"Yeah, Scott," the sniper responded.

I visualized the crime scene photos as I paced the floor. The white male wore a military-style crew cut and was fairly built. The black male was bald with a thick beard. I hadn't handled the investigation, but had read the reports due to the way the men were killed. I remembered believing that the men were killed by professionals, but that theory was never proven. The case went cold, and like a lot of homicides in D.C., was forgotten.

As I started remembering the reports, I curiously stopped pacing and looked at the sniper.

"Wait a minute, something's not right. Scott Duffy wasn't survived by a brother. He only had a sister. His parents were deceased and there was no other next of kin. If I remember correctly, his sister's name was—"

The sniper stood up from the counter and took off the hat and glasses and removed the fake goatee. Her voice rose an octave when she said, "Angela. His sister's name was Angela Duffy."

"Holy shit," I said. My eyes went wide and my mouth hung open. "Now I really need a drink."

Seventy-nine

DUMBFOUNDED, STUPEFIED AND BLINDSIDED were the best words to describe my emotions. I just couldn't believe it. All of my time and energy had been spent looking for a man when, in fact, the sniper was a woman. Brilliant. I looked at the desk and at all of the makeup, wigs, fake beards and now everything clicked. The bodysuit that made her build look broader faked everyone into thinking she was a man.

If she had left the city after killing Faraji, no one would have been the wiser. Every resource had been spent looking for a man.

Now, as I looked at her without costume, I saw the feminine features of her face that I previously hadn't noticed. Her forehead wasn't squared like most men's and her jawline was soft, not rigid. She wasn't as husky as she was in the bodysuit, but I saw that her build was hard under her shirt, as if she were a gym rat. However, the voice—how could she have disguised her voice so I wouldn't have been able to tell that it was a woman trying to sound like a man?

"I can see that you're trying to figure it out," Angela said. Her voice still didn't quite sound like a woman.

"Yeah, you got that right."

"For the past seven months, I've been taking testosterone injections, a hormone that women take when they want to change their gender. I'm not a transgender or anything like that, but I knew that if I made the police think that I was a man, I'd have an easier chance of getting away after I've done what I came to do."

My mind instantly went back to the office building when Harvey Lindenberg had escaped from under their noses.

"So that's how you did it. That's how you got by all the police after the first shooting? You changed into a woman's clothes and walked right out of the building?"

"It would have been much easier if you weren't right there. You've made things more difficult for me these past few months."

"Sorry to have been the thorn in your side," I sarcastically responded. "But you killed a man in cold blood. Doesn't matter what your motive is. You're still a killer and I can't overlook that."

"So what are you going to do?" Angela brought her hands to her front and held them out as if waiting to be handcuffed. "Take me in? Well I'm right here."

"Don't tempt me."

Angela lowered her hands and sat next to him on the bed.

"I'm still not finished. Not until the judge and Nathan Hunt are dead."

"Nathan Hunt?" I asked.

"He's the big guy who killed your wife. He's the judge's trigger man. My brother personally saw him kill two people in the street without even thinking about it."

I felt my heart sink when I thought about Theresa again and what her last thoughts could have been before she died. Was she scared? Did she know that she was going to die?

"I believe Nathan's the one who actually killed Scott," Angela said. She lowered her head and spoke more softly, "but they're all guilty of his death. In my mind, they all killed him, regardless of who pulled the trigger."

She turned to me and I saw her eyes begin to tear. "And then that prick took away my chance to kill Stephen." She slammed her right fist against the bed and turned her face. "I can't wait to put a bullet between his eyes."

"No, you can't do that. There's got to be another way to end this. No more killing."

"How can you say that? They killed your wife and destroyed your life. Those fuckers have to pay for what they've done."

Now it was my eyes that started to tear. What I wouldn't give to steal the last breath away from the man who had taken Theresa's life. But by doing that, I wouldn't be any better than them. I'd be a murderer as well. Then I thought, maybe some people deserve to die. Maybe legal justice just wasn't enough. No, I quickly wiped away the thought. I'd sworn to uphold the law, not break it. My job was to serve and protect the people, not kill them.

"I'm sorry," I said, "I just can't do it. There's got to be a way for me to clear my name and bring those assholes to justice."

"You won't have a chance to. They'll be dead before you figure it out."

"What are you talking about?"

"The judge plans on retiring and leaving the country in the next couple of weeks. My best chance to get to him is now before he disappears."

"How do you know all of this?"

"I told you, I have someone on the inside who's been helping me."

"What...like a mole?"

"You can call it that. She has intimate knowledge of the judge's every move."

I shook my head. "You know I can't let you do that. I can't willingly stand by and let you kill another person."

"I wasn't asking for your permission. Besides, I don't think you're in a position to stop me. I don't want to toot any horns here, but if it wasn't for me you'd be dead, twice. Let's not forget that."

I didn't respond, couldn't respond. The room fell silent with the exception of Henry's sleepy breathing. I didn't want to admit it, but Angela was right. The judge was too connected in the city and any means of trying to bring him down through the legal system would be fought at every angle.

"So let's just say that I agree with you," I finally said. "What do you have planned? And before you answer that, I have to ask a favor?"

"Shoot."

"How good are you at hiding other people's faces with that makeup?"

Eighty

JUDGE FRANK PETERS, FOR the first time in weeks, smiled at someone other than Carmen. Despite the fact that the detective's body still hadn't been found, it was of no concern. It'd wash up at some time or another, or maybe never. Lieutenant Polenski had already confirmed that they had enough phony evidence against the detective that if, by some miracle, he had survived, he'd be locked away for the rest of his life.

But that's not why Frank was happy. He had just signed his retirement papers, and in a few short weeks, he'd be living the rest of his days in Punta Cana, Dominican Republic, where the beaches were always white and the water clear as crystal.

His secretary, Sylvia, stood at the front of his desk with a partial smile across her face.

"Oh, Judge Peters, I can't believe you're retiring. You're the only judge that I've worked for."

"I know, Sylvia. You've been a very good coworker for the last twelve years. But there comes a time when you have to move on. And now it's my time."

Frank noticed that Sylvia was getting ready to cry and he opened a drawer in his desk and pulled out a handkerchief and handed it to her.

"Come on now," he said, "don't cry. It's not like I'm dying or anything. I'm just moving on."

"I know," Sylvia said, wiping her eyes with the handkerchief. "Things just won't be the same here without you."

Frank stood up and walked to the front of his desk and embraced Sylvia. She'd been the true bright spot in this office and he was very appreciative of her work. As he hugged her, he thought about what she really would think of him had she'd known who he really was.

He pulled back from his embrace and wiped her tears with his thumbs.

"I've got something for you," he said. He walked back to his desk and pulled open the same drawer and picked up an envelope and handed it to her.

"What's this?" she asked.

"Promise me you won't open it until after I leave. It's just a little token of appreciation from me to you."

Sylvia took the envelope and more tears fell from her eyes.

"Oh, Judge Peters, you didn't have to."

"Don't be silly. You've earned it."

Sylvia looked at the envelope and then turned and left.

Frank admitted to himself that he hated saying goodbye, but at the same time, he couldn't stop thinking about his new life on the tropical island with Carmen next to him every day. And he felt good knowing that Sylvia wasn't the type of person to go and blow the twenty-thousand-dollar check that he had just handed her.

Eighty-one

I WASN'T SURE IF I could do it. The closer we got to the funeral home, the more I felt like passing out. Sitting in the passenger seat of a navy blue Chevrolet Impala that Angela had rented with one of her aliases, my nerves grew more intense with each passing second. Never in a million years did I think that I would have to attend my wife's funeral at such a young age, in disguise, and with a suspect in a murder that I was investigating.

Theresa and I had planned on moving to the Caribbean when it was our time to retire. We'd talked about having kids and traveling the world. We wanted to see the pyramids in Egypt and travel to the Holy Land to walk in Christ's footsteps. There was so much that we wanted to do as a couple that now I can't imagine living my life alone without her.

The phrase is always used that life is short, but as I looked ahead and realized that I could reasonably live another forty or fifty years, life won't seem short, it'd seem like an eternity. An eternity that I would spend alone, waiting on the time that I'd be able to see Theresa again.

When we arrived at the colonial-style two-story house that was turned into a funeral home in Germantown, Maryland, I saw that the parking lot was half-full. My palms were sweaty and I was having a harder time calming my nerves. My heart raced like I had been shot with an adrenaline needle.

"I don't know if I can do this," I finally spoke. I turned to Angela and my hands were shaking.

"No one will recognize you."

"I should have listened to you. This might be too much to handle."

"Do you want to turn around? It's not too late."

I looked at the small crowd gathered in front of the funeral home, most everyone I recognized. I took a few deep breaths and cleared my mind. I had to see my Theresa one last time.

"No, I can make it."

Angela patted the top of my hand after she pushed the gear shift in park.

"I'll be with you. You'll look less conspicuous if I'm there. If anyone asks, I'm your nurse from a nursing home and Theresa was once your doctor. You've come to pay your respects."

I nodded, and then brought down the visor and looked at myself in the mirror. If I wasn't myself, I wouldn't have recognized me. Angela was a master at disguise, I had to agree. The skin on my face no longer looked smooth and youthful, rather, now it appeared wrinkled and old. A light grey beard neatly blended into the old-looking skin, making me appear closer to my mid-seventies than thirties. My nose was wider than before and my eyelids sagged as if the years of keeping my eyes open had finally taken their toll. My hair and eyebrows matched the color of the beard, and I wore a black derby hat and dark-rimmed glasses with tinted lenses to help conceal my identity.

Angela had also used a synthetic rubber over my hands and applied liver spots to make my hands appear years older than what they were. All of this she had learned from her brother, who had mastered the art of disguise while in the military.

I finally opened the door and slowly got out of the car. I held a cane in my right hand, slouched my upper body slightly forward and proceeded to slowly walk to the front door, using the cane for support with each step. Angela walked next to me, dressed in black slacks and a matching blazer. Her short hair was styled, and with a little makeup, she didn't look anything like the man she had pretended to be months earlier. She held me by my right elbow as we entered the funeral home.

"You okay?" she asked.

I nodded, and thought I was, until I turned to the left and saw the open casket at the front of the room.

"Oh God."

Angela steadied me.

"Don't worry. I've got you."

Eighty-two

LYING IN THE CASKET motionless, wearing a black dress that I recognized as her favorite, her hair pulled back into a ponytail, Theresa looked as though she was simply taking a nap. I wanted so badly to jump in the casket and lie with her. I didn't care about the outside world anymore. I could die right now and I'd be fine with that.

My right hand trembled as I gently glided my fingers over Theresa's stiff hands. How can she be dead? There was a line of people behind me, but I didn't care. I didn't want to leave her side.

"I'm sorry," I mouthed under my breath.

I fought as hard as I could not to cry, but the tears found their way out and streamed down my face.

Then I felt a hand pat my left shoulder. I turned and was shocked to see Theresa's father comforting me. Pops looked like he'd aged ten years since the last time I had seen him. At that time, Pops' eyes were vibrant and alive, in contrast to the tired and sad way they looked at me now. He appeared to be a shell of the man he once was, the man who I had grown to love like my own father.

I wanted to give him a hug and tell him how much I loved him, but I couldn't. I wanted to tell him that what the media said about me was a lie and that I would never harm Theresa. But I couldn't because my life had been taken from me, just like Theresa's was taken from her. The only difference was that I was still breathing and she wasn't.

"Let me help you, old timer," Pops said in a soft and comforting voice.

"She was a great woman," I tried disguising my voice to match my appearance.

"Yes, she was. Where are you sitting?"

I pointed to the back of the room where Angela was sitting. Pops gently led me to my seat and smiled at Angela.

"This is hard for all of us," Pops said. "I appreciate you coming today."

Angela smiled back but I kept my head down. Pops turned and walked back to his daughter's side and comforted others as they said their last goodbyes.

"Do you know him?" Angela asked.

"Yes, he's my father-in-law."

"Oh."

The room rumbled with chatter for a few more minutes before Pops asked everyone to find their seats.

"On behalf of my family, I want to first thank everyone for coming. Theresa was a special person, and she was taken from us in the prime of her life. She will be greatly missed..."

Pops' voice began to fade into the background of my mind, as the only thing I was hearing was Theresa's laughter. I closed my eyes and remembered how her smile would light up the room. I remembered the last night we were together, and how passionately we had made love. She was supposed to go to work, but she stayed home to take care of me and it was one of the best nights we'd had together.

The more I thought about it, the deeper my sorrow grew. She was supposed to be at work. If it wasn't for me, she'd still be alive. I didn't want to believe it, but in some twisted way, maybe I did kill her. She wasn't supposed to be home.

I almost screamed, but my thought was cut off when I heard Angela whisper, "What the hell is he doing here?"

Eighty-three

I NEARLY LUNGED FROM my seat to tackle my now former lieutenant and strangle the life out of him, but I found some semblance of composure and was able to remain in my seat. Lieutenant Polenski and his blond, voluptuous wife entered the room as the service was just starting and sat on the opposite side of the aisle, across the room.

My anger felt like it was going to burn through my skin and melt the prosthetic nose and carry away the makeup that Angela had spent so long perfecting. How dare he come here like this?

My father-in-law's voice no longer carried to my ears. I became deaf to the room and all of my focus was on the man who had helped set me up. A man who I had one time thought was a friend, a confidant, a mentor, but those days were long gone.

"Take it easy," Angela whispered.

I finally blinked my eyes and realized that the pain in my heart must be showing through my face for Angela to say something. I took a deep breath and turned my head back to Pops, who was trying to speak while holding back tears.

"The hardest thing about her death," Pops said, "was that there's no closure. As people, we need closure." He lowered his head and brought his hand to his lips. He caught his composure before he spoke again and addressed the audience. "I just need to know why. But the one man who can answer that is dead himself. So I'll carry this with me to the grave, never knowing why."

The anger that I had just experienced quickly vanished when I heard my father-in-law's plea. My heart sank to a depth that I hadn't known existed. A father wanting to know why his daughter was killed in cold blood would melt the soul of any human being.

I couldn't hold them back any longer. Tears streamed down my face like a river flowing, and all I could do was watch Pops stand in front of the crowd in anguish.

Finally, after a minute of silence, Pops spoke again. "We aren't the traditional type. Never have been. So I'm now going to open the floor to anyone who wants to come up and say a few words about Theresa."

One by one, various people from the crowd made their way to the front of the room and spoke highly of their friend and coworker. About thirty minutes and a handful of people later, Lieutenant Polenski stood and walked to the front of the room. He gave Pops a hug and then addressed the room.

"My name is Robert Polenski and I'm a police officer with the D.C. police department. I was Jacob's lieutenant before he was killed."

A few stirs went throughout the room.

"I knew Theresa and Jacob for a long time," he continued, "and I'm still shocked at how this all ended."

I clenched my fist and narrowed my eyes at my former lieutenant.

"When I first found out what Jacob had gotten into, I contacted Theresa, but never in a million years would I have thought that he would have done what he did."

"Lies," I whispered through my teeth.

"Keep your cool," Angela whispered.

"For a while, I blamed myself," Polenski continued. "I thought that if I hadn't said anything and had brought Jacob in myself, Theresa would still be here."

I stirred in my seat. I exhaled out of my nostrils like a bull ready to charge. "Lies," I whispered again.

"I guess what I'm trying to say is, I just want everyone to know that Metro police are sorry for the pain that one man has caused, and if I could do it all over again, I would."

My inner self exploded with rage and before I could stop it, I jumped to my feet and yelled at the top of my lungs, "LIAR!"

Eighty-four

EVERYONE IN THE ROOM quickly turned around toward me. Their faces appeared startled and confused at the old man who screamed at the top of his lungs. I began to slowly make my way down the aisle while pointing at Lieutenant Polenski.

"How can you stand up there at say those things, knowing it's not the truth?"

"Excuse me," Polenski said, looking a little nervous.

"You dare come here at a time like this and continue to defame a good man's name in front of his wife's family?"

"I'm sorry, sir," Polenski continued, "I don't know who you are, but I assure you I'm not lying."

"Yes you are!" I said as I stomped my foot so that my point was well taken. I didn't move like the old man who first came into the funeral home. "You and Nathan Hunt set up the whole thing so that I'd be blamed for her murder. YOU killed her in cold blood, you bastard."

Pops quickly stood and walked close to me. He stared at me wide-eyed and shocked as if he'd just seen the resurrected Christ.

"My God...Jacob?"

Murmurs floated across the room.

I panned the room and saw some people holding up smartphones, obviously recording the whole thing. I turned back to Polenski and saw that the man's jaw had almost dropped.

At first, my eyes were fixated on Lieutenant Polenski, but then I heard Pops' sorrowful voice say my name and it melted my heart once again. My anger quickly diminished.

"I didn't do what they said I did," I softly responded. "I loved Theresa too much to hurt her. You've got to believe me."

Pops appeared dumbfounded, as if he wanted to hug me and at the same time strangle me. He moved his mouth but nothing came out, almost like his voice had been taken from him.

Suddenly Angela's voice boomed like she was speaking through a microphone. "Jacob, watch out!"

Lieutenant Polenski lunged toward me and caught me with a fist to the chin. My head rocked and I fell to the ground.

"Someone call the police!" Polenski yelled. "We have a fugitive here."

I shook my head and blinked my eyes, but the room felt like it was spinning. Don't pass out, I thought.

Lieutenant Polenski then looked to his wife. "Honey, quickly go to the car and grab my handcuffs."

By now, everyone who was in their seats was standing up, trying to get a look at the commotion.

Lieutenant Polenski went to grab me and place my hands behind my back when Angela burst up the aisle and led with a spinning back side kick that caught Polenski square in the chest. The blow was powerful enough to knock him onto his back. He quickly stood, but Angela caught him with a flurry of kicks that laid him out cold.

She rushed to my side. "Get up, Jacob. We need to go!"

I got to my feet, a little shaky, and looked at Pops.

"I'm sorry. I'll make this right," I said before I ran out of the funeral home.

Eighty-five

POLICE SIRENS ECHOED IN the distance as Angela and I rushed to the car. Angela quickly hopped in the driver's seat and fired up the engine. I was getting ready to get in when I looked across the street and saw a guy on a black and red Ducati pull into the McDonald's parking lot.

I ducked my head in the car before closing the door.

"Go ahead. I've got another plan. I'll lure them away while you get out of here."

"What? No! Get in the car. I can handle them."

"Trust me! I know what I'm doing. We'll meet back at your place."

I closed the door and rushed across the street. I heard the tires on Angela's car squeal as it tore up the road.

"Hey, hey!" I yelled at the man getting off the Ducati. "I need your bike. Police business."

The man pulled off his helmet and looked me up and down.

"Come on, old man, you can't handle this. This is a Superbike 1198—"

I quickly decked the guy in the chin and knocked him out cold.

"Yeah, yeah, don't have time to chitchat."

I grabbed the man's helmet, slipped it on and then turned the key in the ignition and revved the throttle. I popped the clutch in first gear. The rear tire burned rubber as it peeled out of the parking lot and onto Ridge Road just as the first police car arrived.

I shifted to the next gear and the front wheel popped up in the air as I flew by the squad car.

I kicked up the gear again and the bike drove with a power that I hadn't felt in years. When I first joined the force, I wanted to do motorcycle patrol, as I'd been riding motorcycles for about as long as I'd been driving cars, but decided against it when I saw that I had a chance to make detective.

The bike hugged the road like a hand fit a glove. I lowered my body towards the bike and felt the wind pass right over me. Mile after mile, I weaved in and out of cars, driving fast enough that the cop couldn't touch me, but also careful not to do anything stupid, like trying to outrun a cop on a Ducati.

Finally, Clopper Road approached. I turned hard, my left knee inches from the pavement as the bike took the corner with ease. I gunned the throttle again and the powerful engine of the Ducati accelerated like it was a rocket being shot of out a cannon.

By now, there were several squad cars behind me, but they couldn't keep up despite their powerful V8 engines.

I took another hard left turn onto Waring Station Road. I gunned the throttle again, and in the rearview mirror, I saw the police cars getting smaller and smaller the faster I raced. Finally, I ended up at my destination, where hopefully I could lose the police.

Seneca Creek State Park, also known as the Schaeffer Farm Trails, was where I'd gone mountain biking several times with my father-in-law. I knew the trails fairly well and also knew that the cops wouldn't be able to follow me in with their squad cars.

I came to the end of Waring Station Road and turned left into Schaeffer's parking lot, where a dozen or so cars were parked. Some people were pulling their mountain bikes off their bike racks when the Ducati flew past them.

"Hey," I heard someone yell, "you can't take that thing in there."

Too late, I thought. I already am in there.

Eighty-six

THE DUCATI SQUEEZED THROUGH two wood beams about four feet in height and three feet apart from each other at the entrance of the biking trails. I immediately came upon a V in the trail and had to decide if I wanted to go left or right. The sirens from the police cars grew louder as they neared, which caused me to make my mind up quickly. I went right.

The rear tire kicked up dirt, rocks and small tree branches as I gunned the throttle. I looked back and saw that two uniformed officers quickly entered the trails on foot with their weapons aimed. No way they would shoot, but just in case, I zigzagged the Ducati until I was around the first bend and far enough into the woods that I felt protected by the trees.

The narrow dirt path was challenging for a mountain bike, but equally challenging for a 200-horsepower motorcycle as I maneuvered over uneven ground and logs lying in the middle of the trail. Mountain bikers who were already in the trails quickly pulled over to watch the Ducati pass by them. Some people clapped and raised their hands, while most stared, dumbfounded at the unexpected sight.

There were a few times when I had to slam on the brakes to avoid hitting a tree as the trail coiled through the woods. I remembered how much fun we used to have riding the trails on my mountain bike, and how easily I maneuvered around the sharp turns and bends, but it was a whole different story with the Ducati. This bike was truly made for the road.

The rough terrain in the woods continued for another quarter of a mile and then partially opened to a grassy field on my right. I continued on the trail and then, out of the corner of my eye, I saw an officer on a motorcycle crossing the field with his siren blaring.

I quickly turned the throttle and the Ducati revved as it hugged the trail. The woods came upon me again in no time. I remembered that a sharp bend was ahead and slowed just enough to not fly off the trail.

The siren from the motorcycle was right behind me. I glanced in the rearview mirror and saw the officer motioning for me to stop. Fat chance, I thought. More curves to the trail came and went, but I couldn't be as careful as I had been earlier. I knew that if I got caught, the media would have a field day with me, and every good thing that I'd done so far would be thrown out the window.

Above the tall trees, over the roaring sound of the motorcycle's engine, I suddenly heard propellers from a helicopter. The police were up there, trying to get a visual on me. I needed to stay hidden under the trees, but I knew that the trail was leading me back into the open and through a corn field.

There was nowhere to get off the trail, and the Ducati couldn't handle the rough terrain of the woods. So I figured that if I had to be in the open, I might as well make it as quick as possible.

When the last bend of the trail came and went, I gunned the throttle and the motorcycle hit the openness with a burst. The helicopter quickly turned around and was on my tail when I was spotted. I looked in the rearview mirror again and saw that the motorcycle cop was right behind me. I needed to lose one of the two and figured that the motorcycle cop would be the easiest.

Cornfields now flanked me on both sides. Further up, I knew that there was going to be a steep hill which a lot of people on their mountain bikes like to ride down as fast as they can so that they zip down like a shooting rocket. The main difference was that a mountain bike would hit the hill going anywhere from six to ten miles per hour. I looked at the speedometer and was already topping forty. I hoped that the motorcycle behind me didn't know about the hill.

As soon as I passed through the cornfields, the trail widened and the hill was two hundred yards ahead. I moved over purposefully to allow the motorcycle cop to move next to me. And that's exactly what he did.

I looked at the speedometer and saw that I had just hit sixty miles per hour. The cop motioned again for me to stop. Okay, I thought, if that's what you want. Three seconds later, I slammed on the brakes, and before the motorcycle cop had a chance to react, he was airborne over the hill. I spun the bike around, kicked up dirt as the rear tire tried to grip the earth, and rode back the way I came. Now, what to do about the helicopter?

Eighty-seven

LIEUTENANT POLENSKI QUICKLY RECOVERED from the woman's devastating blows. He'd been in plenty of fights in his life, especially as a younger officer, but nothing like the flurry of kicks that had come upon him like a raging tornado.

But the surprise of the day, even more than being knocked out by a woman, was that Jacob was still alive. Polenski had almost fainted when he realized that it was Jacob behind the old man makeup. How'd he managed to survive that night in the bay? And who was the woman helping him?

Polenski's thoughts rushed a mile a minute and he didn't hear his wife calling his name, telling him to slow down. He didn't realize that he was sprinting to his car until his wife's voice brought him out of thought. He quickly spun around as she was trying to keep up in her fitted black dress and high-heeled shoes.

How am I going to explain this to Nathan and the judge? Actually, it wasn't my fault; Nathan was supposed to have taken care of this. Then why do I feel like this is going to fall on me? No, Nathan said that he'd taken care of it. He should be the fall guy. The plan was foolproof. Then again, it wasn't, because the fools were going to have to figure out once again how to get rid of Jacob Hayden.

"Honey," Maggie Polenski huffed, "where are you going?"

"Don't you know who that was?" Polenski quickly responded. "I need to call the chief and let him know what's happening."

Lieutenant Polenski fumbled in his pocket for his keys and within seconds, his car doors were unlocked.

"Hurry up and get in."

The roar of his 300 horsepower sky blue 1967 Corvette Stingray quickly came to life. He turned on the police scanner, hoping to catch the progress of the chase. Maybe he'd been caught by now? Polenski had the feeling that this was far from over.

Dammit, Jacob, why you? Of all people, why you?

Lieutenant Polenski had a fondness for Jacob, but his loyalty was to the judge. Judge Frank Peters had made Polenski into the man he was today, much like he did with a lot of other men. He owed his life to the judge. And because of that, he knew that Jacob had to die.

Voices crackled over the police scanner and Polenski learned that the police had tracked Jacob to the Seneca Creek Park, where he was riding a motorcycle through the bike trails.

Wait, a motorcycle? Polenski almost said out loud.

The Corvette's fat tires squealed as the car raced in reverse out of the parking spot, and then spun again as Polenski shifted into first and cut into the street.

"Make sure your seat belt's on, honey," he said. "Hopefully all of the money I put into this engine won't disappoint me."

He stomped the pedal to the floor and heard his wife scream as the car shot down the road.

Eighty-eight

THE ONLY WAY TO get out without being caught was to dump the motorcycle and get off the trail. The trails all looped around and would eventually send me back to the entrance where everyone would be waiting for me if I was dumb enough to do that.

The helicopter still hovered around, but I temporarily lost it under the cover of trees. When I felt that I had a little breathing room, I got off the motorcycle and ditched the helmet. I peeled the prosthetics off of my face and departed from the trails on foot.

While I ran, I thought about Angela and wondered if she'd gotten away okay. She had managed to escape from an office building full of police, so getting away from this would have been a walk in the park for her.

I kept running.

Fatigue was starting to set in and each step seemed as though it was getting heavier and heavier, like I was running through mud or sand. I needed to stop and rest, but I wasn't sure how far behind the police were.

The police. I'm one of them, or at least, I used to be one of them. I'd been involved in plenty of hot pursuits in my career and the one thing I knew was that eventually the perpetrator would slow down, give up, or make some kind of mistake that eventually got them caught. It happens to everyone.

So what mistakes have I already made? For one, I thought, I should have kept my cool at the funeral home. I shouldn't have let Polenski get under my skin the way he did. Had I been quiet, I'd be heading back to Angela's place, preparing for our next plan. I should have listened to Angela when she said that it wasn't a good idea for me to go to the funeral. But I knew that I couldn't stay away.

I should have been a better husband to Theresa. If I had, she'd be alive right now. When it was all said and done, people may try and tell me that I did all I could, and that there was no way I could have known that she would have been killed. That, unfortunately, was not a good enough excuse. She's dead and it was directly related to me.

Maybe in some twisted way, Polenski had been right. It was because of me that she's dead. So if my work was the reason for her death, then my hands are stained with her blood too.

Damn.

Eighty-nine

MY UP-TEMPO RUN was now a light jog. The trails felt like they were miles behind me, but I knew I'd probably only run about a mile. Running a mile in the woods was much tougher than the average run I'd do on a treadmill. This run felt more like two or three miles, especially given that I was wearing a black suit and dress shoes. My legs felt heavy, like rubber tires. From time to time I'd still feel the slight pain from when I had been shot in the chest a few days earlier. Wow, that seemed like such a long time ago. Almost like a different lifetime.

I thought about Theresa again and knew that if I'd been killed in that basement, she would still be alive. She'd be able to grow old and continue with her career of helping others. I would have left her, yes, but at least she'd be alive. And I wouldn't have minded if, after she mourned my loss, she had found someone else to be her companion in life. That's what life was really about, right? Companionship?

I finally slowed to a walk and then came to a full stop, bending over and placing my hands on my knees to catch my breath. I looked around for the first time and didn't recognize where I was. I'd never gone this far off the trails. I wasn't sure if I was going north, south, east or west. I wasn't sure how far the woods stretched until they got to a road. I wasn't sure of anything, except that coming into the woods was my best bet of getting away. Now I wished that I hadn't dumped the Ducati.

The stress of everything that had happened in the past weeks finally caught up to me and I fell to my knees and screamed louder than I ever had. Once the screams were done, I cried harder than ever before. The kind of crying that caused slobber to hang from my mouth and mucus to drip from my nose. I felt alone, depressed, ashamed and utterly worthless.

I laid on the ground on my back and felt tears roll off the back of my head. With the back of my hands, I wiped my eyes and found myself staring at the tops of the tall trees above. What was life like up there? Majestic? Peaceful? Could I live up there and leave all my problems down here, never to be faced with them again?

I raised my arms and stretched my fingers towards the trees. Now I was looking past the trees, to the bright blue sky that held the heavens.

"I'm ready," I whispered.

More tears streamed from my eyes, but I wasn't sad anymore. I was...ready.

What did ready mean?

A slight wind picked up which stirred the surrounding leaves and grass. For the faintest of seconds, I couldn't breathe. I felt smothered. Something was in the wind. A presence. The wind picked up harder but only blowing over me. My outstretched fingers tingled as the wind blew through them. I felt something touching them, like the fingers of another hand. And then, just as quickly as it came, the wind was gone.

My hands fell to the ground. I took in a deep gulp of air and sobbed again. What just happened? Never in my thirty-four years of life had I experienced anything like it. I'd heard of people who said they've felt the presence of a loved one after they were gone, but nothing ever like this.

I wiped my eyes and sat up. Leaves and dirt stuck to the back of my head and shirt. I was in a state of shock because, in that instant, for the briefest of seconds, I knew that I was with Theresa once again.

Ninety

LIEUTENANT POLENSKI'S CAR WAS parked behind an unmarked police car that was parked behind close to a dozen police cars and media vans in front of the bike trails. He told his wife to stay put while he checked on the status of the search. After speaking with a couple of uniformed officers, Lieutenant Polenski found a spot where he was out of earshot and reached for his cell and punched in Nathan Hunt's number.

He assumed by now, if Nathan was anywhere near a television, he would know that Jacob was still alive. Besides the police helicopter flying over the park, the news helicopters were scouring as well. Jacob hadn't been seen in more than twenty minutes. How did this guy keep getting away?

"Nathan here," the husky voice spoke.

"It's me," Lieutenant Polenski quickly responded. "Where are you?" His voice sounded desperate.

"I'm out. What's with you?"

"You need to get your ass to a TV. Jacob's still alive."

"That's not funny," Nathan quickly responded, almost sounding dismissive. "Is today April 1st?"

"Listen to me," Polenski nearly shouted, but quickly got ahold of himself. His face was red and veins bulged from his forehead and neck. "You said he was dead. You said he was shot. How could you screw something like this up?"

Nathan must have realized that this wasn't a joke because all Polenski heard was dead silence.

"He showed up at his own wife's funeral, for God's sake," Polenski continued.

"Where is he now?" Nathan asked. His voice lacked its usual sarcasm.

"He's in Germantown in the woods. The police have this place virtually surrounded." He looked around to make sure no one was around him. "If they catch him, he'll tell them about us."

"We have all the evidence," Nathan quickly shot back. "It's his word against ours."

"That's supposed to make me feel better? It doesn't matter that we hold the cards. All you need is some snoopy DA out there to look into his allegations and we're in hot shit. I will not go to jail for this bullshit, Nathan."

"None of us are going to jail. Preparations have already been made. We'll just have to speed things up a little."

"Where's Frank?"

"He's packing. I suggest you do the same."

"What am I supposed to tell my wife?"

"That's not my problem. Be at the plane by 9 a.m. tomorrow or else we'll be seeing you in the next life."

"9 a.m.? Where are we going?"

Nathan had already hung up before Polenski got off the last word.

"Jesus Christ," he muttered.

Polenski turned around and headed for his car. He took a deep breath and exhaled.

"What am I going to say to my wife?"

Ninety-one

THE SOUND OF THE helicopter quickly neared. I stood against one of the big trees and tried my best to stay still as the helicopter flew by. The rumbling grew louder the closer it got and then started to fade as it quickly made its pass and continued its search. After it passed, I continued on.

My mind was still trying to deal with what had just happened. Had I really felt Theresa? Was my mind playing tricks on me? In my emotional state, it was very possible that that was the case. But I had felt her, just as if she'd been standing right next to me and grabbed my hand. That's how real it felt. I'd heard of phenomena just like this too many times for it not to have been real. Theresa had communicated with me and let me know that she was alright. I missed her dearly, but if she was alright, then I needed to move on and make sure I got out of this alive. Theresa would want me to move—

"Hey, I see him," a loud voice came from behind.

I quickly turned around and saw an officer fifty yards away start to run towards me.

"Stop right there!"

My heart skipped a beat and adrenaline suddenly overcame me. A wave of intense fear caused my muscles to suddenly wake. "Oh shit."

I spun and dug my feet into the ground. With a burst that I hadn't felt since my high school track days, my legs stretched to their fullest length and stomped and stomped and stomped across the wooded terrain until I was nearly at full speed, blowing by tree after tree.

My fingers were extended with each long stride. My legs felt light and strong. I was running fast in a straight line, almost as if a path had been created for me. Trees blew by in a blur.

More voices came behind me.

"Stop."

"There he is."

"I see him. He's running."

"Over there."

They were coming in droves, and fast. Soon, I knew, the helicopter would be overhead and I doubted that I'd be able to lose it again. What made things worse was the thing that I feared would happen happened. I heard them barking. Multiple dogs, multiple dog voices. Their barking was almost conversational, as if they were betting on who could take me down first.

There was no more time for thinking. All I could do was run. I ran as fast as I could. I didn't want to feel razor-sharp teeth pierce through my flesh, so I continued running.

I looked up ahead and noticed that the denseness of the woods was starting to thin out. A road must be near. I believed that it was probably Darnestown Road. If I could make it, maybe I had a chance. But what real chance? I'd be out in the open and exposed. The dogs would have their target set like heat-seeking missiles and they would shoot after me and wouldn't stop until they'd taken me down.

I burst through the woods like I was shot out of a cannon and quickly came upon the road. I turned left and ran down the center double line. The irony came to my mind. Months earlier, I had chased a coked-up Mexican down the middle of a road, pleading for him to stop, and now I was being chased by a pack of dogs who were probably telling me in their language to stop. I looked back and saw the first of the dogs, a large German shepherd, come through the woods, and then three more immediately followed. When they saw me, they flashed their teeth and licked their chops and then let out flurry of barks as they turned on their burst.

The dogs came fast. It didn't matter how fast I ran, the dogs ran three times faster and would be on me in a matter of seconds. I looked up to the sky and thought just the slightest of thoughts, you helped me once, can you do it again?

The barking grew louder. I was scared to look back, as I knew that they were right behind me. I could hear their breathing and imagined their saliva dripping from their mouths in anticipation of taking off my arm.

For the first time, I felt the fire building in my lungs. I didn't know how much longer I could run at this pace. My legs were starting to feel heavy and my muscles ached. I was sweating profusely and knew that at any second, my trek would be coming to an end. Maybe the judge would win. They won't believe my story and the bastard will get away with murder. Just as I finished my thought, I heard a dog snarling on my heels. But I also heard something else, a roar that was louder than the dog's barks.

Ninety-two

TIRES SCREECHED AND A dark blue sedan slid to a stop. The passenger door flew open. I instantly recognized the car but couldn't believe that it was there. Of all the cars in the world, of all the drivers, Pops was behind the wheel. He didn't need to tell me to jump in, that was the natural reaction.

"Hurry up, Jacob!"

Once in the car I took breaths in gulps until my body slowly started to realize that I wasn't running anymore. I was hot and extremely sweaty. The muscles in my legs ached and I could feel them start to cramp.

"How...how...did you know I'd be here?" I asked.

Pops didn't take his eyes off the road. His hands were firmly wrapped around the steering wheel at the ten and two o'clock positions.

"When it was reported that you had entered the trails, I started thinking of different areas that you could come out. I've been driving around for the past half hour, hoping I'd see you. And here you are."

My breaths were coming much easier now.

"You might want to put your seat belt on, son. We're not out of this yet."

"Pops—"

"No need to say anything, Jacob." He took his eyes off the road for the first time and looked at me. "I believe you. You and me were always straight with each other, and when you looked into my eyes, I knew you couldn't have done what they said you did to Theresa."

"I loved her," I responded. "Still do."

"I know, son. So do I. Now, we've got to get you outta here so you can tell the world what really happened."

"You know these roads better than I do. How do you suggest we do that? The police will have the whole area shut down soon."

Pops hesitated before he responded. "Did I ever tell you of the time that I was accused of stealing from a liquor store, and that me and my friend Harry had to outrun the police around these parts?"

"No, you didn't."

"It was before I met Theresa's mother. 1962, to be precise. This area wasn't as liberal to us back then as it is now. These were all country roads back then."

Pops took a sharp right off of Darnestown Road and shoved the pedal to the floor.

"My friend Harry and I stopped in to the local liquor store to buy a bottle of rum. You see, we had two hot dates that night and we knew that a couple of shots of the good stuff would loosen up all of us."

A stop sign caused Pops to brake hard, and then take a quick left. The tires squealed as they sped off.

"The owner, Mr. Fleming, a white man who wasn't too fond of us colored folk back then, said that we'd stuck a carton of cigarettes in our pockets after we paid for the rum. Of course we said that we didn't, but that didn't stop Mr. Fleming from calling the cops."

The road began to zigzag, which caused Pops to slow and accelerate from time to time.

"We knew that even though we didn't take nothing, if the police came up and saw us there, we'd have been taken to jail. So we hopped in my '58 Chevy Impala and got the hell out of there."

Another side road came up on us and Pops took a sharp right.

"You said that they chased you?"

"Sure enough, they did. As coincidence had it, Sherriff Anderson was pulling up to the liquor store right when we sped off. We saw old man Fleming point at our car and then Sherriff Anderson came chasing after us."

Pops turned left at the next side road.

"So what happened?" I inquisitively asked.

"I made a few turns, took a couple of side roads, lost Sheriff Fleming and then ended up right here."

I wasn't paying attention to where we were headed, but when I looked out the front window, I was surprised to see where we were. A restored-looking farmhouse painted a pale yellow with white shutters next to the windows was in front of us. Over the years, houses had been added to the neighborhood, but the old yellow farmhouse was one of a kind.

"But this is your house," I responded.

"Yep. Although back then it wasn't."

Ninety-three

THE ROOM WAS AS dark as a room could be, with no windows or lights. I stayed still, just like I was told to. I even tried to make my breathing quieter in case someone put a stethoscope against the wall, listening for any sound of human movement. Well, that was an exaggeration in my mind, but I still tried to be as quiet as possible.

I heard their voices when they came into the house. Though they were muffled, I knew they were the police and they were looking for me. I told Pops that his house would be the first place the police would check. Pops suspected the same thing so he put me in a secret room in the house that only Pops and Mama J knew about.

I heard Pops' muffled voice, and then heard feet climbing the old wooden stairs. The stairs creaked when they were walked upon. Pops never got them fixed because he wanted to hear when someone walked up or down them. Especially when Theresa became a teenager and was prone to do what teenagers were known to do.

"She could try to sneak out or sneak a boy in," Pops would say, "but she wouldn't make it far."

The feet stopped at the top of the staircase and I heard multiple sets of footsteps walking along the top floor. There were probably at least two or three officers searching the rooms, I thought. Someone came into the bedroom and I heard them open the closet door. I tensed and held my breath. There was no way the officer could have known that behind the wall in the closet, I sat in a room the size of a large walk-in closet, hoping that I wouldn't be found.

I had been to the house dozens upon dozens of times. I helped them move their heavy wooden bedroom furniture around and never once noticed that the ceiling fan had three cords hanging down from it. Most ceiling fans have two cords: one for the light and one for the fan. The third cord opened a small seamless door in the closet that led to the hidden room.

After a few minutes, I heard footsteps going down the stairs. My nerves relaxed and I felt like I could breathe. I started to look around the dark room. I couldn't see anything, but I was sitting on what felt like a leather-wrapped chair. The chair was actually pretty comfortable. Why do they have a comfortable leather chair in a hidden room? More importantly, why do they have a hidden room in the first place? I suspected that the room was probably built by the original owners, and that anyone who lived here had the luxury of having a secret room. But what's with the chair?

As a matter of fact, when I was rushed into the room and before the door closed, I thought I saw clothing hanging from the wall. I stood up from the chair and reached my hands out in front of me and felt for the wall. When I reached it, I walked along the wall until my hands ran into garments which felt like leather pants, maybe a shirt. I continued moving along the wall until I felt a chain.

"What the hell is this?" I whispered.

There's got to be a light in here. I began searching for a light switch and found it hanging in the middle of the room. I pulled the cord and a red light turned on. If I wasn't in my in-laws' house, I would have thought that I had stumbled into a brothel. Full-body leather clothes with masks, whips and chains hung on the wall.

"What kinda freaky mess is this?"

Out of the corner of my right eye, I saw someone standing next to me, which made me jump. It was just my reflection from a large mirror behind the leather chair.

"Jesus," I pointed at myself in the mirror, "you almost caused me to crap my pants."

Who would have ever thought that the people I'd come to know, who were so sweet and innocent, were into the kinky stuff.

Just then, the door opened and a flood of light filled the room. Pops and Mama J stood there staring at me. I stared back at them.

"What can I say?" Mama J said. "I'm a dominatrix."

I looked back and forth at both of them.

Pops nodded with the slightest of smiles, "She is."

Ninety-four

TWO HOURS HAD PASSED SINCE the police left. At least, the initial officers who had searched the house left two hours ago. I peeked through the bedroom window and saw an unmarked police car parked across the street from the house. I expected that the police would have the house staked out. I would have done the same. I knew that the house phone would be tapped by now, as well as Theresa's parents' cell phones.

The day was coming to an end and the sun was nearly gone. I sat at the edge of a king-sized bed. I let myself sink into its softness and then laid back. It felt like forever since I had laid in a bed. My body was sore and tired beyond belief. I wanted to take my shoes and clothes off and fall asleep forever inside this comfortable house that had so many warm and loving memories.

I closed my eyes and my mind instantly began to think of Theresa again. She was alive and we were in our bed at home, naked and laughing, without a care in the world. Theresa pulled her hair behind her ears and blew me a kiss. I reached for the floating kiss, grabbed it and blew one back to her. Then she put her head against my chest and wrapped her arms around my body. We just laid together, in awe of each other, naked and enjoying every minute of our time together. I rubbed my fingers through her hair and she made little circles on my stomach with her fingers. Everything felt normal. Life had returned to normal.

Then something unexpected happened. I saw someone out of the corner of my eye. I turned my head and saw Nathan Hunt enter the room. I quickly jumped from the bed and leaped toward him, but passed through his body like a ghost. Nathan laughed.

"You never learn," Nathan said.

Then he reached for Theresa and threw her over his shoulder.

I grabbed the closest object, which was a lamp, and swung it at Nathan's legs, but the lamp passed through as well.

Nathan began to leave the room with Theresa on his shoulder.

"Let her go, you bastard!" I yelled.

"Too late for that buddy," Nathan responded. He laughed as he carried Theresa away.

My eyes shot open and the bedroom was dark. I was shaking and sweating heavily. For a moment, it felt like air escaped my lungs and I couldn't breathe. It was only a dream, I told myself. I calmed a little and caught my breath. How long was I asleep? I had no clue what time it was or what time it had been when I dozed off, only that there was still daylight in the sky before I closed my eyes.

Just then, the bedroom light turned on and Pops and Mama J stood in the doorway. Theresa's mother was holding a plate with two turkey sandwiches stacked on one another and a glass of apple juice.

"You must be starving," she said as she sat next to me. Her voice was as loving as it always had been towards me. "Eat this. You'll feel better when you're done."

I didn't realize how hungry I was until my eyes came upon the two sandwiches stuffed with turkey, lettuce and tomatoes. I inhaled them before I had a chance to think about it.

"Slow down," she said, "you don't want to choke to death."

"Jacob," Pops said, "what you saw in our hidden room, Theresa never knew about."

I raised my hand while still chewing on one of the sandwiches. "That's none of my business."

"I know," he responded, "but it's something that we've kept to ourselves for a long time. The room was actually there when we bought the house, so naturally it was a great space to keep our little secret from Theresa."

"I get it," I looked at both of them. "It's just hard to imagine the two of you dressed up like that, you know."

We all laughed which made me wince a little due to my facial wound. I gulped down the apple juice. Mama J was right, I did feel better, more alert and energized.

Even though the dream caused me to feel jittery and unnerved, the short rest was welcome and much needed. For the first time in a while, my head felt clear and I was able to think, probably because I was somewhere that I felt safe from the outside world.

Mama J took my plate and glass and placed them on the bed. Then she wrapped her arms around me and lightly sobbed. When she pulled away, I felt dampness on my shoulder from where she had left tears.

"Jacob, do you know who did this to Theresa? I didn't believe for one minute what the papers said about you. You're too good of a man to have done what they said you did."

I nodded. "I do." It was hard for me to look into her eyes, but I did when I continued. "They were after me. It was the case I was working on, and apparently, I was getting close. They came to kill me and she just happened to be there. Normally, she would have been at work, but she asked another doctor to cover her shift so she could spend time with me."

Pops reached over and placed his hand on my shoulder. "It wasn't your fault, son. Don't carry that burden. It'll only tear you up inside."

I nodded and agreed, but it didn't mean that I could let it go.

"So what options do we have?" Pops asked.

"We don't have any options," I quickly responded. "These people are dangerous and I won't allow you guys to get involved."

"We're already involved," Pops said. "They took away our beloved Theresa, and I'll be damned if I let them get away with it."

I stood and turned to my father-in-law. "Pops, I'm sorry, but you can't get involved. They nearly killed me and I couldn't live with myself if they did the same thing to you guys as they did to Theresa. I'm sorry, but this is something that I've got to do alone. This is personal between me and them now."

"Well then, if we can't get involved, I guess we can't help you get back to your lady friend who helped you at the church," Pops responded.

"Angela?"

"Yep. She found me while you were on the run and told me where to meet her if I got you."

"She found you?"

"Yep."

Ninety-five

DETECTIVES STEPHEN HERNANDEZ AND Scott Piler of the Montgomery County Police Department sat in their unmarked cruiser across the street from Jacob's in-laws' house. Detective Hernandez was dark-skinned, with a shaved head, a thick neck and a thin beard. He was sitting in the driver's seat. Detective Piler was his total opposite, with creamy white skin and red hair. He couldn't have weighed more than a hundred and fifty pounds on a six-foot-one frame. Detective Hernandez, on the other hand, was round and closer to two hundred seventy-five pounds on a six-foot frame.

The police radio chattered from time to time with voices from dispatch or other officers communicating back and forth with each other.

"This is the part of the job that sucks," Hernandez said. "I mean, we've been sitting out here for nearly six hours. The guy's probably clear across town by now. No way he'd show up here."

Hernandez reached into the back seat for a plastic grocery bag where a couple of candy bars and water bottles were. He grabbed a Snickers and tore off the wrapper.

"You sure you want to eat that stuff?" Piler said. "Stuff's got enough sugar to last you all week." He patted his partner's belly. "Thought you were trying to shed a few pounds."

"I am. Haven't you ever heard of the candy bar diet?"

"Whatever. Five years from now, you're going to be crying to me because you've got Type 2 Diabetes. And I'm going to bring this conversation back up."

"You kiddin' me? Five years from now, they're going to be calling me the Rock." Hernandez flexed his bicep.

Just as he finished his joke, the garage door opened and a sedan slowly backed out.

"Look, we've got something," Piler says.

Hernandez picked up the radio and spoke into it. "We've got movement. Dark blue sedan exiting the garage, license plate, Bravo, Roger, Sam, three, zero, nine."

A deep male voice crackled back. "Got it. We'll tail it when it passes us."

"10-4," Hernandez answered.

"What do you think?" Piler asked.

"Could be nothing or it could be something. Maybe they're going to the grocery store for some milk and cookies."

The dark blue sedan backed out of the driveway and slowly drove away. Just as one side of the garage door closed, the second one opened and a white Lexus SUV slowly pulled out of the garage.

"Something's going on," Hernandez said. He reached for the radio again and spoke into it. "We've got a second car coming out of the garage. Looks like it's probably the wife."

"10-4," came the same deep voice. "Stay on her tail and see what she's up to."

"10-4," Hernandez replied.

The white Lexus SUV slowly pulled away from the house and Detectives Hernandez and Piler followed behind.

Ninety-six

ALL OF THE LIGHTS in the house were off. I watched from the living room window as the unmarked car followed Mama J out of the neighborhood. My adrenaline was pumped again. I felt refreshed and renewed. I'd been able to take a shower and change clothes. Luckily Pops and I wore the same size. With the dirt and grime from the woods off of me, I was ready to get back into the city and reclaim my life. The life that had been stolen from me.

I waited a couple of minutes after the cars left before leaving the house. I told my in-laws that there would most likely be another team set up down the road, ready to tail whoever left the house. That's why the plan was for them to leave in separate cars and at separate times. Now, no one would be around to see me leave the house.

I had to admit that Angela was as tenacious as anyone I'd ever met. She must have seen something in Pops' eyes at the church that led her to believe that he could be trusted. Angela had saved my life twice, three times to be exact, but had also taken the lives of others. I hadn't thought about it much, but once my name was cleared and I was back to being a detective, how would I handle Angela? Would I turn her in or let her go? She'd done good by helping me clear my name, hopefully clear my name, but she also killed men in cold blood. I'd have to cross that bridge if ever I made it there.

I left through the back door, pushing Angela's fate to the back of my mind. First, I had to get to her in order to finish the game that was started.

Luck has a way of making itself available at the most opportune time. While I was trying to figure out a way to get back to the city, Pops mentioned that old man Smitty who lives down the street was on vacation and always left the house and car keys with my in-laws until he got back. The old timer was pushing eighty-five years old but was still sharp as a whip. He'd gone down to Louisiana to visit his daughter and her grandkids and wouldn't be back for another week.

We decided that once the police were led away, I would run down the street, fire up the white '85 Cadillac Eldorado and make my way back to the city. And that's exactly what I did. I left the neighborhood slow and easy. No cops in sight, no flashing bright lights in the rearview mirror. The great white hope of the Eldorado was going to lead me back home.

Part Seven: The Avenged

Ninety-seven

CARMEN VALERA SAT AT the edge of her plush bed, waiting for the driver who was supposed to pick her up and take her to the judge's house, where plans had been made for them to take a chartered flight out of D.C. Things were moving faster than expected.

She called Angela's phone but got an automated voice response. She left an urgent message for Angela to call her back immediately.

Two suitcases sat by the front door, packed with all of her clothes. Either way, she wasn't coming back to this apartment. Her life of living a lie would end tonight. But she must decide which life she wanted to live.

When she first met Angela, she was immediately attracted to her. Angela was tall, with long blond hair, an hourglass physique and eyes that could take the breath away from any man, or woman. Carmen didn't think that she could fall in love so fast, but she had. Angela was her goddess, who was sent from heaven to be her life partner, friend and lover.

They'd shared intimate secrets with each other, secrets that no one else knew. Then Angela's brother had been murdered and everything changed. Angela grew obsessed with getting back at the men who had killed her brother. She started working out more and taking testosterone. She pushed her body to its physical limit; running, weight-lifting, mixed martial arts seven days a week for hours upon hours. She began losing her womanly figure and started bulking up and looking more like a man. She cut her hair and then started growing facial hair. She wasn't the same person that Carmen had fallen in love with. But she was still in love with Angela, so much so that she agreed to go with her plan.

Angela believed the best way to get to the judge was to get to him from the inside. So Carmen posed as an upscale call girl and met the judge at a political gathering in Washington, D.C. Once the judge got a look at Carmen, it was a no-brainer. Carmen was able to learn about the law firm, Faraji Owusu and Stephen Carter. The next target was supposed to have been Nathan Hunt, and then finally the judge, but the plans got screwed up when the detective, Jacob Hayden, had gotten involved.

Carmen was still able to seduce the judge to the point that he had asked her to marry him. Truth was, when he proposed, she became a little excited. She'd been sleeping with him for over six months, so it was only the natural progression that she'd start to have some kind of feelings for him. To her, he was gentle, kind, compassionate, almost picturesque if there were such a thing. He was the first man she'd been with since she was a teenager dealing with her bi-sexuality, before she realized she was a lesbian. No man could arouse her the way a woman could, except the judge. At first, she had faked it, but eventually their sexual encounters became very pleasurable.

Could Angela ever please me that way again? She hadn't seen Angela in nearly two months, and the distance between the two had started to tear at her heart. Love conquers all, right? At least that's what she'd always been told.

Just then, she heard a horn beep outside her bedroom window. She looked and saw that the car was there to pick her up. She waved and at the same time, her cell phone rang. She looked at the caller ID and saw that it was Angela.

"Hi, baby," she said.

"Hey," Angela replied. "He's on the move, isn't he?"

"Will be in a few hours. He's chartered a private jet. Told me to pack my bags for a one-way trip. I don't think he plans on coming back."

"Shit, I knew this was going to happen."

Carmen still hadn't gotten used to hearing Angela's lower voice from the hormones. She missed the way Angela used to talk to her.

"What do you want me to do?" Carmen asked.

"Stay on course. I'm meeting Jacob and then I'll get you out of there. Tonight. It all ends tonight."

"Ok. I love—"

Angela had already hung up.

Carmen didn't curse or complain. She simply reached for her bags, turned off the lights and left the apartment.

It all ends tonight, she thought. She had just confirmed who she was going to be with.

Ninety-eight

IT WAS GOOD TO see Angela again, I admitted to myself. In the most twisted turn of events, she was the person I was trying to apprehend for committing a cold, calculated murder, yet she was also the one I needed now more than ever. She'd been able to blend into the crowded city for the past few months while experienced police officers searched for her, so I knew that she was the one person who'd be able to help me get my life back.

I managed to get out of my in-laws' neighborhood without incident and made my way back to the city, where Angela was waiting for me in the parking garage on 10th Street next to the Catholic church were Stephen had been killed. I saw the humor in her picking that particular parking garage. That was the place where she had caught me from behind, handcuffed my hands behind my back and told me to leave the case alone. She was trying to warn me even back then to drop the case, but I hadn't listened.

I spotted her car on the third level and parked a few spaces from it. She was waiting for me, just like she said she would be. The garage was full of cars this evening, which was good. It gave us more cover to blend in and not be noticed.

"Hey," I said, getting into the front passenger seat.

"Good to see you made it out alive."

"Don't know what I would have done if my father-in-law hadn't been there. Guess I would have been dog food for those hungry German shepherds."

"You're one crazy SOB, if I do say so myself. I mean, what made you think you could get away in the woods on a motorcycle in the first place?"

"Worked, didn't it? I'm here."

"Barely. Next time, you need to stick with me. Would have saved the both of us a whole lot of time and heartache."

"You were worried about me, huh?" I teased.

Angela smiled, and for the first time I saw a beautiful woman.

"You're just lucky that someone else was on your side."

I thought about the experience I had in the woods and couldn't have agreed more. Seconds later, Angela turned serious again.

"My inside contact informed me that the judge is going to be on the move. He's chartered a flight. If we want to catch him, we need to do so soon."

"Any idea where he is?"

"His place."

I rubbed the stubble of my facial hair as I thought about the situation. The detective in me wanted to call the police and have this end legally. The problem we'd face was that we couldn't prove anything. We couldn't prove that they had killed Theresa and we couldn't prove that the judge was tied to the law firm. Plus, with the judge's connections to the judicial system and, apparently, the police department, they'd discredit anything I said and make me appear to be a loon ready for a straightjacket.

The other alternative, the one that boiled in my veins, was to seek revenge and kill the bastards that had killed Theresa. The bigger question that filled my mind was could I really do it? Could I really kill a man in cold blood, even when revenge seemed like it was the only option?

Angela started the car and backed out of the parking lot. I'd know my answer pretty soon.

Ninety-nine

THE JUDGE'S HOUSE WAS to our left. Angela had parked about a block away twenty minutes ago, and I instantly felt that something was wrong. The neighborhood was quiet. Manicured yards with A-frame brick homes lined the peaceful street. An upstairs light in the judge's house was on, but there weren't any cars in the driveway and there wasn't a car parked in front of the house. From where we sat, we couldn't tell if there was any movement in the house. Angela tried texting Carmen several times with a symbol that they both understood to mean "text me back," but the return text never came.

My anxiety level was high and I started to feel as if the judge and his entourage had somehow made it to the airport before we got to the house. If the judge got away, how could I get my life back? How could I ever be the person I used to be?

I looked at my watch and saw that it was a quarter to ten. I was antsy and knew that I needed to calm down. Watching the house reminded me of the anticipation I used to feel right before a raid. Jumpy nerves, high intensity, pumping adrenaline, the rush of barging into a house and not knowing what was waiting for me on the other side.

"We need to move," I said. "Something's not right about this."

"Yeah, I was thinking the same thing."

Angela raised her Glock and twisted a silencer onto the front of the gun. I did the same. I looked around the neighborhood before I got out of the car. Everything was clear. The neighbors didn't notice that we were there, or at least gave that impression.

"We go in through the back door," I said. "How good are you at picking locks?"

"Kiddin me? Picking locks is my specialty."

I knew how to pick locks as well, but something told me that Angela was probably better at it.

"When we get inside, don't shoot to kill," I reminded Angela. "We need his confession first."

"He's not going to confess, Jacob. That prick would want nothing more than to go to the grave knowing that he still has you by the balls."

"Well, at least give him the chance to confess. If he's dead, he's no good to us."

Angela rolled her eyes, but agreed. She wouldn't kill the judge. Not now, at least.

We got out of the car and quickly walked across the street, managing to stay in the shadows of the darker night. We reached the back of the judge's house within seconds. Angela pulled out a pocket knife and picked the back lock quicker than I could have imagined. There was a slight click and the knob turned.

We entered the house like thieves, walking on eggshells. Neither made a sound. The main floor was dark and quiet. The whole house was quiet. This wasn't good.

My hands were tightly wrapped around the Glock and I had it firmly aimed in front of me. My index finger rested on the side of the gun, but I could have it on the trigger faster than a blink.

Angela and I cleared the main level and carefully walked up the stairs to the second floor. In the dark hallway, the bright light from the lit room glowed under the closed door. There were two other rooms and a small bathroom that were clear. If they were in the lighted room, they sure were quiet, I thought. Could they have heard us enter the house? Maybe there's a posse of men waiting on the other side of the door with guns aimed, ready to shoot at the slightest turn of the knob. It was a possibility, but highly unlikely.

Angela and I each stood on either side of the door. I placed my ear against the door and didn't hear anything. I reached for the knob and gave Angela the signal. I turned the knob and both of us burst into the room with our guns aimed, ready to take on the world. But taking on the world would have to wait because, just like the rest of the house, the room was empty. The bed was neatly made and the closets were bare. The judge and his goons had managed to pack up and scatter from the house before Angela and I had a chance to catch them.

I turned to Angela, who looked like she'd just gotten punched in the gut. Her voice was steady and calm when she spoke. "That bitch told him we were coming. She betrayed me."

I looked around the room in disbelief. I sat on the edge of the bed and allowed my head to fall into my hands. What now?

The room felt like it was starting to spin. My world was quickly coming to an end and I didn't know what else to do. The judge had beaten me and now I felt like I was alone, without anyone to help me. Angela had done her best, but now, even she had run out of luck. Her lifeline to the judge was just cut off. How could things have gone so wrong?

I thought that just a few months ago, my life was nearly perfect. I had a great job, a beautiful wife and a loving home. Everything had changed when Turtle met me that afternoon in Dupont Circle with a scoop on a corrupt judge. I wished that I had followed my gut feeling and left when Turtle was late that afternoon. I wouldn't have been there when Faraji Owusu was killed and therefore wouldn't have been put on the case. Charlie would still be alive. Theresa would still be alive. Everything would have been as it was before Turtle brought this horror into my life.

Then, as if a time bomb went off, it clicked in my head. Something that the most entry-level of detectives would have followed up on. Turtle knew a guy on the inside, and I'm willing to bet that whoever Turtle knew probably knows how to reach the judge.

Goddammit, I thought. All this time, Turtle had a guy on the inside but I was too wrapped up in my own mess to follow up on it.

"We need to go," I said. "Luck may still be on our side."

"Where to?"

"To find a turtle. Hopefully he won't be hiding in his shell."

One hundred

U STREET WAS JUST as crowded as ever. The trendy neighborhood was filled with popular restaurants and nightclubs that often caused a bit of a traffic jam. I knew that U Street was Turtle's hangout and hoped that I'd get lucky and spot him amongst the crowd of people along the sidewalks.

Angela's car crept slowly behind a line of other cars, which would normally frustrate me, but tonight I was glad it was crowded because it gave me a chance to look at each face we passed. Lines of people waited in front of various nightclubs, waiting to get in. The bass of hip-hop music filled the street, and because there were so many nightclubs lined along U Street, it almost sounded like an outdoor concert.

We slowly passed the historic restaurant, Ben's Chili Bowl, which President Obama had famously visited early in his presidency. I'd eaten there countless times and had never seen it not crowded. On our right, we passed the even more historic Lincoln Theatre, in which great names like Duke Ellington, Billie Holliday and Nat King Cole had performed regularly. Red and blue police lights suddenly flared in front of Angela's car, which caused both of us to become tense for a second, but then we realized that the cop was only trying to get a double-parked car up ahead to move.

The busy part of U Street was starting to fan out, and I told Angela to turn around so that we could make another pass through. We slowly crept in the other direction and luckily, a parking spot opened up where all of the action was happening. We quickly nabbed it and we were able to see everyone that passed us. Ten minutes quickly turned into forty-five minutes, and then an hour turned into two. By now, it was past one in the morning. U Street was just as crowded as it had been over two hours earlier, without any sign of letting up. I thought that maybe we would give it another half hour and then we'd either have to call it a night or look for Turtle somewhere else. Luckily, we didn't have to wait much longer.

Coming out of one of the night spots was Turtle with an attractive brown-skinned girl around his arm. I quickly sat up in my seat and pointed, "There he is."

"Jesus, about time."

Turtle and the young girl walked by Angela's car without giving us any notice. I got out and followed behind them. A couple of times, I saw Turtle stumble, which led me to believe that he'd been drinking and was probably drunk. Hope he didn't think he's getting behind the wheel? They crossed U Street and walked to a side street filled with parked cars. The girl reached into her purse for a set of keys and opened the door to a silver Honda Accord. She and Turtle talked for a few minutes and then kissed and waved goodbye.

Turtle watched the car drive away and then started heading back the way he had come. I lowered my head and Turtle passed me without even looking and I smelled traces of alcohol and marijuana as if he were wearing it as cologne. I followed Turtle for another block and saw him reaching for his keys to a black Ford Crown Victoria.

"I know you don't plan on driving."

Turtle turned around and was apparently getting ready to say something when his eyes widened and his chin nearly dropped to the ground.

"Oh shit, Jacob, is that you?"

"Yeah, man, it's me."

Turtle's face beamed with excitement and he reached out and hugged me.

"Man, I've been buggin ever since I heard you were dead."

"Well, as you can see, I'm not."

Turtle backed away and looked me up and down, smiling as if he had won the Mega Millions. "Oh shit, Jacob, what the hell happened? I knew you couldn't have done what they said you did. You know I don't trust no cops, but you've always been a straight-up dude. I knew you couldn't have killed your wife." Turtle's face suddenly turned solemn. "Sorry about your wife, man."

I nodded. "Appreciate it. Means a lot. Listen, man, we need to go somewhere and talk. Somewhere safe."

"I feel you, I feel you. We can go back to the crib. Nobody's there."

"What about your mother?"

"Oh, she's over her boyfriend's house. She won't be home til tomorrow."

"Okay. I've got someone with me. She's cool though, so I don't want you to get all freaked out."

"No sweat." Turtle smiled and lightly punched me in the arm. "Man, it's good to see you. I was startin to think I was going to have to find somebody else to hook me up."

"I'm not back yet. Still got some unfinished business to attend to."

"Bet," Turtle responded. "Whatever you need, man, I got your back."

We slapped five. Turtle opened the driver's door and was getting ready to sit down.

"Oh, no, I'm driving. I could smell the alcohol and weed a mile away."

One hundred one

I WAS RELATIVELY SURPRISED when I first stepped into the Victorian row house. The place was nicely updated but kept the Victorian look. Brown wood floors that looked like they'd recently been refinished covered the first floor. To the right of the foyer was an expansive living room with two modern leather couches neatly across from each other in front of a fireplace. I looked around the room and nodded my head with approval.

"What, you expected this to be a hole in the wall?" Turtle uttered.

"Well, not a hole in the wall...but I must say, I'm impressed."

"Yeah, this is pretty nice," Angela added.

"Moms and I like to live in comfort and style," Turtle said as he expanded his arms to show off the room.

"All right, all right, don't get too ahead of yourself," I retorted.

We both smiled at each other and then sat on the couches.

"So what do you need to talk about, man?" Turtle started.

I thought about the meeting at Dupont Circle, the one that had started the downward spiral of my life.

"I want to talk about our meeting in Dupont Circle. You know, the one where the man was shot in front of us."

"How could I forget? Never seen nothing like it in my life."

I wanted to glance over at Angela, but decided not to. I didn't want to let on in any way that she was the one who had actually killed Faraji Owusu.

"So before that happened, we were talking about Judge Peters and you said that you had some inside information that he was dealing arms and that a law firm was a front to launder his money."

Turtle looked at Angela and it appeared that he was debating if he should say anything in front of her. "You sure she's cool?"

"Yeah, she's cool."

"She a cop?"

"No, she's not a cop." I snapped my fingers to get Turtle's attention, get him refocused. "Let's focus on that conversation. Who'd you get that information from?"

Turtle began shaking his head and suddenly he didn't seem that confident anymore. "I don't know, man. Jacob...this is some serious shit you're asking me. I mean these dudes don't play. I was serious when I asked for protection if I'm going to be giving up this kind of info."

I leaned forward in my seat and I was beginning to get unnerved.

"Turtle," I held back my frustration, just a little. "This isn't the time to be thinking about yourself. These guys have killed people. Now I need to know who your source is."

"I know they killed people. Why the fuck you think I'm hesitant to tell you?"

"They killed my wife," I blurted out. Tears started to fall from my eyes. I wanted to scream out in frustration, but fought the urge. I had to keep my cool if I was ever going to find the judge.

"Turtle, I'm asking for your help. Man to man. I need to know your source."

Turtle reached in his front pocket for a pack of cigarettes and quickly lit one. He took a long drag and then let the white smoke slowly drift from his mouth.

"It's this white dude I sell weed to. He's a lawyer over at the courthouse."

"I knew you were selling," I said. "When I get my life back, me and you gonna have some words."

Turtle rolled his eyes and took a puff from the cigarette.

"A defense attorney?" Angela asked.

"Yeah. Name's Tim Johnson. One night, we was smokin up and he was high as a kite. I only had a couple of drags, so I was cool. He started telling me about some crazy shit this judge was into and that the judge saw to it that Tim would defend certain people in order to get them off. People that were connected to the judge."

Turtle took another long drag and then let the smoke drift out of his mouth.

"I didn't care at first. I thought he was just another crazy white boy talkin shit, you know. Tryin to impress the local drug dealer. Until he started talkin about this kid I knew, RoRo, who was killed. He didn't know I knew RoRo, so he was just runnin his mouth about how Judge Peters had RoRo killed because he thought RoRo was becoming a liability."

"By RoRo, you mean Ronald Jackson?" I asked. "The nineteen-year-old who was shot and killed in South East earlier this year?" I remembered the name.

Turtle took another drag, "Yeah, that's him."

"But another teenager was busted for the murder. The gun that was used to kill Ronald was found in his bedroom. Ballistics matched the bullets to the gun."

"Yeah, that was Swift. Claims he didn't do it. Said he was being set up. Guess he was right." Turtle took another drag from the cigarette. "RoRo was a friend of mine. He was a good dude."

Turtle mashed the half-smoked cigarette in the ashtray.

"After I found that shit out, I was like, damn, we got to get this dude. So that's when I called you."

And that's when my life turned to hell, I thought. I leaned back on the couch and let the softness of the cushion absorb my tension.

"Does the name, Tim Johnson, mean anything to you?" I asked Angela.

She shook her head. "No, my brother never mentioned him. He wasn't someone on my radar."

By radar, I understood that to mean hit list. So now we had to track down Tim Johnson, hoping that he knew where the judge had gone. Luckily, Turtle gave us some much-needed help.

"Well, if you guys need Tim, you're in luck. Tomorrow's his pick-up day and he's always on time. I love selling weed to white boys."

Bingo, I thought. Finally, one of them will be coming to us.

One hundred two

THE NEXT DAY'S WORKDAY couldn't have come to an end any sooner. Tim Johnson's court-appointed client was the last of the day's docket. A sixteen-year-old kid who'd been caught shoplifting from the Macy's on F Street. It was his first offense, so the city accepted his no-contest plea to the charge and he received sixty days of community service. Tim shook the kid's hand as he left the courtroom and knew he'd see him back in a couple of weeks for getting caught doing something else. Most of these kids didn't learn their lesson, unfortunately, and usually got caught doing something worse than they had done the first time. No doubt Tim would see the kid again.

He loosened his tie as he left the courthouse on Indiana Avenue and walked across the street to the Judiciary Square Metro station. Today was one of those days he wanted to forget. He couldn't wait until Judge Peters gave him the word to leave the public defender's office. But until then, he patiently waited, defending nickel and dime scumbags who kept getting in trouble.

Don't these idiots learn their lesson? If they did, then he'd be out of a job.

The train was crowded as usual around rush hour. He wanted to sit and close his eyes for the few stops that he'd be on the train, but no one looked interested in giving up their seat. He pulled his BlackBerry from his pocket and punched in a text to Turtle that he was on his way. After a day like today, a little of the good stuff would calm his nerves and help him relax. Hopefully, Turtle would throw in a little extra for free. Sometimes that's a perk of being in his position; they give him what he wants and in return, he helps them out if necessary.

Turtle texted back and said, "Cool."

He looked around the train and happened to catch a picture on one of the local papers that someone standing across from him was reading. The title of the article read, "D.C. Detective Not Dead After All" and included Detective Jacob Hayden's profile picture from the police department. Tim didn't need to read the article to guess what it said. The detective's reemergence had been the hot topic of the city for the past day and a half. The local news stations, four, five, seven and nine covered the story as if he were the Prince of Wales making a sudden visit to the District. Most of the people in the public defender's office knew Detective Hayden and couldn't believe that he had killed his wife and then gone on a rampage and killed those drug dealers.

Yeah, well, you're all right, Tim thought. He hadn't killed his wife or the Gomez brothers.

Tim switched trains at the Gallery Place-Chinatown station and hopped on the green line for a couple of stops until he got to the Shaw-Howard University station. He walked about ten minutes until he got to Turtle's house. Turtle must have seen him coming because he opened the door as Tim started up the front steps.

"How's it going, my lawyer friend?" Turtle asked.

"Better, soon as I can get a hit."

"No doubt, no doubt. I got some good shit this time."

"You always got some good shit, Turtle. That's why I keep coming back to you."

Turtle stepped back from the front door and Tim walked in. He saw that there were a man and woman inside, sitting on the couch. He nodded his head and thought they were customers just like him. He'd been there before when people were getting their weed before him. Usually they stayed for a few minutes and then left. But when the man stood up, Tim's eyes nearly fell out of their sockets.

"So you know who I am, Mr. Tim Johnson," Jacob said. "I think we need to have a little talk."

One hundred three

"TURTLE, WHAT THE HELL is going on?" Tim asked. His voice was full of nerves.

"My man thinks you might have some information for him."

I walked close to Tim Johnson, who stood nearly five inches shorter than me. Usually, I'm not an imposing figure. My demeanor doesn't give off that I'm a badass, but today was different. I needed information that Tim probably had.

I looked Tim up and down and then gritted my teeth. I wanted Tim to be scared of me, which I believe I accomplished. He looked like he wanted to pee in his pants.

"No one knows you're here," I said smoothly. "No one knows that Turtle's your weed guy. I know because a man in your position who wants to work his way up the ladder wouldn't let anyone know that he does drugs, especially with a black kid from the inner city. Do you get my point?"

Tim nodded.

"Now, I know you know my reputation. I've never had a complaint of police brutality filed against me and I've never been accused of being dirty. I've always been a good cop. You know that. You work in the public defender's office and they know shit on a lot of cops, but not me. I mention all of this to say that I might be on the straight and narrow, but my female friend behind me is not."

Angela stood up with her silenced Glock 9 millimeter in her hand.

"Oh shit, Jacob, what's this shit?" Turtle quickly asked.

I ignored Turtle but was glad for his reaction. That made the setting all the more uncomfortable for Tim Johnson.

"So I'm going to ask you some questions and you're going to be straight up with me. Is that fair?"

Tim nodded again. His eyes looked past me to the butch-looking woman holding the gun. I turned around and saw Angela's cold eyes throwing ice darts at Tim.

I motioned with my arm for Tim to sit. I wanted to make the man nervous but also allow him to relax a little. I didn't want Tim so uptight that he might forget important details. I'd used that method plenty of times during interrogations.

"So, let's start with the easy questions first. Now remember, some of the questions I already know the answers to, so don't start lying. I'll know when you're lying," I assured him. I paused for a few seconds to let that thought settle in Tim's mind. "Do you work for Judge Frank Peters?"

Tim didn't immediately answer, and that's when Angela took a step closer, letting Tim get a better look at the gun in her hand.

"It's a simple yes or no answer," I said.

Tim looked down, "Yes," he said in nearly a whisper.

"Good, you see, we're making progress. The next question will be tougher, but I know you'll do just fine. How does the business work?"

Tim started shaking his head like he was getting ready to say he didn't know, but I quickly stopped him, "Ah, ah, ah, remember, I don't want to be lied to. My friend is pretty good with that gun, and she can make the bullet enter your body in ways that'll make your death long and painful. Now, do you want to start over?"

Tim shook his head. He took a breath before speaking. "I don't know all of the details, but I do know that the money and weapons go to Mexico and parts of Africa. He partnered with drug cartels in South America and insurgents in the Sudan and other hostile African nations to supply them weapons."

"The cartels use the weapons to protect narcotic production from the Mexican government," Angela said.

"And the law firm?" I asked.

"It's a front. The judge launders the money from the weapons sales and makes it appear that the money's coming from negligence claims and car accidents."

"How much of it is a front?"

"About forty percent."

"How does he get the claims through insurance companies if they're bogus?"

"He has a dummy insurance company that's incorporated in Delaware that pays out the false claims. That's about all I know."

"And how do you fit into all of this? What do you do for the judge?"

"If someone affiliated with the business gets arrested, I'm the court-appointed defense attorney that represents them. Usually, they're misdemeanor or low-level offenses. Before Stephen was killed, I was going to leave the Public Defender's Office and work for the firm."

I slapped Tim on the knee. "See there, Tim, you're doing a great job."

Tim started sniffling and then he let out a faint whimper.

"Is he crying?" Angela asked. "What a wimp."

"Tim, Tim, there's nothing to cry about," I said. "You're doing just fine. A few more questions and we'll be done."

Tim raised his head and his eyes were bloodshot red. He looked like a schoolboy who'd been sent to the principal's office and then found out that the principal had called his parents.

"You don't seem like the type of person who's cut out for this kind of business. How'd you get involved?"

"The judge did a few favors for me when I was in law school, and he told me that one day he might need favors from me. I didn't know at the time that I'd be caught up in this."

"What'd he do for you?"

"I was caught drinking and driving and had marijuana in my system. I could have lost my scholarship if the judge hadn't stepped in. I was clerking for him at the time." He started crying again. "I didn't know I was giving my soul to the devil."

"And let me guess, he said if you tried to leave, he'd have you killed?"

"I know he would. I've seen people who tried to cross him get killed. Seen it with my own eyes."

"Like RoRo?" Turtle asked.

Tim shook his head, no.

I thought about Melvin Johnson, the kid who had been shot and killed near his house and who had access to a storage facility in Maryland where Charlie and I had found crates full of weapons. Could he have been working for the judge, too?

"What about Melvin Johnson, better known in the streets as Gimmick?"

"Yeah," Tim responded, "Nathan paid a visit to him. And when Nathan pays you a visit, usually you don't live to tell about it."

"Goddamn him," I said under my breath. "So where is he now? How do we find the judge?"

"He went north to Rhode Island. He has a house on the beach. He said he'd contact me soon but didn't say when."

"Rhode Island?" I said.

"Smart move. Who would look for him in Rhode Island?" Angela asked.

"What's going to happen to me?" Tim asked.

I nodded to Turtle and Turtle tossed me a small tape recorder. I waved the recorder in Tim's face.

"We have your statement on tape. You're going to stay here with Turtle until this gets figured out and then I'm guessing the Feds will want to have a word with you."

"You mean you're not going to kill me?"

"No. Unfortunately, I still need you to help clear my name."

One hundred four

THINGS HAD BEEN MOVING fast for the former Judge Frank Peters, but it was nothing that he couldn't handle. His old life was now a thing of the past. Twenty-plus years on the bench and ten before that as an attorney seemed like a distant memory. He had hated being a judge, but the perks of the position had outweighed his misery, and it allowed him to run his business with the authority he wouldn't have had if he hadn't been a judge.

No more 9 a.m. calls for all to rise whenever he entered his courtroom. No more having to read tedious legal briefs that he couldn't care less about, and no more sitting in boredom, listening to arrogant attorneys arguing points of law. The old ways were a thing of the past. Now it was time for him to live his new life.

A cool breeze from the Atlantic Ocean blew by his face as he stood at the edge of his deck, staring at the lowering sun getting ready to touch the horizon of the massive sea in Barrington, Rhode Island. Normally in November, temperatures would already be in the thirties, but a recent warm front had caused the surrounding area to almost feel spring-like, with temperatures hovering close to sixty. The once-clear sky was beginning to fill with grey rain clouds. Behind him was his beautiful four bedroom Colonial beach house which, like many things he owned, wasn't in his name and couldn't be traced back to him. He took a sip of Scotch and then puffed on a Cuban cigar. Life couldn't be any more perfect.

It'd been two days since he found out that detective Jacob Hayden was still alive. He had to admit that even he was a little shocked by the news and couldn't believe the detective's resilience. If the detective wasn't such a square, Frank would have offered him a job. He was the kind of man that Frank needed; someone focused and persistent, not like the losers currently working for him. If he wasn't so emotionally invested in Nathan and Polenski, he would have shot them himself when he found out that the detective was still alive, proving his point that business and relationships don't mix.

He'd known the two of them since they were teenagers. He had guided Polenski's career in the police department and taken Nathan under his wing as his right-hand man. He trusted them more than he trusted anyone else, but he was starting to think that maybe they were becoming more of a liability than an asset.

He puffed on the cigar again.

So many things were going through his head, so many decisions that he'd need to make in the coming weeks, beginning with Carmen.

What to do with her? Could he trust her? Maybe she can be trusted, maybe she can't. He never would have guessed in a million years that she was a pawn in a plot to assassinate him. Now at least he knows why Faraji and Stephen were killed. He would have been next if it weren't for Carmen. She threw everything away for him. That must count for something? Maybe she could be trusted. He hoped so. He'd fallen in love with her after the first few weeks they'd been together. No woman had ever had an effect on him like she did.

What really scared him was that he had nearly let himself fall into a trap. He should have seen it coming, but didn't. He was a man who prided himself on seeing things from all angles, but he had missed this one, and it almost cost him his life. If he had a daisy, he'd pick off the petals and recite the rhyme, "she loves me, she loves me not," and whichever was the last petal he believed would be the truth. But he didn't have a daisy.

Maybe he could do what Two Face does in the Batman stories and let a coin decide her fate. Heads, she lives, or tails, she dies. Could it really be that simple? In his sixty years of life, he had never felt more betrayed and loved at the same time. Maybe she really does love me? She could have easily not said anything and let the plan play itself out. But she didn't. She gave up her past life for me. She does love me.

He turned around and looked as she sat in a recliner chair, wearing blue jeans and a brown sweater, reading a book. She noticed that he had turned around, so she smiled at him. Frank smiled back. The breeze from the beach blew part of her hair across her face. She pulled it back behind her ear and then blew him a kiss. He reached out and grabbed it and placed his hand over his heart. He loved her and he believed that she loved him back.

He turned back to face the beach and reached into his pocket and pulled out a quarter. He tossed it in the air, caught it and put it on the back of his other hand. Heads she loves me, tails she doesn't. He believed she did but wanted to check with fate and get its opinion. He removed his hand from over top of the quarter and saw what fate thought of his love.

He looked at Carmen and then looked back at the quarter. He put it back in his pocket and then walked behind Carmen and rubbed her shoulders. He leaned down and gave her a kiss on the cheek.

"You really do love me."

"Of course I do."

"I know."

Fate doesn't lie.

One hundred five

THE WIND PICKED UP and the temperature had dropped about fifteen degrees since night had fallen. It took Angela and me close to eight hours to drive north to the small beach town in Barrington, Rhode Island. We learned that the judge's house was off of Nayatt Road, a two-lane road that paralleled Barrington Beach. Clever, I thought. This is one place that I never would have guessed the judge would use as a hideout. No one from the south travels north to the beach in the winter, especially to a place known for its frigid temperatures at this time of year, like Rhode Island.

The eight-hour trip gave us plenty of time to talk and plan the best way to take down the judge. Angela wanted to hit them hard; rush them in a blaze of glory and take down anyone and everyone who was in the house. I started to get the feeling that Angela had a death wish and that maybe she wanted to die in a gunfight.

I thought it better to take them down one at a time when they weren't together. They'd be more vulnerable that way. Tim Johnson confirmed that both Lieutenant Polenski and Nathan Hunt had left with the judge, so I knew that trying to take all three down at the same time would be a suicide mission. Even though Angela was able to catch Polenski off guard at the funeral, Polenski was in excellent physical shape, a good fighter and a better shooter. We needed to be smart if we wanted to get out of this alive.

But I also realized that trying to take them down one at a time would be difficult at best, especially given the fact that we were in an area that we weren't familiar with. I doubted that, with their heightened security, the judge and his men would chance being apart from each other for very long, even though they probably weren't expecting us to track them to Rhode Island. Angela and I had gone back and forth about what we should do, and we decided that they were most vulnerable when they slept and that that was the best time to hit them where it counts.

Sprinkles of rain began falling on the rental car that was parked on a side road about a quarter mile from the judge's beach home. I looked at the clock and it had just turned to twelve a.m. Stroke of midnight. What kinds of crazy things happened at the stroke of midnight?

"We drove by the house three times and all the lights were off. Either they're not home or they're asleep. Either way, I say we make our move now," Angela said.

I was hesitant. I wanted to wait longer, to stake out the house until I was sure the time was right. Being a homicide detective, I'd done dozens of stakeouts, and the one thing I truly learned was that patience was a virtue, if ever there was a meaning to a saying. But I also realized that this may be our only chance to catch them off guard. I nodded my head and then Angela pushed a button on the side door and the trunk popped open. She got out and when she returned, she had an arsenal of loaded weapons. She handed me two black Ruger 380 pistols with mounted lasers, a sawed-off Remington shotgun and a nine-inch Bowie hunting knife.

After we checked our weapons, Angela turned to me. "Last chance to back out."

I didn't hesitate to answer, didn't need to think of the response. "Let's go. Tonight we get our revenge."

Ten minutes later, we were standing behind trees, looking at the dark house. The property was large. I estimated the house sat on a half-acre of land, not including the beach behind the house. The sound of waves crashing against the shore was clear from where we stood. I smelled the salty sea in the air. There was a black iron rod fence along the front of the property that tapered off once it got to the wooded area of the yard where Angela and I stood. A U-shaped cobblestone driveway was in front of the house, empty of any cars. The property, along with the house, was dark.

"We'll try the back door again like we did in D.C.," I whispered.

The sounds of the sea were more prominent when we reached the back of the house. I wondered if we had just traveled eight hours to find out that we were on a wild goose chase and that the judge was already gone. Angela picked the lock in a matter of seconds and the back door clicked and opened. We hunched over low when we entered the dark house with our weapons aimed. As I took my second step, a light flicked on and a familiar voice was already waiting for us.

"Well, well, well, Detective Hayden. We meet again."

One hundred six

WE WERE OUTNUMBERED AND outgunned.
Judge Frank Peters stood in front of Nathan Hunt,
Lieutenant Polenski and another bull-looking man with a
head the size of a cinderblock who had weapons trained
on us. I quickly realized that the slightest inappropriate
move would surely end our lives.

"So I guess you and your little girlfriend thought
you could just sneak into my house and do away with me?
Is that it?" Frank said.

Angela glanced at me and before she could put the
thought into her head, Frank had already interrupted it,
waving his pointer finger in the air. "Ah, ah, ah. I
wouldn't do that if I were you. You see, I want to spend
some time with the two of you before these guys put
bullets between your eyes. But if you move the wrong
way, that'll be the end of it. So I'm only going to say this
once and then you'll have two seconds to decide what
you're going to do. If you do nothing, they'll shoot you. If
you raise your weapons, they'll shoot you. And, in case

you're wearing Kevlar vests, they won't aim for the body like that dipshit did in D.C. So, let's see how this will play out. Drop your weapons. The clock starts now."

I didn't have time to think about it. I dropped the shotgun that was in my hands and also the two Ruger pistols that were holstered to each leg. I slowly pulled from the back of my pants the hunting knife and heard it clink as it fell onto the floor. Apparently, Angela wasn't going to try and shoot it out in a gun battle like I thought, because she did the same.

Frank smiled and looked back to his guys. "There, you see, even the wild can be tamed."

He reached in his pocket and pulled out a smartphone, punched in a code and read a text. "Judge, Detective Hayden knows where you're at. Should be there in a few hours. Tim." Frank looked at me. "Technology's the best, isn't it?"

I scrunched my eyebrows and immediately thought about Turtle. Did he double-cross me? Was Tim Johnson able to get away? The answer didn't matter anymore because I knew I'd be dead soon.

We were in a room with walls that were covered with expensive-looking wood paneling, hardwood floors, leather sofas, glass end tables and wood beams crossing the ceiling. Everyone appeared tense except for Frank, who stood with a grin on his face and a cigar in his right hand. He wasn't wearing a suit like the past few times that I had seen him. He was wearing a red and blue flannel button-up shirt and blue jeans. The shirt outlined the broadness of his chest and arms, which I hadn't noticed before.

Frank took a puff from his cigar and then a dark-haired Hispanic-looking woman came into the room. She stood next to Frank and hugged his arm and then looked at Angela with eyes that appeared to say, I'm sorry. From Angela's description of her, I knew this was Carmen, her ex-lover who was supposed to help her take down the judge. Frank's smile broadened and then he winked at Angela.

"Guess she wanted a real man after all," he said to her. To Carmen, he said, "go ahead and grab the weapons."

Carmen carefully walked over to me first and grabbed my weapons and put them on the sofa. Then she walked to Angela, bent down and grabbed her weapons from the floor. When she stood up, she stared at Angela, leaned over and kissed her on the lips. Angela backed away and wiped her mouth with the back of her hand.

"Don't you ever touch me," Angela hissed.

"Don't worry about that," Frank said, "I'll make sure she won't be able to anymore. You can't touch someone when they're six feet belowground."

"Kiss my ass," Angela demanded.

"You sure you want to tempt me?" Frank laughed.

"So what are you going to do with us?" I cut in.

"Don't you worry about that. Just know that this time, your guardian angel won't be able to save your black ass."

The men behind him laughed, but I obviously didn't find the comment funny.

"So, before I allow my guys to kill you, why don't we have a little chat."

He motioned for us to move to the couch.

"No need to be uptight about this."

"I'll stand," I said.

"Me too," Angela said as well.

"Suit yourself."

He grabbed a barstool from the nearby kitchen and casually sat, as if he were about to chat it up with old friends. He inhaled his cigar and then blew the smoke away.

"You've got some balls, I have to admit," he said to me. "And you've also caused me some problems. You and your lady friend." He smiled as he puffed again. "You probably thought because I wore a robe to work every day that you were just going to be able to push me around and I'd give in. Is that it?"

I didn't answer. I wanted so badly to lash out at the man, but the guns aimed in our direction made the argument against it pretty easy.

"So now the cat's got your tongue, is that it? You drove all this way to see me and now you don't want to chitchat. Okay, I'm fine with that. But the look in your eye tells me something different, detective. If I were a betting man, I'd say that you want to take a swing at me. Am I right? At least give me that much."

"You're right," I said. "I'd like to knock your head off."

"So, you do have some balls after all. You're a man after my own heart."

He stood up from the barstool and rubbed his chin as if he were in thought. "Contrary to what you may think of me, I am a pretty fair man. So here's what I'm going to propose." He pushed the barstool back with his foot. "I'm going to let you take a swing at me. If you knock me out, I'll let you live and kill only your friend."

I was caught off guard by the judge's proposition, and my face showed it.

"I see you pondering the proposition. Just to show you that I mean what I say, let me take off my shirt."

He stepped back and pulled his flannel shirt off, revealing his hard and muscular body. When he put up his guard in a fighting position, his biceps looked like two rocks had been sewed into his arms.

"Come on. Don't chicken out on me," he taunted. "I'll give you one swing."

I didn't move. I didn't want to be a part of this charade that he was putting on. I knew that the minute I raised my hand, I'd receive a bullet in the head.

"Oh, come on, don't be a pussy." He lowered his guard and stuck out his chin. "Here, I'll make it even easier for you."

I fought back the urge with all my might. Nothing would have given me greater pleasure than to strike that son of a bitch right across the face. But I knew that he wouldn't let me live, regardless of what he said.

He was starting to get irritated that I wouldn't swing. He moved closer to me, taunting me even more, but I didn't budge. Finally, he stood right in front of me and I could smell the tobacco on his breath.

"I would love to have been there when Nathan killed your wife. You know what he told me? He said that he snapped her neck like he was breaking a twig. Was she that fragile? Did you used to have to give it to her gentle because she could break?"

I'd never felt hatred towards a man until now. I fought back the tears that were forming in my eyes because I didn't want to give him the gratification of defeating me.

He stepped back and put up his guard again. "One last time, detective. Free shot for your life."

I didn't move. But he did. He struck me across the face with a powerful blow that knocked me down.

"Enough games," he said. "I gave you a chance. Maybe we aren't cut from the same cloth, you pussy."

He turned to Nathan Hunt and said, "Take them downstairs and end this shit."

One hundred seven

NATHAN HUNT LOOKED AT the large Bowie knife in his hand, turned it around a couple of times and then aimed it at Angela and me, who were now tied to two chairs in the cellar of the house. The room was cold, lit by a single hanging lightbulb in the center of the room. The bulldog man, appropriately named Rex, struck me again with brass knuckles wrapped around his hand. My left cheekbone felt fractured and I'm sure my left eye looked like a bruised balloon. After Rex finished with me, he took the brass knuckles off, turned to Angela, and slapped her repeatedly with an open hand.

I tried to speak up in her defense, but only mumbled words found their way from my mouth.

Rex finally stopped the abuse and then Nathan stepped forward. He waved the knife in my face and then moved the blade to my chest and let the tip dig into my flesh. I screamed, and then with a yanking motion, Nathan slid the blade across my torso. Bright red blood soaked my white T-shirt. I'd never felt pain like that before.

"I'm not sure how you got away from me the first time," Nathan said, "but it won't happen again."

He took the blade and swiped it along my right arm, causing blood to splatter against Angela's shirt. I screamed again in agonizing pain.

"Did you think you were going to stick this knife in me?" Nathan asked. He swiped the blade again against my shoulder.

"Stop it!" Angela screamed. "Why don't you try that shit with me?" Her skin was cranberry colored from the open-hand smacks that Rex had laid on her.

"Oh, don't you worry about that. I'll deal with you in good time. Besides, someone has to teach you what it's like to be with a real man."

Angela screamed and tried to stand from the seat, but Rex moved quickly to knock her back down.

I tried to focus and not pass out, but I felt like I was going to lose consciousness and I wasn't sure if I'd regain it again.

Nathan swung the knife a few more times, touching my flesh that hadn't been exposed, until I sulked in the chair, beaten and ready to die.

"I love my job," he said.

Next, he turned to Angela and blew her a kiss. "So what should we do with you?"

"I've got some ideas," Rex said.

"I'm sure you do, big boy. How 'bout I leave the two of you alone to work on those ideas."

He patted Rex on the shoulder and then leaned close, "Shoot them between the eyes when you're done with her. Oh, and have fun, but don't take too long. We're going to have to bury the bodies before daybreak."

Nathan walked from the room and placed the bloody knife on a small table by the door.

One hundred eight

CARMEN DIDN'T THINK THAT seeing Angela again would have affected her the way that it had. When she had walked into the room and saw Angela and the detective standing hopeless at Frank's will, her heart nearly dropped. She wanted to run into Angela's arms and hug her the way that she used to, but she knew that that life was now a thing of the past. So she gave her a kiss, hoping that Angela would be able to forgive her in some way. But Angela wiped her lips and told her never to touch her again. Those few words hurt more than anything else.

Carmen was in the basement, down the hall from the cellar, standing in a dark bathroom, and heard every horrifying crunch that Rex's fist made against the detective's face. She heard Angela try and speak up for him, and then she heard the continuous slaps that Rex's hand made against Angela's face. Nathan laughed and then Carmen heard Jacob scream as if he were being tortured. She didn't know what was causing the detective to scream, but she could only imagine how Nathan was terrorizing him to death.

A part of her wanted to run away. Tears fell from her eyes at the awful thought that Angela and the detective were going to be killed soon. Had she made the right decision? She loved Frank; loved his warmth and compassion, but he was a monster. She had known that before she fell in love with him, but his affection confused her heart, and before she knew it, she'd fallen head over heels. What would he think of her if he caught her in the bathroom listening to the torture? Frank and the lieutenant had stayed upstairs while Nathan and Rex beat Angela and the detective.

Then she heard something that crushed her heart even more. Nathan told Rex to have fun with her. What did that mean? Was the detective already dead? She held her breath when she heard Nathan walk down the hall and pass the bathroom. He didn't notice that she was standing there, confused and scared. Seconds later, she heard his footsteps travel up the stairs and then close the door that separated the basement from the kitchen.

"So how do dyke bitches like it?" she heard Rex ask.

Angela didn't answer and Carmen was scared for her life. Would he rape her? Could she stand by and listen to Angela being raped? Rex laughed and Carmen heard what sounded like Angela's shirt being torn off.

"Don't touch me!" Angela screamed.

Rex smacked her again. "Baby, I like it rough. The more you fight, the better it'll be."

"You touch me again and you're a dead man," Angela responded.

"I've got to give it to you. For a dyke bitch, you've got some awesome tits."

Carmen heard more struggling, and then Angela screaming to get off her. She didn't know what to do. She couldn't just stand there and let Angela get raped by some crazed madman who was going to kill her afterwards. She started crying harder. Angela screamed and then Carmen heard Rex say, "That's it, that's it. Take it like a big girl."

Everything in her wanted to lash out, but she wasn't sure if she was strong enough. Angela continued screaming at the top of her lungs but then the screams turned to whimpers. Had she already been defeated?

Carmen slowly stepped out of the bathroom and quietly walked along the hallway until she reached the cellar door. She saw Rex on top of Angela with his pants down. The detective was slouched on the chair, not moving, and Carmen thought he was dead.

"Is that how you like it, baby?" Rex taunted again.

Carmen sniffed and Rex quickly turned around. "What the fuck?"

She raised her arm, holding one of the Rugers that she had taken from the detective. She'd slipped it under her shirt when no one was paying her any attention. She squeezed the trigger two times and bits of the top of Rex's head blew off. His body fell on Angela.

Carmen dropped to her knees in disbelief at what she'd just done.

"Carmen...Carmen," Angela called. "Untie my hands. Hurry, before they come down."

Carmen rushed over and reached for Angela's hands. "The knots are too tight."

"Over there by the door. Use that knife. Hurry!"

Carmen retrieved the bloody knife and worked its sharp blade until Angela's hands were free. When Angela stood up, she kicked Rex three, four, five times, and then spat on his corpse.

"I told you you'd be a dead man if you touched me again."

Angela quickly put on her pants and then took the knife from Carmen and untied Jacob.

"Angela, I'm sorry," Carmen cried.

"Stop it. Not now," Angela replied. "Let's get out of here first."

Angela bent down and lifted Jacob's head, "Jacob, can you hear me?"

Jacob moaned and opened his one good eye.

"Can you stand?"

"I think so."

She helped Jacob to his feet and he nearly fell back down in pain.

"I got it," he said. He pushed himself back up and looked at Rex. "What happened?"

"Long story," Angela answered. "We've got to get you out of here. You're no good in this condition."

"No," Jacob quickly responded. "We need to end this tonight. I can manage."

Carmen walked over and picked up the gun from the floor. "This is all we have."

Angela twirled the knife in her hands like a skilled hunter. "We have this." She turned around and kicked Rex's body again. "And this dead son of a bitch has a Glock strapped to his leg."

Just then, Nathan yelled from the top of the stairs, "Hope she was worth it."

One hundred nine

LIEUTENANT POLENSKI WASN'T SURE how he felt. He had just heard the gun go off two times and knew that Jacob must now be dead. A part of him was happy that it was finally over, but another part was sad that he had lost a former friend. Despite everything that had happened over the past few months, Jacob was indeed one of his friends. He'd eaten dinner at Jacob's house, and counseled him when he and Theresa were going through marital problems because of the drinking. Jacob was a good and honest man, Polenski thought. The world needed more men like Jacob Hayden.

Now he was dead and Lieutenant Polenski felt a somberness in his heart.

"Robbie," Frank said, "you gonna be up to burying this guy tonight? You don't look so good."

Polenski turned around and looked out the kitchen window. It was dark out, but he could hear the beating of the rain against the house.

"Sure we should do it tonight? Mud's gonna leave tire impressions in the ground."

"Don't you worry about that. I just need to know that your head's in the right place."

"I'll be fine."

Nathan moved to the basement door, opened it and yelled down, "I hope she was worth it." He closed the door and walked back into the kitchen.

The kitchen was of moderate size, with stainless steel appliances, an L-shaped beige granite counter, and cherry wood cabinets with a center island. Polenski leaned against the island and sipped on a bottle of apple juice while Nathan sat on a barstool across from him.

"After we tie up this loose end, I want you to make plans for us to be in Mexico by next week," Frank said to Nathan. "And Robbie, I want you on the phone with Gregory Bines in the morning with the next shipment order."

"Got it," Polenski responded.

"What's taking that prick so long down there?" Frank asked. "You think he's fucking a corpse?"

Nathan laughed, "Wouldn't surprise me if he was."

"Robbie, go check it out. I don't want no weirdos fucking dead people in my house."

Polenski placed his juice on the counter and walked to the door. When he opened it, the last thing he saw was Angela aiming a handgun and then he heard a bang. Everything around him quickly faded to black as his lifeless body slumped to the floor.

One hundred ten

"HOLY FUCK!" I HEARD Nathan's voice cry out. I climbed the stairs behind Angela, wincing at every step but determined to push on. I could only see out of one eye, and the left side of my face felt like it was going to fall off.

Angela fired again when she was at the top of the stairs and stepped over Polenski's body. A male voice screamed in pain and then I heard footsteps run across the floor. I finally reached the top of the stairs and looked at Lieutenant Polenski's dead body. Angela was a good shot. A bullet hole was where his right eye used to be.

"Nathan ran to the front of the house. The judge went out the back door. Think I hit Nathan in the arm," Angela said.

I looked around the room and saw our guns on the kitchen counter. I grabbed one of the Rugers.

"I'll go after the judge," I said. "I have a bullet in my gun with his name on it."

"Be careful."

"You too."

We split up and seconds later, I was in the pouring rain. The beach was less than one hundred yards from the house, and I saw the tail end of Frank's feet turn a corner into the woods.

I ran as fast as I could, each step sending piercing shockwaves of pain through my beat-up body. I entered the woods with my gun aimed, but my vision wasn't any good. My breath came in quick intervals and my heart pounded like a beating drum in my chest. I wasn't sure which way the judge had gone. I turned around in circles, aiming the gun in every direction, hoping for a glimpse of the madman, but he wasn't there. Then, as if I was hit by a train, Frank swung a large tree branch the size of a two-by-four at my legs and knocked me down. I crashed to the ground with a thump and the gun flew from my hand.

"You think you can take me down, detective!"

Frank swung the branch again and I moved just as the branch struck the ground, missing my head by less than an inch.

"I'm gonna kill your black ass!"

My left tibia felt broken, but I knew if I didn't try and move, the judge would kill me for sure. I turned around and tried crawling away, but wasn't able to move very fast.

"Ha, ha, ha, I'm gonna enjoy this," Frank taunted.

I struggled to move. I dug my fingers in the ground, trying to take the pressure off my legs, but Frank stepped on my butt and pushed me back into the ground.

"You never should have come up here. Now you're gonna be with your dead wife in hell, you sonofabitch."

I continued reaching and struggling to cover any ground when my hands felt a thick stick. I grabbed it, turned around and swung with all of my strength. I struck Frank on the side of his face, which clearly caught him off guard. He looked like a boxer who'd been caught with a right hook he wasn't expecting. His legs wobbled and he dropped the heavy tree branch. I struggled to my feet, but when I did, I swung the thick stick again and again, over and over, hitting Frank on the back of the head, shoulders, arms; anywhere I could cause some kind of pain.

Frank finally fell to his knees and spat out blood. He looked up at me, half-grinning.

"Fuck you."

In the background, three gunshots rang through the air in the direction of the house. I turned around and wondered who had been shot, Nathan or Angela. When I faced the judge again, a fist connected with my fractured face and knocked me down with horrifying pain.

I rolled over and covered my head, expecting to feel the stomp of blows from the judge, but none came. I turned around and saw the judge limping towards the beach. I pushed myself up and saw the gun that I had dropped next to a tree. I quickly grabbed it and pursued Frank again, this time catching him from behind and knocking him down. I punched him in the back and heard an "ugh" escape from his lungs. I stood up and aimed the gun at the back of his head.

The air was cold and the rain fell harder, causing my body to shiver. I had never killed anyone before, but I knew that was about to change. Frank turned around and looked at the gun pointed at his head. I wanted to shoot, but something inside of me wouldn't let me pull the trigger. Deep in my mind, I heard the echoing words that told me justice could still be served. No, it couldn't. Despite the fact that revenge was the whispering rationale that plagued my inner soul, my conscience wouldn't let me end this man's life.

After everything that had happened and after all that I'd been through, I suddenly doubted myself and tensely lowered the gun. As I did, Frank smirked. He got to his feet and flipped me the finger.

"I knew you didn't have the balls to do it, you weak-ass pansy."

My brows curled, and white rage suddenly demolished any doubt. My skin reddened as I sharply extended the Ruger once again. I clenched my jaws together, but the deep wounds that had torn at my heart screamed to be released.

"You don't deserve to live!"

Frank's smirk widened to a full smile and then he spat at me. I became engulfed with blind rage and swung my right leg, kicking Frank between the legs. He grunted and toppled over to the ground in pain.

"I should kill you right now, you son of a bitch," I yelled. "You took everything from me!"

I raised and aimed the gun. Frank climbed back to his knees and eventually stood in a hunched over position holding his balls. He coughed and then slowly stood to his full height. With rain pellets beating him in the face, his cold eyes spoke before his mouth opened.

"And I'd do it all over again if I could."

The lasts words were too much for me to handle. I yelled as a rush of adrenaline burst through my veins which caused my finger to squeeze the trigger. I continued squeezing, each bang becoming more deafening than the first, until there were no more bullets left to shoot. Yet, as the riveting sound from the jolting gun slowly died and the adrenaline eased away, my eyes glossed over with fear as I stared at the end of the barrel, disillusioned by what I had just done.

Judge Frank Peters' body was on the ground, riddled with bullet holes.

One hundred eleven

KILLING JUDGE FRANK PETERS didn't bring
Theresa back. Killing him didn't make me feel any better.
Actually, it made me feel worse. I took the law into my
own hands and killed a man in cold blood. Was it in self-
defense? It didn't matter. I had taken an oath to serve and
protect the people, not kill them.

I kneeled next to Frank's corpse and looked into his
vacant eyes. He would have killed me if he could have, I
tried to rationalize with myself. He wouldn't have thought
twice about it. I sought and found my revenge, but it
wasn't a sweet taste like some say it is.

Feet running across the wet ground caught my ears
and I quickly turned around and raised my gun. With
only one good eye, I couldn't make out the image through
the dark and rain. Could it be Nathan, ready to kill me
once he was close enough? Was it Angela? The person ran
fast, and I feared that it was Nathan coming to end my
life.

"Jacob!" Angela called out.

I breathed a sigh of relief. I lowered my weapon and fell into Angela's arms when she got there.

"It's finished. We can go home now," she said.

Minutes later, Carmen was with us, and we hugged each other on the beach in the midst of the rainstorm.

One hundred twelve

Two Weeks Later

DAYLIGHT POURED INTO THE hospital room that I was checking out of. I'd spent the past two weeks at the Washington Hospital Center, healing from the beating that I'd taken at the judge's beach house in Rhode Island. I underwent eight hours of reconstructive surgery to fix the damage that was done to my face. The doctors weren't sure if I'd ever regain full sight out of my left eye, but they were optimistic.

During the eight-hour trip back to Washington, Angela told me that Carmen had saved her life twice that night. After I went after the judge, Angela turned to find Nathan, looking in every room of the house, but she couldn't find him.

"It was like he had just vanished," Angela said.

She was making her way back down the stairs when Nathan came out of nowhere and elbowed her in the face. She fell down and dropped the gun. He picked it up before she got her bearings and was getting ready to shoot when Carmen stabbed him in the back with the hunting knife that Nathan had used to cut me up. Angela was able to maneuver the gun away from him and then put three bullets in his chest.

When we got into the city, I told Angela to drop me off a block away from the hospital. I was going to turn myself in and didn't want them implicated in any way in the killing of Faraji Owusu or the judge and his men.

"It'll work itself out," I said. "I'll be ok."

"I can never repay you for what you've done for me and my brother," Angela said.

She wrapped her arms around me so tight that I cringed in pain.

"Sorry," she said. Her eyes were filled with tears.

"You're the one I can't repay," I responded. "I'd be at the bottom of the Potomac right now if it weren't for you."

"Take care of yourself," Angela said.

"You too."

I closed the door and Carmen blew me a kiss goodbye.

When I entered the Washington Hospital Center, some people gasped at my grotesque apperance while others just stared as I limped to the information desk.

"My name is Detective Jacob Hayden. I need help." Then I fell to the ground.

One hundred thirteen

CHIEF RODNEY WATERS, a thirty-one-year veteran of the police force, entered my room wearing his blue and grey police uniform. Chief Waters was a large African-American man of six feet four inches and close to two hundred sixty pounds. He was known for being a hard-ass and running the department straight by the book.

For the past two weeks, two Metropolitan officers had stood in front of my door while the department investigated the claims I made about Judge Frank Peters and his money laundering and weapons smuggling business.

I was sitting at the edge of the bed when the Chief walked in. I instantly stood, but the Chief made a motion with his hand for me to sit.

"How you feeling, Jacob?"

"Better, sir."

"Your face is healing nicely, although I don't think you'll be hearing any catcalls from women anytime soon."

I smiled. Two weeks after the surgery, my face was still bruised, but a lot of the swelling had gone down. The doctors told me that I'd need to go through months of rehabilitative therapy and that most of the scarring would go away, but not all of it.

"Jacob, I'm going to cut to the chase. May I sit?"

"Sure."

Chief Waters pulled a chair from across the room and sat in front of me.

"The department has decided not to press any charges against you, and the DA has decided not to indict you. After careful research, we dug deeper into your claims and found out that Judge Peters had a network of operations going all through North and South America. Frankly, I don't know how he was never on anyone's radar after all this time." The Chief cleared his throat. "Because of you, nine officers have been arrested as accomplices of Lieutenant Robert Polenski, two of whom were detectives at your station.

"We were able to subpoena Stephen Carter's flash drive from Bank of America, which itemized detailed transactions over the past six years. I'm not sure if you knew this, but Stephen had recorded conversations between himself and Judge Peters that directly implicated the judge in almost every transaction that was recorded on the flash drive."

"No, I didn't know that, sir."

"We're also holding Tim Johnson in protective custody. He knows the names of others who are implicated in this goddamn mess." Chief Waters leaned closer, "Frankly, Jacob, you've opened a can of worms that will not only affect the Metro Police Department, but several departments across the country."

Chief Waters stood and pushed the chair back to its original place. He walked over and extended his hand. "You've done a fine job, Jacob. I'm just sorry that you had to endure so much pain. No one on the job should ever have to go through what you went through to stop a criminal."

"Thank you, sir. That means a lot coming from you."

"No, thank you, Jacob. My door is always open for you."

Chief Waters turned to walk out, but then stopped before he left the room, "Oh, and there's a car waiting for you downstairs to take you home."

"Thank you, sir."

Forty-five minutes later, I climbed out of a black stretch limousine in front of my house. I hadn't been home since that awful night of Theresa's murder and was wondering how I'd react to being there again. I turned the front doorknob and immediately, Henry barked and jumped up and down.

"Henry, how'd you get here?"

I knelt down and picked up the growing chocolate Lab. Henry licked me all over my face and even got his tongue in my mouth once or twice.

"Okay, okay, I'm glad to see you, too."

I put Henry down and sat on the living room couch. "You can do this, Jacob." I looked to my right and stared at the spot on the floor where I had tripped over Theresa's body. My heart sunk but I didn't let myself cry. Be strong for Theresa, because she'd do the same for you.

I walked to the kitchen and saw a stack of mail on the counter. I knew that my in-laws had probably come by the house in anticipation of my return. I sifted through bills and junk mail and then came upon an envelope the size of a card. I opened the envelope and pulled out a card with a large heart on the front, and the only words were a handwritten message that said, "Thinking of You." There wasn't a return address on the envelope and I knew that the card must have come from Angela. I hadn't heard from her in two weeks and suspected that I'd probably never hear from her again.

I sifted through more junk mail until I came upon an envelope that didn't have a return address, but had my name and address handwritten on the front. The envelope didn't have a postage stamp, so I wondered how it had gotten mixed up with the rest of the mail. I opened the envelope and saw that a letter had been written to me.

Dear Detective Hayden,

Let me introduce myself by saying that I cannot tell you my name. You do not know me, but you waved to me once, which really made my day. You see, I've been following your career for the past few years and you've really made an impression on me. That's a good thing. Before I get into the meat of this, I want to say that I'm sorry for the loss of your wife. I know you loved her very much. I also know that you were able to kill the bastards that did that to her. Good for you. You and I might be cut from the same cloth. Time will tell on that, though. Now, to get to the good part.

You've been chosen, Detective Hayden. Just like the rest of them. I've chosen you. And I only choose the best. Let's just say that you will soon be a part of a game that I like to call "Life or Death." No one has ever beaten me at this game. How can they? I'm the one who made it up. The rules of the game are simple: if you beat me, then you live. If not, then you die. But don't worry, Detective Hayden, I won't start the game with you until you are one hundred percent ready. I know that you've just come home from the hospital and that you need your rest. So rest up, my friend, and give little Henry a big hug for me. You just might be the first one to beat me.

Sincerely yours,

Anonymous.

P.S. I thought that of the others, but I was wrong.

I put down the letter and saw that Henry was staring at me. "Did you write this?"

Epilogue

I DIDN'T SLEEP MUCH my first night home. The house didn't feel the same without Theresa there. The bed smelled too much like her even though it'd been weeks since she passed away, so I tried to sleep in the guest room, which wasn't much better. I dozed off from time to time, only to quickly wake up in cold sweats. I saw every hour pass: three, four, and then five. Finally, at six, I got out of bed.

I took Henry for a walk around the neighborhood. The New Year had recently passed and some of the houses still had their Christmas decorations up. I'd received cards from some of my neighbors while in the hospital, which reminded me that I needed to stop by and thank them once I got my strength up. My emotional strength more than physical.

The morning air was cold, so I was happy that Henry took care of business pretty quickly so that we could hurry up and get inside. I knew the next few weeks were going to be tough because I'd not only have to endure physical therapy, but I'd have to begin the process of packing away Theresa's belongings. How could I do that? I hadn't decided what I'm going to do with them, but knowing Theresa, she'd probably want me to donate them to Goodwill or a similar organization that would give the clothes to the less fortunate. She was truly a saint.

Now in the kitchen, I leaned against the counter and sipped on a cup of coffee. The house was quiet. Too quiet. Even when Theresa was at work and I was home alone, the house never seemed this quiet or empty. I had noticed yesterday when I came home that there was an emptiness that I'd never felt before. I thought about it for a while and decided that when Theresa was alive, her energy was alive as well, and radiated throughout the house even when she wasn't here.

I started to think some more and my mind was taken back to Camille Johnson, the mother of the teenager, Melvin Johnson, who had been murdered in his neighborhood over five months ago. I remembered how heartbroken she was over the loss of her son and how I told her that I'd find the man responsible for killing him. I had made a promise to her, and now, more than anything, I understood the importance of closure.

I grabbed my keys, and fifteen minutes later, I was in front of her row house. It was almost seven in the morning, not an appropriate time to visit someone, but I felt she needed to know who had killed her son and why. As I got out of the car, I saw her open her front door, wearing dress slacks and a black button-down coat. She didn't notice me at first, but when she did, she stopped dead in her tracks.

"Detective Hayden?"

"Hi, Ms. Johnson, it's been a long time." I walked up to her and shook her hand. "I've got some information for you regarding your son's death. Do you have a minute?"

"Of course. I was getting ready to leave for work, but I can tell them I'll be a few minutes late."

She looked at me and I could tell that she wanted to say something about the bruises on my face.

"I'm okay," I said. "It's just been a long six months."

"Well, why don't we get out of the cold and maybe you can tell me about it."

She turned around and headed back to her house. As we walked up her porch, I asked her, "So how have you been?"

"There are good days and bad days. I miss my son. But the one thing that gets me through all of this is," she stopped and turned to me, "the one thing that I can never forget, is that one day I'll see him again."

I nodded and smiled, "I understand."

I really did.

The End

Acknowledgments

Thanks to Steven Cribby, Lewan Hutchison and Sherman Gray for taking the time to read and offer your insights into making *The Avenged* a more complete novel.

Other Books by Charles Prandy

Jacob Hayden Series
Book 2: Behind the Closed Door.
Book 3: The Game of Life or Death (Coming in March of 2014)

Stand-Alone Novels
The Last of the Descendants

To be notified of future works by Charles Prandy, please go to www.charlesprandy.com.

About the Author

Charles was born on November 14, 1973, and grew up in Derwood, Maryland, a small city about twenty-five minutes outside of Washington, D.C. His neighborhood was typical of small-town suburbia; he had great friends, played sports and got into mischief. He graduated from the University of Maryland University College with a degree in Legal Studies. He attended Wesley Theological Seminary for two years, and it was there that he got the idea to write his first novel, *The Last of the Descendants*, which was published in May, 2008.

He's currently working on the next novels in the series and will continue to write until his brain goes numb.

Made in the USA
Lexington, KY
31 March 2014